# CLOAK OF

# CLOAK OF CONTROL

JACKIE BUTTERWORTH

Tate Publishing & *Enterprises*

Published by Tate Publishing & Enterprises, LLC
127 E. Trade Center Terrace | Mustang, Oklahoma 73064 USA
1.888.361.9473 | www.tatepublishing.com

Tate Publishing is committed to excellence in the publishing industry. The company reflects the philosophy established by the founders, based on Psalm 68:11,
*"The Lord gave the word and great was the company of those who published it."*

Book design copyright © 2007 by Tate Publishing, LLC. All rights reserved.
*Cover design by Jennifer L. Fisher*
*Interior design by Isaiah R. McKee*

Published in the United States of America

ISBN: 978-1-60462-555-4
1.Fiction: General: Contemporary: Spiritual/Spiritual Abuse
2. Fiction: Religious: General

08.02.15

Ian
Blair
Rebecca and
Cameron

*The Lord bless thee, and keep thee: The Lord make his face shine upon thee, and be gracious unto thee: The Lord lift up his countenance upon thee, and give thee peace. Numbers 6:24–26 (KJV)*

# ACKNOWLEDGMENTS

There are many people I would like to thank who have helped me, in so many different ways, to write this book. My husband and best friend, Ian; my children, Blair, Rebecca, and Cameron; my mother and father, Shirley and Paul Duval; my brother and sister-in-law, Stuart and Lynette Duval; my mother and father-in-law, Joy and Ray Butterworth; my sister-in-law and brothers-in-law, Trish and George Miliadis and Jason Butterworth—all have played a special part in my life and I value their support and unconditional love. I am also grateful to the many friends who have shown genuine interest and given real encouragement, especially Rose Williams—thanks Rose, you've been a real blessing.

I would like to give special thanks to Dr. Kevin Dyson and his wife, Joy Dyson, who introduced my husband and me to God's grace and freedom, and instilled in us the excitement of God's Kingdom. To the many members of God's family we have met around the world—your love and acceptance have meant so much.

I would also like to thank the wonderful team at Tate Publishing. Thank you for your invaluable help, support, and encouragement throughout the whole process.

Most of all, I want to thank the Lord for all he has done in my life. Where would I be without him? I pray that he will bless this book and place it in the hands of all who need to hear its message.

# PREFACE

This book is about the practice and subsequent effects of unhealthy control and spiritual abuse over the lives of people. To be spiritually abused and legalistically controlled within any church, where one should feel safe and secure and should find freedom and healing, can be a devastating experience. Leaders practising such abuse have much to be accountable for, for not only does it bring confusion of identity, fear and pain, but also, sadly, the experiences from these negative human role models are more often than not transferred onto God. As a consequence, many people's images of God have become distorted and twisted, and the good news of the gospel has become, instead, a negative message and a heavy burden. God is seen as an abusive bully or one whose standards are so impossibly high that some people spend the rest of their lives anxiously performing to reach them and earn his approval. They feel inexplicable guilt, shame and condemnation, and for many, God's face is seen as perpetually angry and disapproving. Unfortunately, it may take years for some to discover the true identity of their God, if ever, and for others they simply fall by the wayside, weary and discouraged.

Yet God, in his deep understanding, does not give up on us. He desires that his people be one, that they be healed and free and walking victoriously under the banner of his grace and love.

It is my sincerest prayer, therefore, that as you read this story you may be encouraged that no matter how deep the pain and confusion, our God is a God of *love, truth,* and *grace.* His arms are open to you today to heal and to restore and to lift the heavy burdens laid upon you by men. He truly will replace man's *cloak of control* with his own *robe of righteousness.*

Jackie Butterworth

*They tie up heavy loads and put them on men's shoulders…*
*Matthew 23:4 (*NIV*)*

# BEHIND CLOSED DOORS

Zara clutched her coat around her slender shoulders and braced herself as she stepped out into the stormy winter night. A haunting wind moaned around the darkened, empty buildings, accentuating her solitude; tonight, at the church office, she was all alone. Carefully checking the alarm system, she switched off the lights and pulled the heavy office doors closed to lock them. It always took some minutes for the auxiliary night lights to come on, and so Zara waited, huddled against the tall concrete walls to protect herself from the driving rain, waiting for the welcome lights that would guide her to her car.

As she stood in the darkness, she surveyed the buildings that surrounded her, normally so familiar, but now barely visible through the stormy night, so formidable and foreign. The offices that stood behind her were several stories high, yet just a small part of a much larger complex. The church itself, an evangelical church simply called The Light, was designed by an architect who, in his time, had been quite radical, for its structures were angular and contemporary. In fact, apart from one dominant stained glass window at the front and a small bell tower to the side, there were few clues that this was indeed a church; to the casual observer it could be a convention auditorium or a business centre. *One thing was for sure*, Zara thought, *there was no lack of money*. Tonight, however, this opulence was overshadowed by the shroud of darkness, and the sharp, concrete buildings cast strange and ominous shadows. Zara could imagine that the walls held many dark secrets, and she shuddered involuntarily; not as a reaction to the cold, winter winds that whipped strands of auburn hair across her finely chiselled face, but rather a shudder that came from deep within her. There was something about this place, something she could not yet put her finger on, something that was not quite right.

She had been working at the church office for two years now, ever since she had left community college and ever since she had joined the church. Zara remembered that night well. It had been a Sunday evening similar to this when she had first encountered a group from The Light huddled on a street corner in the town giving out tracts. They were inviting people to their meetings and, unlike the weather, had seemed so welcoming and warm that Zara had been persuaded to join them. That same night after an altar call, she gave her life to Christ, and under the guidance of a counsellor had signed on as a member of the church. In the weeks that followed she'd expressed her desire to go to university to gain a bachelor's degree in law, but instead had been encouraged by her church counselor to become more involved in the work of the church. University, she had been told, was a worldly place and women were discouraged from going there. Within days she'd been offered a job at the office as a typist; the strong undertone of a message being that "this was God's will." Zara had assumed that attending university would lead to humanistic pride, and as a new Christian she had genuinely wanted to do what was right. How could she argue? But that was the problem. No one did argue, not publicly anyway. If the leadership said it should be so, it was.

Zara sighed. She had so many questions and already suspected she was being viewed by some as a "loose cannon"; a fact that was only being tolerated because she was still a relatively new church member. But she wondered how long this tolerance would last. From what she could observe independent thinking seemed somewhat of a threat. The fact was she was beginning to feel like she didn't fit in. Oh, everyone seemed friendly enough; they smiled, they laughed. Yet no one ever really spoke of their problems. Was it possible that they didn't have any? Zara couldn't help but feel there was more to it. Despite the outward appearance of perfection here, there was an unspoken, pervasive feeling that hung like a thick cloud over this church. Was it fear? Fear of what?

A sharp clap of thunder suddenly jolted Zara from her thoughts and moments later the night lights finally flickered on, flooding the car park. Thankful, Zara pulled her coat collar around her face and with head down dashed to her VW; the bright, canary yellow a comforting sight against the bleak backdrop. Safely inside she encouraged its reluctant motor to turn over, and then slowly chugged away through the large wrought iron gates, headed for home.

But as her car disappeared down the winding, tree-lined avenue and out of sight, two darkly-clothed figures stepped out from the shadows and into the dim light of a solitary street lamp. They watched her with distrust as her car faded into the distance.

"She's gone," one muttered to his silent partner.

⚢

Ruth Henderson sat slumped over the kitchen table, her weary head resting on her arms. All was quiet in her teenage daughter's room, but the evening had been as turbulent as the weather beating incessantly against their shabby, wood-framed bungalow. Now, as she listened to the rain pounding heavily onto the window panes, Ruth strained to hear more, hoping to hear a car pull into the driveway, desperate for her husband's footsteps to come up the footpath. He had not come home yet; the hour was late, and she feared the worst.

She had needed her husband tonight; needed him to back her up as she had faced the torrent of teenage emotions. For Ruth had tried to explain to her daughter, Emily, why it was not God's will that she go to a school social event. Dancing, drinking, and mixing with non-Christians (especially non-Christian boys) was strictly forbidden at the church of The Light, and they would not grant their approval. Her daughter had seen things differently, and had argued and screamed into the night before slamming her door in anger. Ruth listened in pain as Emily sobbed in her room before eventually falling asleep and Ruth felt so alone, so confused.

She remembered fondly her own youthful days when she had attended parties and danced into the night. It was at one such party that she met and later married her husband, Jack, and they had been such happy times. But she was a Christian now and wanted to do God's will for both herself and her family. The church of The Light had many rules, which they insisted were based on Scripture, and if obeying them meant God would be pleased, Ruth knew she must carry them out, although she admitted that doing so had not always been easy, as tonight had proved. Ruth sighed as she recalled the difficulty she experienced on other occasions when trying to enforce the church's rules in her home. It had been hard, for example, to suggest to her husband, who was not a believer, that they should no longer have a television; and to her daughter that she could no longer listen to worldly music on the radio, or visit the cinema, as these were forbidden. Her family was resistant at first to give up these pleasures, but knowing how important the church was to her, they unhappily yielded. They had even agreed to give up travelling, as this was a luxury that was also frowned upon by the church; for any trip, overseas or other, meant being absent from the meetings. In most services it was preached from the pulpit that their church, The Light, had the whole truth, and they, unlike any other fellowship, were the only truly enlightened ones. Ruth certainly didn't want to be absent nor backslide from such a place as this. She just couldn't help but think how things seemed so much simpler, so full of joy, when she'd first become a Christian, before she'd ever joined this church. Why did it all feel like such a burden now?

The sound of crunching footsteps on the pebbled pathway outside caused Ruth to lift her head and freeze. Then the fumbling sound of a key finding its way into the lock had her on her feet in minutes, anxiously stumbling toward the front door. Her husband! She glanced at the clock in the hallway. 2:00 a.m. Would he be sober tonight? His drinking had become a problem of late, so much so that she had made an appointment with the pastor at church to ask for his advice and help; something she had never done before. After tonight's tumultuous episode maybe she should mention her daughter's rebellious attitude as well. It could do no harm—could it?

❡

Laying his reading glasses gently on his Bible, Leonard McKenzie rubbed his weary eyes. His wife of forty years lay peacefully sleeping in the bed beside him, her white, curly hair tussled on the pillow and her aging cheeks pink from the warmth of the duvet that enveloped her. He should be sleeping as well, but he felt troubled in his spirit and many things were racing through his mind so sleep was far from him. Leonard leant over and quietly turned the table lamp off then sat still in his bed, listening to the wind and rain outside, which seemed to match his melancholy mood. There was no moon tonight and his room was in complete darkness.

Complete darkness. Leonard couldn't help but consider the irony of this phrase as he compared it to the meeting he had attended earlier that day at the church of The Light. It was a meeting of the elders with Milton Whitfield (the pastor of The Light) to discuss upcoming events, church business, etc., but Leonard was amazed at how one-sided and perfunctory these meetings always were. There seemed to be little opposition to anything Pastor Whitfield suggested, even though some courses of action seemed not only bizarre, but downright wrong. Was he the only one who could see it? He had often wondered if it could it be healthy to have no Board of Governors to be accountable to, for surely this would ensure the safety of the church. To have only one man at the top surrounded by "yes men" must truly be endangering them all. He admitted that he was indeed one of these men as he himself had been an elder at the church for many years, but why could he not speak up? Why could he not share his concerns? In honesty, who would listen? There had been so many things over the years that he had doubts about; things that he couldn't understand and, as yet, had had no proper explanations as to why these practices existed. He had tried to raise his objections personally to this elder or that, but they seemed almost fearful to rock the boat, happy to bury their head in the sand as it were.

Take the wearing of hats. For as long as he could remember the women in the church had been told to cover their heads whenever praying in the presence of men as a symbol of their submission to them. This was based on the passage of scripture in 1 Corinthians 11 where the apostle, Paul, forbade women to pray or prophesy with their heads uncovered. However, even Leonard recognised that the specific instructions given by Paul were cultural and an observance of a social custom at the time. As for the issue of submission that Paul referred to, of course these principles were timeless and necessary for order and the smooth running of any business, government, or family. However, such submission was never intended to mean surrender, withdrawal, or apathy, and certainly did not mean inferiority. It was so much more about mutual commitment and cooperation, and about the respecting of different roles and responsibilities, only Leonard was not convinced that the church understood this. Their women were forbidden to teach, preach or to song lead in general meetings whenever men were present, and were not even permitted to meet together in small groups, whether at church or at home, lest they gossip. From Leonard's observations the women certainly were not treated as equals.

Then there was what was loosely termed as the "boy/girl" issue, where single men were forbidden to mix with, or talk to, single women, whether they liked it or not. Leonard shook his head as he reflected on this unhealthy situation. During the meetings single men and women sat on separate sides of the church so as not to be distracted from the sermon. They went to separate camps during their holiday breaks, and even at Youth Club each Saturday night they performed their different sports or activities in separate rooms. If a young man was interested in a young lady, he would have to seek the pastor's permission first and arrangements would be made for them to meet if the pairing was approved. Such a couple would then be said to be "talking," and this phrase was very appropriate considering they were not allowed to do anything but, for dating was also strictly forbidden, and all courting took place within the church grounds only, where the couples could be watched and chaperoned by all and sundry. Leonard was thankful that he had met and married his lovely wife, Marjory, many years before joining The Light. Their courtship had been a beautiful time and a memory he would treasure forever. How sad that the young people of this church were being robbed of such a precious time in their life that could never be repeated and yet was such a basic building block for a solid and lasting marriage.

Leonard pulled the blankets up around his chin, feeling a little chilled, but his thoughts continued to race and would not be dampened. He reflected again on the day's meeting.

The scripture had often been quoted to him, "Obey them that have the rule over you, and submit yourselves: for they watch for your souls, as they that must give account . . ." (Hebrews 13:17, KJV). Yet the accounting of souls Leonard had witnessed today had been questionable. Names were mentioned of those suspected of not tithing ten percent of their income, thus affecting the building project; those who were questioning the leadership; and even worse, those who were not attending 100% of the many meetings and prayer gatherings held at the church during the week and in the weekends. Phone numbers were distributed between the elders to give "encouragement" to those souls whose performance for God's Kingdom could be further improved, and if a little more than encouragement was required, then they would not hesitate to take further steps to what, in Leonard's mind, amounted to sheer thuggery. But let's face it, Leonard thought cynically. People were needed in the pews to receive the regular brainwashing-type sermons that he was so opposed to; messages that often bound the people in fear. It seemed to be their way of maintaining control over the church, for few people dared leave this place for fear of going to hell. Leonard had often read about the use of control through fear and "mind control techniques" but had always associated these with cultish practices.

Leonard shuddered despite himself. He must be tired. What was he thinking? The Light was well known as an upstanding, evangelical church, not a cult! But even as he settled down to sleep under the warmth of the duvet, he knew that he was not so sure anymore.

✹

"Thank you, Peggy…yes, I certainly will. Take care now and God bless you."

The phone clicked and Gladys Jones put down the receiver, feeling very pleased with herself. A smug smile spread across her aging face, and with an air of self righteousness, she settled down in her wing-backed chair before the warmth of the fire and resumed her knitting. Her tortoiseshell cat, Zebedee, stretched lazily against her feet. He was Gladys' sole companion these many years, as she was a spinster. Not that her solitude both-ered her this bleak, wintry night, for her thoughts were occupied elsewhere. She had become privy to some information that few, as yet, knew, but her friend, Peggy Percival, had shared with her tonight in order that she pray for the person involved. It seemed that elderly Sister Hoyland had been reported as sponsoring an African child through an outside missionary agency, something wholly unacceptable at the church of The Light, as members were to bring all monies into the church alone, and were not to distribute funds to any outside organisations under any circumstances. It was Pastor Whitfield's prerogative to decide which missionary agencies should be supported, if any, and he alone was responsible for giving them money. Heads would surely roll and Sister Hoyland's repentance would most certainly be required. This was indeed a matter for prayer, and as a prayer concern, Gladys reasoned, this could not possibly be classified as gossip; gossip was a sin, and Gladys did not sin. In fact she prided herself on living the type of Christian lifestyle that was a testimony to all who observed her. She attended every meeting at church, including prayer meetings beforehand; she taught Sunday school; tithed more than ten percent, with an offering; was on the flower roster and cleaning roster, and her most noteworthy Christian deed was to have no fellowship with those who had left the church. She was the champion of ignoring and plain snubbing the poor souls who had abandoned the church of The Light and were, according to the pastor, "out of God's will and on their way to hell." *Yes*, Gladys thought to herself, as she pulled the wool away from her playful cat's paws. She was the epitome of a Christian, and she *would* pray for this latest incident...right after she had thought about who else she could phone to share the news with. Well, after all, this *wasn't* gossip, and the more people praying, the better! Right?

# MILTON WHITFIELD

Milton Whitfield stared sullenly out of his study window. The day was grey, and the sea below him was dull and choppy. Several small yachts had ventured out into the ocean and were being swept across the waters, their sails billowing in the wind as their owners struggled bravely to control them. Milton shook his head irritably at their foolishness. He was a keen fisherman, but only a madman would be out on the water on such a day as this. Adjusting the heating dial on the wall, Milton returned to his desk where the Saturday morning newspaper laid open. A large photograph of a man in his sixties dominated the page headed by the title, "Veteran Faith Healer, Phillip Townsend, still attracting thousands." Seating himself in his black leather chair, Milton reread the ensuing article, his face pained and bitter. He suddenly seized the page, screwing it up with disgust, and threw it into the nearby wastepaper basket. His gaze was once more drawn to the large window in front of him as he stared miserably out at the blustery day, lost in the pain of his thoughts.

✟

Milton Whitfield's childhood had not been easy right from the start. Born and raised on a dairy farm with his elder brother and two younger sisters, he had been set to work as soon as he was old enough to hold a pitchfork. His father, Edward Whitfield, a staunch, fundamentalist Christian, had been a hard man, although his work ethics were impeccable, and his mother, Claire, a more genteel lady, had become worn down over the years of marriage to a man who provided little emotional support. As a result, she had developed a cutting and critical tongue, and it seemed there was little Milton did that ever met with her approval. Growing up in such an environment had often been difficult for young Milton, who had been full of life and dreams. In fact it seemed from the day he was born his personality clashed with that of his parents. Milton's many creative ideas were often scoffed at and put down, not because his family meant to be harsh on the young lad, but more because they didn't understand him. New ideas were a threat, and it seemed much safer to stick with the tried and true. Perhaps this was why Milton's elder brother, Byron, seemed the favoured one time and time again. He was far more serious and conservative, and talked of being a minister when he grew up. Their father was uncompromising in the home when it came to matters of religion. He would have his family in church as often as the farm allowed it, and at home strict Bible reading and prayers were always observed around the table. If the children disobeyed the many rules imposed on them by their father, they knew the rod would be their punishment, and Milton was often the recipient.

As Milton grew older, therefore, the matter of choosing a career became a bone of contention. It seemed that farming or religion were the only two acceptable choices in his family and he was drawn to neither. Byron, on the other hand, followed his dream of becoming a minister and, after his schooling was complete, he enrolled at university to study theology. Edward and Claire Whitfield had been so proud when Byron eventually graduated with honours. Not so with Milton. His creativity and gift for speaking had led him into sales, his bent being more toward the business world. Edward Whitfield had been quick to voice his disapproval and repeatedly raised Byron up as the example that should be followed. Feeling pressured and keenly rejected for his innovative business ideas, Milton made the decision to attend a Baptist Bible college to gain some degree of parental approval. But even this failed. Although the Bible college was well known and excellent in its delivery of teaching, it did not, in Edward and Claire's eyes, match up to the standards of other universities, and, more to the point, it was Baptist. The family had always been Methodist and they held nothing but suspicion toward his efforts.

It was, however, at this Bible college that Milton made his first serious commitment to Christ and experienced the true transformation of a born-again life. Ignoring his father's disapproval, he channelled his creativity into Christian endeavours; his salesmanship made him a natural evangelist. It was at this Bible college that Milton also made several other lasting relationships. He made good friends with a couple called Leonard McKenzie and Marjory Stewart, and later had the privilege of being best man at their wedding. And it was at this college that he met Nancy.

Nancy was a skilled violinist who often played during the morning devotional sessions at the college. Milton found he could not take his eyes off her as she played with such passion and devotion, and he saw within her a deep and obvious love for the Lord. He also learned that she had a deep love for children. When the opportunity presented itself for a team to travel to a city known for its disadvantaged street kids, Milton was quick to volunteer. He knew that Nancy would be going. Making sure he was seated beside her on the bus, the two began to talk. They talked about their families, about their interests, about their dreams. Both had a desire to extend God's Kingdom, Nancy working with youth and Milton as an evangelist. Both had a love and passion for life, for God, and soon after, for each other. It was not long before they were married.

Feeling it necessary to move away from the influence of his parents and Byron, who by now had accepted a ministerial position in a well-established traditional church, Milton and Nancy decided to relocate to a larger city farther south. They were hearing good reports about a certain young preacher who had started holding meetings there. His name was Phillip Townsend. Apparently a new wave of the Spirit was beginning to flow where folk were being healed and delivered, and Nancy and Milton were keen to be a part of it. It was at one such meeting that they both received a word directing them toward pastoring a church themselves. It was not something they had considered before, but spurred on by the encouraging prophetic words and the support of those around them, they began looking into its possibilities. With the help of a loan from the bank and the meagre savings from a sales job Milton had picked up, they purchased a small plot of land, and their first humble church building was erected. Together, arm and arm, Nancy and Milton had stood on its small grass frontage and thanked the Lord.

It was not long before the little church began to grow. Drawn to Milton's charismatic style and Nancy's friendly manner, numbers soon doubled and Milton realised he would need the added help of two trusted friends. Leonard and Marjory were quick to respond, even though it meant changing location, house and job, and Leonard McKenzie became the first elder to serve at the church that was called The Light. In no time at all they were celebrating the church's tenth anniversary.

Many other churches in the area were also growing strongly; not the least being the church of Phillip Townsend. Unlike Milton's evangelical thrust, Phillip's ministry was devoted to healing; meeting after meeting crowds were drawn to see the miraculous workings of God. Milton even encouraged his own congregation to attend some of these meetings, and many brought back reports of their own personal healings. On a monthly basis, all the ministers of the area would meet to share their burdens and dreams—Methodist, Pentecostal, or Baptist— and all enjoyed the mutual fellowship. Milton only wished his own family could be this open and accepting.

It was during this time that Milton received a phone call from

his brother. Unbeknownst to Milton, his mother had been struggling with breast cancer for a number of years and her time was
now drawing to an end. Hurt and angered that he had not been
informed sooner of her illness, Milton would never understand
the reason why this had been kept from him. He and Nancy
quickly flew home to be with her in her last hours. Milton was
shocked to see the frail frame of his unconscious mother lying
before him on the hospital bed, and tried in vain to relay to his
family the wonderful messages of healing and hope he had witnessed at Townsend's meetings. However, his stories were stonily rejected by both Byron and his father who were suspicious
and anti the Pentecostal movement, and Milton had watched
helplessly as his mother passed away.

On returning home, however, Milton and Nancy faced a
deeply personal problem of their own. Having been married for
twelve years, they still had not been able to conceive and Nancy
was desperate for a child. Recent tests had revealed that once
again she had failed to become pregnant. So, with the support
and prayers of their congregation, they decided to go forward
for special healing prayer at Townsend's meetings. And it was
indeed a miracle. Several months later the wonderful news was
announced. Nancy was expecting her first baby!

Milton would never forget the joyful time of preparation
as they awaited the birth of their first child. Nancy was simply
aglow with the love of life and her God as she knitted and sewed
baby garments and purchased the crib and teddy bears. Milton
set about decorating the nursery for their long-awaited arrival—
wallpapering, painting, and putting up shelves. Yet this was not
his only project. Major construction work had also begun on the
church buildings in order to accommodate the many people
now attending. These were indeed busy days, but for Milton
and Nancy a most exciting time in their lives.

As the days and months of her pregnancy passed, however, Nancy was growing indescribably tired. This was to be
expected, of course, with all that was happening, yet to be on

the safe side Milton insisted that she give up her responsibilities at the church and spend more time resting. His suggestion was gladly accepted. The doctor, however, was deeply concerned. The baby did not seem to be developing as well as it should be and dark bruises had appeared on Nancy's thighs. He insisted on a series of tests being carried out and it was during this process a discovery was made that all was not well. Nancy's blood tests were showing some disturbing discrepancies. She was diagnosed with an acute and rare type of leukaemia. Fearful for her child and adamant the baby remain unharmed, Nancy refused all treatment.

Devastated, Milton called upon Phillip Townsend and the elders of The Light to stand with him in prayer as they sought the Lord for her healing. Members of The Light started a 24-hour prayer chain to constantly cover the couple in prayer. Over the following months many took it in turns to fast and pray for several days at a time as a point of intercession. Milton himself spent many sleepless nights pacing the floor, begging God to save his wife's life. But despite all their efforts and petitions before the throne of God, Nancy and her unborn baby son died.

Milton sunk into deep depression. The devastation of losing the two most precious people in his life cut to the very core of his being. He understandably took time off from ministry to allow himself space to heal, and Leonard McKenzie stepped in to run the church for a period of six months. But during this time a profound change came over Milton Whitfield. In the depths of his despair he began to question everything he had ever known. He questioned his ministry, his own abilities, and the people that surrounded him. He was plagued by thoughts from his past, where his own parents had seemed to criticise his every move; his own brother outdoing his every attempt to succeed. He was tired of being perceived as weak; tired of being second best. He would do better. He would prove to the world that he could be successful. His ministry would become powerful—even more powerful than Phillip Townsend's. His own brother would have to acknowledge his success. And he *would* succeed—only Milton would do it his own way and *alone*. He would not ask again for the help of other ministries that, in his hour of need, had failed him. He would *not* instruct his congregation on the unreliable teachings of faith healing that had allowed his precious wife and child to die. He would teach his people the way of hard work, discipline, and obedience to the age-old wisdom of pure Scripture alone. *Never* would he, or anyone else under his care, be hurt in this way again!

Milton had been sitting in his study for over an hour now as he painfully pondered his past. He glanced again at the newspaper that was discarded into the rubbish bin. Although twenty years on, the pain of those memories was as poignant today as yesterday, and with bitter frustration he rose to his feet. So, Townsend's meetings were still flourishing. He moved across the room to a table where a red velvet cloth covered a large glass case. Removing the cover, Milton looked possessively at the model of his modern multi-million dollar church complex with its tennis courts, conference hall, and fitness centre. Proudly he counted again the many properties and shops that he had purchased surrounding the church, before replacing the cover almost reverentially. Then slowly he turned and leaving the study, headed down the corridor toward a closed door at the end of the hall. Hesitating, he slowly turned the handle and, pushing the door open, stood for a moment surveying the room. It was tastefully decorated in creams and lemons. Frilly curtains adorned the windows, below which sat a wooden rocking chair. Shelves displayed toys and teddy bears, though covered in dust, and in the centre of the room sat an unused crib. Tentatively Milton moved toward the little cradle and with his aging hands gently began to rock it. Then lifting a picture frame from its quilted centre he held it tenderly in his hands. As he looked at the young and beautiful face of his wife, he stroked the photo gently.

"I'm doing this for you, Nancy," he whispered. "Just for you."

# OBEY THOSE WHO RULE OVER YOU

A wintry sun filtered weakly through the windows of Zara's two-bedroom flat, and stirring sleepily she tried to remember what day it was. Thank goodness—it was Saturday. Zara turned her feather pillow over, pummelled it a little, then sank lazily back under her covers, relieved and content that she did not have to get up for work. Outside she could hear the hum of a lawn mower as her neighbour started his weekend chores and inside the comforting rattle of pots and pans as her flatmate, Kate, busied herself with the dishes. Zara sighed. She really should get up and help her with the cleaning.

Cleaning! Zara sat upright in her bed with a jolt, all traces of sleepiness suddenly gone and her contentment quickly replaced with alarm. She'd forgotten. She'd been rostered for Saturday morning cleaning at the church and Sister DeVreeze would grant no forgiveness for tardiness. DeVreeze was like a Sergeant Major who ensured the cleaning was undertaken in exactly the same manner as was in keeping with the ethos of the church: perfection, discipline, and obedience. There was no choice. If you were rostered to clean—you cleaned—no questions asked; no excuses—for cleanliness was next to Godliness.

Leaping from the comfort of her bed and grimacing at the chilled air that greeted her, Zara hastily grabbed a T-shirt, then sweater, and still pulling her jeans on, stumbled into the kitchen.

"Kate! Quick! Where's the coffee, I'm running late!" she

groaned, rummaging frantically through her handbag for an elusive lip-gloss.

Kate looked up from her labours at the kitchen sink where she was attempting to reduce a pile of dirty dishes left there from a busy week before.

"Good morning, Zara," she grinned affectionately, her cheery round face lighting up at the sight of her friend. She knew Zara did not do mornings well at the best of times. "What's all the hurry?" She dried her hands on a kitchen towel and reaching for a mug, obligingly poured Zara a cup of strong coffee.

"I've only just remembered that I'm supposed to be doing cleaning at the church. *DeVreeze* has put me down to scrub basins and toilets in the ladies' cloakroom," Zara complained, pulling on her sheepskin boots. "I forgot completely until now and you know I can't get out of it. I'm so sorry to leave you with all the housework. I really was intending to give you a hand this morning." Zara twirled her long auburn hair up and held it in place with what looked like black, wooden chopsticks. Rushed or not, she still looked attractive.

Kate held up her hand. "Don't give housework here another thought," she insisted good-naturedly. "Anyway, it's my turn. As I recall, you did all the work last weekend while I was relaxing at a friend's wedding. Speaking of which . . ." Kate pulled out a stool and sat down with a mysterious air at the small kitchen table, handing Zara the mug of coffee. "You've still got a few minutes to spare haven't you? Here—take this and drink it. I've got something to tell you before you go that just can't wait until this afternoon. I was longing to tell you last night, but you were asleep when I got home."

Zara glanced at her watch. Yes, she still had another five minutes and something about Kate's manner had aroused her curiosity. Studying Kate's face, she waited for an explanation. Come to think of it, Kate did seem a little different this morning—she was almost glowing. Zara thought she could guess the reason.

"Has this got anything to do with a certain Dan Marshall by

any chance?" She smiled as she, too, pulled up a kitchen stool and perched on it. Maybe Dan had given her an early birthday present.

Kate blushed a little sheepishly, but then unable to conceal her news any longer bubbled with excitement. "He proposed! Dan Marshall proposed to me last night—and of course I said *yes!* Zara, I'm going to be Mrs. Dan Marshall!" She let out a squeal of delight. "We'll be getting engaged as soon as we can—and we're planning to get married in six month's time!"

Zara was unsure if her shock was due to the strong coffee she'd just swallowed, or from this unexpected news. She stared at Kate in stunned disbelief. Dan and Kate had only been seeing each other for *three* months. Could this be possible? Wasn't this all a little rushed?

"Proposed...?" she finally spluttered. "Where?"

The delight on Kate's face faded slightly at Zara's hesitance and seeming lack of enthusiasm, but she tried to hide her disappointment. She knew Zara had many questions about the courting procedures at church, as they'd had many discussions on this subject before. Looking earnestly at her friend she tried to explain.

"Zara, I know Dan and I haven't been seeing each other for long, but we both sincerely feel this is God's will...and to answer your question—well, he proposed to me over the phone, last night while I was at my mother's. He wanted to do it differently—actually he had a candlelit dinner all planned at a restaurant in town—but, you know how it is. The pastor wouldn't permit us to go out together—so he had to content himself with proposing to me over the phone. Well, he wasn't going to do it in the church car park with everyone watching!" Then quickly in Dan's defence, "Over the phone or not—it was every bit as romantic as it possibly could be."

Kate was beginning to feel frustration rising within her. She could see what Zara was thinking, but what choice did she and Dan have? Sure, it would have been nice to have been proposed to face to face, with flowers and chocolates and all the trimmings, but it hadn't been allowed, and if they wanted to continue seeing each other they had to abide by the rules, no matter how restrictive and unfair. She had never been one to question as Zara often did, perhaps due to the fact that Zara was still relatively new to the church's ways. Kate simply reasoned that if going along with what the church said meant staying out of trouble she was willing to do it, no matter how hard or inconvenient.

And she was right. Zara could think of many romantic ways to be proposed to and "over the phone" did not feature high on the list, but by the defensive look on Kate's face she knew this was neither the time nor the place to argue. No, for her friend's sake, she knew for now she must put aside her personal objections and show her support. Getting up she put her arms around Kate affectionately and embraced her.

"I really *am* pleased to hear your news. Congratulations. You know you're going to make a gorgeous bride."

"You'll be my bridesmaid, won't you?" Kate pleaded, relieved at her friend's approval.

"Nothing would please me more," Zara beamed genuinely. "How about I pick up some bridal magazines on my way back from cleaning this morning and we'll talk all about it this afternoon when I've got more time."

Zara waved to her friend from the window of her VW until she was out of sight, then fell into thoughtful silence as she weaved her way through the narrow backstreets heading toward the church. She hadn't meant to dampen Kate's excitement, yet she couldn't deny her own feelings of concern. The church certainly did have unusual ways of doing things—things that didn't feel quite right. Maybe she would just have to learn to adjust, but it was all so bizarre. Kate was getting married to a man that she had never been on a single date with, never even seen outside the church walls, and certainly never had any physical contact with. She had only been able to talk to Dan twice a week in the church car park after meetings and occasionally over the phone. How could they possibly know each other? From the start Kate and Dan had seemed like such an odd couple; Kate being so bubbly and sweet—Dan, so serious and reserved. They didn't even seem to have much in common. But, they *had* been assured by the leadership that this was God's will and his doing and so how could you doubt? Yet Zara did feel doubtful and somewhat confused. She genuinely wanted to know what was right, to know God's will and leading just as much as Kate did. She just couldn't help but wonder how much of "God's will" had actually been the "church's will," or perhaps more accurately—a desire to play divine matchmaker. Although she would never tell Kate, she had heard from a mutual friend that the pastor had said Dan and Kate were only suited to each other because of their dysfunctional home backgrounds. Was this really the basis on which the pastor had allowed them to be together—the deciding factor which had made this "God's will"? It just didn't seem right.

Zara parked her car on the street, ensuring it was well locked and still preoccupied with her thoughts, walked briskly across the road to the church. She knew that divorce was absolutely forbidden at the church of The Light and that marriage was therefore a long term, life decision. She just hoped desperately for her friend's sake that she was doing the right thing.

✟

After the promise of sun earlier that day, the afternoon had turned grey and depressingly damp, and Ruth shivered as she sat in the opulent, though insufficiently heated, reception room of the church office, watching the clock and wondering how much longer she would have to wait. An appointment was made with Pastor Whitfield for two o'clock on this Saturday afternoon, but it was now 2:40, and with every passing moment she felt growing apprehension. It was no wonder. The pastor's office was like the inner sanctum to which, it seemed, only the privileged or the troublemakers were ever summoned, and it had a reputation for being "a place of reckoning." Like so many others at the church, Ruth had never been into Pastor Whitfield's office, and in fact had never actually spoken to him before either, although she had been a member of the church for over ten years. Pastor Whitfield kept aloof from the congregation, choosing instead to surround himself only with his elders and a select few wealthy members. He had often preached that "God's anointed should not be touched and must be addressed and treated with the utmost reverence." This knowledge only served to add to Ruth's tension as she rehearsed over and over in her mind an appropriate greeting.

Glancing uneasily at her watch she saw that it was now three o'clock. What could be taking so long? Shifting awkwardly in her seat, she tried to calm her nerves by distracting her thoughts onto her surroundings. The décor in the waiting room was not unpleasant, being tastefully arranged in pinks and burgundies with modern furniture and colour co-ordinated accessories, yet the atmosphere was somehow heavy and dark—a fact that was hard to define. Maybe it was the grey winter's day that was visible through the windows, or the fact that the room was only lit by one solitary table lamp. But whatever the reason, the sensation of oppression was almost tangible and felt more like a funeral parlour than a church reception.

"Ruth Henderson?"

At last. Sister Percival, the pastor's prim and sombre secretary, appeared at the door, speaking out her name in a hushed but officious tone. Her greying hair was tied back severely in a bun, and she peered at Ruth over the top of her half-rimmed glasses.

"The pastor will see you now."

Ruth stood uneasily to her feet, relieved that the wait was over. But as she headed uncertainly toward the door that led into a hallway from which stemmed a maze of offices, she suddenly realised that she did not know which one was the pastor's office. Returning to the reception desk she enquired hesitantly of the secretary who had seated herself there.

"Uh...I'm so sorry, but which office does Mr. Whitfield . . ."

"*Pastor!*" Sister Percival snapped abruptly, startling Ruth. "He is referred to as *pastor.* Please show some respect for God's anointed. Come this way, please."

Tight lipped, she beckoned with her hand and, mortified, Ruth followed the woman down the narrow hallway in an almost reverential manner, afraid to speak another word. Rich, soft carpet lay beneath her feet, and a range of offices, large and small, branched off in several directions either side of her, quiet and empty now as it was Saturday. Ruth was ushered through the last door on the right and, a little overawed, found herself in a large, luxurious office that smelt of polish and leather. Dark wooden bookcases lined several walls while another was covered in large paintings surrounded by heavy-gilt frames. Persian rugs were scattered over the already luxurious carpets and deep leather chairs were positioned around an ornate mahogany desk that dominated one end of the room. Behind this desk sat Pastor Milton Whitfield—a slender man of medium height, though slightly stooped, with thinning black hair and spectacles perched precariously on the end of his nose. In fact he appeared more like a shrewd businessman than a man of the church. Whitfield looked up as she entered, his piercing brown eyes coolly studying her for a moment in a seemingly distant and unfriendly manner.

"Sister Henderson, I presume? Please, take a seat." Pastor Whitfield leaned back in his chair and removed his glasses. "How can I help you?" he said with little intonation.

Feeling somewhat intimidated, Ruth sat gingerly on the edge of an ostentatious leather sofa. "I...I...that is—thank you for seeing me . . ." she stammered uncertainly.

"Yes, well, what was it that you've come to see me about?" he smiled dryly. "You do know that we are here to help you, don't you?" Pastor Whitfield glanced at his watch, none too subtly.

Ruth's heart began to pound within her chest and for a moment her mind went alarmingly blank. "Yes. Yes, of course," she managed nervously, her mouth feeling unnaturally dry. Clearing her throat, she sat upright and took a deep breath in an attempt to gain her composure. Although she felt deeply uncomfortable in his presence, she believed in her heart that she was doing the right thing by being here, for if she could not find help and support within the church, then where else could she go? This man was the anointed leader of the church of God, so surely this was a safe place for her to confide, despite her fears. She felt confident that he could be trusted to give her the best advice for her precious daughter and much-loved husband. For the next ten minutes she explained to the pastor, to the best of her ability, her concerns regarding her husband's drinking problems and her daughter's resistance to the church rules.

She may not have felt so trusting, however, had she known that Sister Percival sat within earshot on the other side of a sliding door, pen and notebook in hand, taking down every word that Ruth uttered. To be the bearer of news to the church gossips, whether that news be good or bad, placed Sister Percival in an enviable position of power, and it was a position she would not easily relinquish. Equally, within the walls of the office where Ruth sat, her safety and confidentiality were not assured. For she may not have shared so freely had she known that the pastor reached slowly beneath his desk and pressed a button that read "Record." The practice of manipulating taped information to back up whatever course of action he deemed to take at a later date was a habit Whitfield had long fallen into, and one he felt to be entirely necessary for his own security. Oblivious to these facts, however, Ruth unburdened herself for several minutes more before pausing.

"So," Pastor Whitfield took the opportunity to cut in, "in

short you are saying that both your daughter and your husband are rebelling against God and this church?"

Ruth was a little taken aback at the bluntness of this statement and unsure as to how to respond. "Well...they...that is, Emily...she's just a normal teenager—she's not a bad girl really. It's hard when you're young and all your friends are going to parties and . . ."

Again Pastor Whitfield cut in abruptly. "But, Sister Henderson...surely you know her so-called friends at school are of the world and are on their way to hell. She should be having no fellowship with them. Her soul would benefit more from deeper involvement *here* at the church. Are you disciplining your daughter and ensuring that she attends all of our meetings?"

"Well, yes!" Again Ruth felt alarmed at his directness and seeming disapproval. She was quick to reassure him. "I attend every meeting and encourage my daughter to do the same. And of course I try to ensure discipline at home—only my husband, Jack, is not a believer and therefore doesn't always see things the same way as we do, but . . ."

"Yes, your husband—the alcoholic who criticizes my church," Whitfield muttered cynically.

Ruth felt a little shocked and somewhat hurt at the manner in which this last statement was uttered. "He hasn't always been a heavy drinker," she said in his defence. "In fact, he is a talented salesman and has always been a steady provider for us. It's only in the last year . . ."

"Yes, yes." Pastor Whitfield waved a hand impatiently. "You can label your family as you wish. But there seems to be one thing you are forgetting," he narrowed his eyes and stared directly into Ruth's, "*you* are the Christian in your home and a privileged member of this elite church. It is up to you, therefore, to *pray*, to *memorize Scripture* and to *quote* it to yourself over and over for your family. You should be rising early each morning to *read the Bible* for at least an hour and be obedient to the word." Whitfield thumped his desk as though to accentuate this prescription for Christian living.

Once again Ruth was aghast at the harshness in which his words had been delivered. "But...but I have been doing these things, Pastor. I read the Bible daily; I pray constantly; I praise God for my family . . ."

"So, like your daughter, you are questioning my advice?" the pastor's eyes flashed impatiently. "It is becoming clear to me where the problem lies in your family. The problem obviously lies with *you!*"

"With me?" Ruth uttered timidly, looking perplexed and anxious.

"Your questioning proves you have a rebellious spirit also. It appears to me you have your own issues with authority and therefore with God." Whitfield turned and looked sullenly out of his window in reflection. "You have sat here in self pity and depression—signs in themselves that you are not completely yielded to God—and you are obviously not trying hard enough in your home to be obedient to the word." He turned back to Ruth. "For if you had been in complete submission to your husband and this church, your family would not be in the chaos that it is today. The Bible clearly teaches that a woman brings her unbelieving husband to Christ by her meek and submissive spirit, and the fact that your husband is an alcoholic and still unconverted, and your daughter is in such a rebellious state proves to me it is indeed *you* who is at fault."

Ruth sat in stunned silence, feeling a wave of confusion, condemnation, and guilt sweep over her. Was it true? Was she really the reason for the problems in her family? Ruth bowed her head in shame, her face hot with humiliation, and her lips beginning to tremble. She had thought she was doing her best for God, the church, and her family, but obviously it was not good enough. She must try harder.

Seeing her total dejection, Pastor Whitfield leaned back in his chair somewhat triumphantly and looked toward the ceiling as though deep in thought. Ruth instinctively remained silent as she waited anxiously for him to continue. After what seemed forever he turned to her again.

"I have heard all I need to hear." He looked at her strangely, and then rose abruptly. "Leave this matter with me. Despite your errors, I think we can be of help to your family."

Ruth rose a little shakily, feeling perplexed at his last statement. How did he intend to help her family? Yet there was no time to ask and having received such a harsh rebuke earlier, she dared not question further. She was ushered quickly into the hall and the door was shut firmly behind her. The meeting was over.

Moments later Ruth stood outside the church buildings, buttoning her coat against the wintry afternoon winds. She felt such a failure and somehow so substandard. A lump rose in her throat and reaching for a handkerchief she dabbed tears from her eyes with trembling hands, aware of a familiar ache deep within her. She had done what she thought was best by submitting herself and her family to the leadership of the church as she had been taught to do, and yet she felt so uncertain, so wretched. The pastor had said he would help her, yet why did she sense that all was not well?

Turning, she walked slowly toward her car, unaware that a curtain had twitched behind her and that a shadowy figure watched her every move.

"Sister Percival," Milton Whitfield mused moodily as he looked down on Ruth from his office window. "Get me Leonard McKenzie's number."

⚜

Dragging his wheelbarrow from the garden shed along with tools and a rake, Leonard prepared to tidy his extensive and normally well looked after property. Being a retired business-man had its advantages for he was a keen gardener. However, the storm last night had left debris and leaves scattered all over his yard, and it would take a good few hours this chilly Saturday afternoon to clear. The sumptuous lunch he had just eaten did not help; his wife, Marjory, was famous for her cooking, and Leonard sighed as he glanced at the stomach that refused to sit unnoticed beneath his shirt. The exercise would do him good.

With hands on hips he surveyed the damage done. Many years ago he planted apple and plum trees, which had long since matured and spread their branches like a canopy over his lawns. Several of these branches, bereft of leaves, had snapped and would need trimming and clearing. A white wooden bench, which normally sat beneath the trees giving welcome refuge in the summer months from the heat of the sun, was overturned and lay awkwardly amongst his rose beds. Leonard peered farther down the yard, beyond the trees, to where his treasured vegetable garden lay. He had spent many happy hours in this patch, but for now, in winter, it lay fallow, waiting for the spring planting. Apart from scattered leaves that would need raking, he could see no further disruption there. His only other job then was to clear the flower beds from food scraps and rubbish that seemed to have been blown from his neighbour's overturned rubbish bin.

Pulling on his gloves, Leonard picked up his pruning shears and headed toward his roses. He feared he would have to prune these back severely on account of the damage and he paused for a moment to look at the tags. One was a white, heavily scented rose he had planted for his wife on their thirty-fifth wedding anniversary.

"Leonard!" Marjory's familiar voice disturbed his thoughts as she called to him from the patio. "Leonard! There's a phone call for you. It's Pastor Whitfield."

*The pastor?* Leonard groaned inwardly. What could he want with him on a Saturday? He put down his tools reluctantly and headed back toward the house to take the call. Removing his coat and work shoes and wiping his hands on a towel he picked up the phone from the kitchen bench.

"Hello, this is Leonard."

The voice on the end of the phone sounded impatient and gruff, and Leonard listened intently as the pastor talked on for some time. Marjory carried on with her baking, carefully spooning mixture into greased baking tins, for she'd heard elderly Sister Welham had had a bad fall that morning, and she intended to take muffins to her before the afternoon was out. Nevertheless, as she worked, she kept a watchful eye on Leonard for, although she could not hear the content of the telephone conversation, she could guess by the sober expression on his face what it was about. They'd had these calls before. No doubt Leonard was being asked, yet again, to do something he did not agree with. Marjory placed the muffins into the oven and began scrubbing her dishes with more vigour than was necessary, feeling frustration rising within. For some time now Leonard had been sharing with her his concerns about the church of The Light, and she had to admit she was beginning to agree. They'd been faithful members of this church for more years than she cared to remember and had many treasured memories and dear friends, but lately her perspective was changing, and a righteous anger was stirring in her soul over the many things she was witnessing that did not seem right.

The telephone conversation appeared to be coming to an end, and although Leonard had made several futile attempts to interrupt and object, it was to no avail. He put down the phone and stood in silence, facing the wall for several minutes as he processed the call. Marjory noticed that he was shaking slightly and she placed a steadying hand on his shoulder.

"What is it, Leonard. More trouble? Who is it this time?"

Leonard turned slowly to her and with an air of resignation shook his head. "It's Ruth...Ruth Henderson."

# DIVISION MAKERS

When Ruth arrived at the church early on Sunday morning, Gladys had already made a start on the flowers. They both had been placed on flower duty that day and were asked to arrange a large display of lilies and agapanthus to sit in a prominent position just below the pulpit. It was well known that Gladys prided herself on her flower arranging abilities and, although Ruth was also talented in this area, she felt it better not to interrupt or advise her. She chose instead to busy herself laying newspaper over the plush carpet beneath the vase stand to catch anything that should perchance fall, and to hand flowers to Gladys from the buckets as the need arose. They had two hours in which to complete this task before the start of the Sunday morning service, but for Ruth the time could not go fast enough. She had much on her mind and was not in the mood for Gladys' non-stop prattle, or dared she say, gossip.

"Have you *heard*, Ruth?" Gladys whispered almost secretively. "Jenny and Phil Johnson are expecting their first baby! They've only been married for six months and personally I think it is *ridiculous*. They are *much* too young—they'll never manage—pass a bit of greenery will you, dear? I mean to say, Jenny is not like Melanie Rutledge—you know the one who has just had twins. Now *there* is a capable girl if ever I saw one. Her babies are *always* immaculate when she comes to church, as is she, and she *never* misses a meeting. Such a lovely girl—another lily please, Ruth. Oh—and I hear that Matthew Kelly has spoken to the pastor about seeing the Clayton's youngest daughter. What *is* her name? Amy—yes, and she is *only* seventeen. Very pretty, but I'm afraid not too intelligent. However, I'm sure the pastor will agree to them seeing each other. I mean she is an elder's daughter after all, and that always counts for something. I'm positive this is God's will." She paused for a moment. "I think we need some more agapanthus in the front here, don't you?"

Ruth handed a flower to her, about to reply, but Gladys quickly continued.

"Did you know that the Robinsons have just bought a new car? *Scandalously* expensive I hear, but I suspect they may be trying to keep up with the Joneses—which in this case, my dear, is the McLachlans. They've just finished building a new home in a very well-to-do area, you know. I saw Judy McLachlan at the hat shop just last week and she was buying a *very* expensive hat—with shoes and a bag to match!"

Ruth was not particularly interested in the spending habits of the McLachlans or the Robinsons, but she listened politely and smiled appropriately nonetheless, despite herself. She did not feel so gracious, however, when Gladys moved on to what seemed to be her favourite subject; namely, who had left the church or was about to leave, and who were the latest victims of her snubbing. In her heart Ruth had never really supported this idea of ignoring or being rude and unfriendly to those who had chosen to leave the church. Besides, if they truly were lost, should they not rather be sought after, reconciled, and brought back in to the fold? No, it didn't make sense and she certainly did not want to discuss the issue this morning. So when Gladys lent over to rearrange a stray lily, Ruth grabbed her opportunity to change the subject.

"The flowers are looking lovely this morning, Gladys. The way you have arranged them and the effect of the greenery is just perfect. You are very talented," Ruth said in genuine admiration, for she was not often insincere, but the reaction she received was most unexpected.

Gladys stopped short in her tracks, obviously unsure as to how to respond to such praise. Then awkwardly she clasped her hands together as though in prayer and looked heavenward. "To God be all the glory. Praise be to his name. It is through his doing and his alone," she gushed sanctimoniously.

Ruth was taken aback and more than a little surprised at this almost comical display. A simple "thank you" would have sufficed. Besides which, from the pleased, although somewhat embarrassed expression on Gladys' face, Ruth wondered just exactly who *was* receiving the glory. Gladys quickly regained her composure by resuming her repertoire of stories, but for Ruth this had become background noise. She was more concerned with her own thoughts on this matter at hand.

She had heard the pastor solemnly preach on many occasions that God was to receive all glory for all things for "without him we could do nothing"; we were but "worms whose righteousness was as filthy rags." But it seemed strange that one was not able to accept even simple praise for the obvious God-given talents within us. Surely God was not opposed to this, as long as we humbly recognised the source of our talent? Yet the pastor was adamant we must *never* take praise unto ourselves under any circumstance, lest God be angered. This seemed to give such a confusing picture to her of the God she thought she knew. However, even as she considered these things, Ruth felt a wave of guilt flood over her. She was questioning the church's doctrine again, perhaps even God, just as the pastor had said she was inclined to do. Feeling perturbed with her inability to submissively obey without question, she resolved within herself to better her performance.

Stooping to pick up a flower that had fallen to the ground, Ruth was suddenly aware that Gladys had stopped what she was doing and was staring at her intently, waiting for a reply to a question she had obviously just asked. Ruth shook her head.

She had been so tied up in her own thoughts she had not heard her.

"I'm sorry, Gladys, what did you say?" she said apologetically.

"I *said*," Gladys emphasised impatiently, "*how* are your daughter and husband?"

Gladys was silent now for the first time that morning and by the full attention she was giving Ruth seemed determined not to move until she had gained the gossip she so obviously knew was in the offing. Ruth was a little shocked. How could this be? She had only spoken to Pastor Whitfield yesterday afternoon about her family and only in the strictest of confidence. She had not shared this information with anyone else. The pastor had assured her he would help in their situation but she had heard no more. No, she must be imagining things. Gladys could not possibly know her problems. Perhaps she was merely asking after her family out of politeness.

"They're fine," she opted to reply, a little unconvincingly.

But by the strange look that crossed Gladys' face Ruth knew there was more to her questioning. Gladys knew something!

⚜

Arriving their usual thirty minutes before the Sunday morning service, Leonard and Marjory warmly greeted friends and fellow members of The Light as they made their way through the foyer and up to the main auditorium doors. With Leonard in his dark, three-piece suit and Marjory in her new blue-feathered hat and matching dress they looked a striking couple, despite their age.

"Hello, Marjory," Sister Smith gushed, grasping both her hands. "My, you look lovely today in that colour. Is that a new hat?"

"Good morning, Helen, how are you...yes, it is new, thank

you. Tell me, will you be joining us this week for the retirement home visits? We could really do with your help."

"Oh, no…I don't think I can make it, Marjory. I've been asked to help serve afternoon tea at the McLachlan's house-warming party. Were you not invited, my dear?"

Leonard waited patiently as Marjory chatted, stepping back slightly to observe the people surrounding him. To the casual observer it would seem all was as it should be on this busy Sunday morning as everyone arrived for the meeting, but to Leonard's trained eye he noted that a chosen array of couples had been strategically placed around the foyer to "meet and greet" all who entered. This was a rostered duty under the supervision of Brother Henry, who stood ready to prod and pressure those chosen for the task, if all was not performed to standard. Leonard chuckled despite himself. *Woe betide a newcomer*, he mused. For Brother Henry would have one of his minions pounce on them as soon as they entered, having them signed and committed as members before they knew what had struck them. Interesting, he reflected, how easy it was to get in to this church, but not so easy to get out. Glancing at his watch he gently tapped Marjory on the shoulder then guided her by the elbow in the direction of the main doors. It was time to settle for the service.

In contrast to the hustle and bustle of the foyer from which they had just come, an eerie silence greeted them as they walked into the main auditorium; apart from the dreary sound of the organ playing no one breathed a word. Everybody understood that idle chatter and needless movement were frowned upon in the sanctuary, and Leonard often felt confused as to whether he had come to a funeral service or Communion. Reverential stillness in a church was one thing but this was different. A high expectation of perfection had been placed on the people to the point of control. The fear that governed this total performance was so strong that all eyes stared rigidly to the front without any movement, lest they receive a reprimand or be shamed amongst the members and therefore God. For this was *his* house and one must be utterly silent before *his* authority and omnipotence, doing only what was directed by the leadership.

Before taking his seat on the padded pews, Leonard observed that two of the church "heavies" had been positioned at the rear of the auditorium. He knew from the elders' meeting he had attended earlier that week that they were there to keep an eye on Jeff Rawlings. Jeff, of late, had developed the tendency to raise his hands in worship, unprompted by the song leader— and the church ruled that hands could only be raised when, and only when, the song leader indicated. If Jeff refused to abide by these rules this morning, he would be physically removed from the meeting. Leonard sighed. Did it really have to be this way?

The service was soon underway, and three hymns and a collection later Leonard settled down for the morning message. He longed for some good, solid spiritual food and wondered what they would hear today. Pastor Whitfield could barely be seen from his high pulpit, but the sound system was the latest and his voice could be heard clearly throughout the auditorium.

"Our reading this morning will be taken from Romans 16:17– 19," he announced dryly.

The rustle of leaves filled the building as everyone turned obediently to the scripture indicated. Leonard thumbed through the pages of his slightly yellowed Bible, well worn from years of faithful use, and soon lighted upon the portion to be read. Scanning the page he quickly recognised the passage and groaned in his spirit. Not again!

"Now I beseech you, brethren, mark them which cause divisions and offences contrary to the doctrine which ye have learned; and avoid them." The pastor paused and looked around the congregation for effect before continuing. "For they that are such serve not our Lord Jesus Christ but their own belly and by good words and fair speeches deceive the hearts of the simple" (Romans 16:17–19, KJV). He closed his Bible dramatically and peered down at the people, pausing for some time.

"For many years now you have been privileged to receive

excellent doctrine and teaching here at this church. Men, like myself, have given of their time and effort to dig deep into the scriptures and present to you the truth of the word of God. The very name of this church is The Light, given because we *have* the light—divine revelation and illumination that no other church has. I tell you, we *alone* hold the whole truth which is presented to you faithfully each week. This is the doctrine which you have heard and learned, and by which we run this church. Yet there are those amongst us who would talk contrary to this doctrine! Recently a well-known Brother and Sister left our midst after having been with us for many years. They sat under our ministry and we looked after them in the Lord. Their children went to our camps and Youth Clubs and even taught in our Sunday school. Yet they questioned our doctrine, our divine revelation, and left us for another fellowship. I tell you they are taking second best. They are in danger of backsliding and will end up in hell! They are like rats who have abandoned the ship; like weeds that have been pulled up out of God's garden. Unfortunately when weeds are pulled up they disturb some of the good planting and so for many this has been an unsettling time. For just before they left they started asking questions and undermining this church. They were reported as going to this one and to that saying: 'What do *you* think?'; 'Does this church *really* have the whole truth?'; 'Are all these rules *really* of God?' I tell you they are what the Bible calls 'division makers'! But there are those amongst you who are saying, 'They were our friends, we have known them for so long—what do we do if we see them?' I say to you that because they are division makers you must *avoid* them. Have *no* fellowship with them. Do not have them home for coffee because they will poison your minds, and soon you will find yourselves asking if what they say is right. Others are saying, 'But they look so happy and content.' I tell you it is because God's conviction has lifted from them. They are happy because they are no longer conscious of sin and can do as they please. I hear of this church and that church doing such wonderful things. But I tell you they lack *discipline*. They may hug each other and jump around in praise and worship, but all manner of deception and the flesh is at work. I say again…we are the *only* ones with the truth. Have no fellowship with any other church, or with *any* who have left our midst!"

Leonard began to stir in his seat. He was uncomfortable with this interpretation of Scripture and with the manner in which people who had left the church were being treated. Marjory and he had never had children, but how awkward and painful it must be to have a family member leave and to be faced with the possibility of never fellowshipping with them again—as was often the case.

As though to confirm his thoughts a muffled sniffling sound could suddenly be heard from farther along his row and glancing sideways Leonard saw that it was Sally Lawson. Tears were running down her checks, although she was doing her best to conceal them, and Leonard searched his thoughts as to their meaning. Reading his mind Marjory hastily scribbled a note and discreetly pushed it into his hands. Of course—Sally's mother had recently left the church to join another and here she was being told from the pulpit to have nothing more to do with her. Leonard watched as Marjory kindly passed a pack of tissues along to Sally. It all seemed so harsh, so unnecessary.

He glanced at his watch. Talking of harsh and unnecessary, he reflected that he, too, had an unpleasant task to perform after the meeting—one he would not take pleasure in, nor, yet again, agreed with. By now he knew that Ruth Henderson would have received a note that told her to meet the pastor and himself in the church office at 1:00 p.m. They were to sort out her daughter Emily's problems. Leonard felt uneasy as he recalled yesterday's phone call and he could not bring himself to look up at the pastor as his sermon droned on and on. He wondered if Ruth had any idea of what was about to happen.

# THE ROD OF IRON

It was five o'clock in the evening before Emily finally saw her mother's red Ford station wagon pull into the driveway. She'd been waiting at her friend's house all afternoon while her mother had been to some meeting or other at the church and, Emily thought to herself, *She sure had taken her time.*

Waving goodbye to her friend, Joanne, Emily climbed into the car and threw her bag and a magazine onto the back seat. "What took you so long?" she chided as she turned to look at her mother.

Ruth started the car and pulled out onto the road to make the short journey home. It had been a harrowing afternoon; spent mainly waiting alone in the church reception, as Pastor Whitfield and several elders had sorted out the "details" of his proposed help to her family. She now looked pale and anxious, and her hands were trembling slightly. Emily noticed that the makeup on her cheeks was patchy and stained, and she suspected she'd been crying.

"Mum, are you okay?" she asked in surprise. "What's the matter—where have you been?" She knew her mother and her had been arguing a lot lately, but didn't all teenagers? She still deeply loved her family and wouldn't want to see them come to any harm.

Ruth took a deep breath, desperate to keep the truth from her, longing for all to be normal again. "How did your afternoon go at your friend's place?" she asked bravely, trying to keep her voice cheery and calm.

But Emily would have none of it. Her mother was obviously upset and she wanted to know why. "Mum, what's wrong? Why have you been crying?" she persisted. "Is it Dad? Has he hurt you?"

Feeling her daughter's concern, Ruth struggled to contain her already fraught emotions. "No," Ruth's voice began to tremble. "No, that's not it."

"Then what?" Emily pressed, feeling alarmed. She had never seen her mother like this before and it worried her. "Tell me what has happened!" she insisted.

Ruth knew that the road ahead would soon split into two and that the street on the left would lead to their home—but she could not bring herself to turn. Whether she liked it or not she knew she would have to give an explanation to her daughter first. For at this very moment two elders waited at their house at the direction of Pastor Whitfield, and Ruth felt her stomach turn as to the reason why. How could she do this? Her daughter meant everything in the world to her and she would never do anything to harm her. How had this situation become so complicated? Surely other families had their moments of turmoil and questioning too. Why did it feel as though hers was the only one being dealt with so harshly? Maybe it was because she was such a weak and sinful Christian, as the pastor had suggested. She had failed in her marriage and as a mother and this was all her fault. Overwhelmed, she pulled into a small public car park and brought the car to a stop. The emotions she had been suppressing all afternoon finally overflowed and she broke down into tears. How had her life come to this?

Emily put her arms around her mother's shoulders and waited patiently as she wept. Her mind was spinning as to the cause of such distress and she, too, felt sick in her stomach. Eventually, Ruth reached for a tissue and sitting upright, attempted to compose herself. Whatever happened, she must try and support the church and the leadership, no matter what her personal thoughts were. She must not allow her "rebellious spirit" to influence her daughter. Turning to Emily she feebly tried to explain.

"Your father's drinking problems have been getting worse," she started hesitantly. "He's been coming home later and later each night, quite often in an aggressive mood and I never know what he's going to do." Ruth reached for another tissue. "He threatened me with a knife last week. He didn't hurt me and I know he doesn't mean it, it's the alcohol speaking—but at times he can be quite frightening. Not only that, but he's been using all the housekeeping money for his drink and the bills have been mounting up. I...I've tried to keep a lot of this from you, but it's really been worrying me."

Emily waited as Ruth wiped away more tears. She'd suspected all was not well with her dad and she was angry at his actions, but she felt there was more to it. She was sure it was not only her father's problems that were causing all this grief. "Go on," she coaxed gently.

"Well...lately you and I have been arguing a lot—then there was the dispute last week over why you couldn't go to the school party . . ."

"Mum . . ." Emily protested.

"...and you know you've been questioning the church rules," Ruth persisted. She looked at her daughter's perplexed face and hesitated for a moment, conscious of her own guilt; was she not also questioning the church's ways? Ruth bowed her head and continued. "The truth is, Emily, I just couldn't cope any more—not with all the added stress and worry of your father. So...I decided to go to the leadership at church to ask for their help and advice. They promised they would help...and in fact, they've been sorting something out this very afternoon. That's where I've been."

"Wait—you went to the church about me and Dad?" Emily wanted to make sure she'd heard right. This couldn't be good. "So what did they say?"

Ruth dropped her eyes, unable to look at her daughter. "When I told them about our arguing and about your dad's drinking—well...they...they only want what is best—they would only do what they think would be most beneficial for us as a family and . . ." she stalled.

"Mum!" Emily interrupted. "What did they say?" Emily felt panic rising within her. What advice could they possibly have given her mother to make her react the way she had?

The tears began to flow again down Ruth's cheeks as she forced herself to continue. "They think we are unfit parents to take care of you...they say we are not disciplining you enough and they think your apparent rebelliousness needs to be dealt with." She paused for a moment, looking despairingly at her daughter. "They want to remove you from our home this evening—and place you with another family in the church, where they feel you will get better care...and they are refusing to allow your father and I to have access to you."

"Mum! You're not serious, are you?" Emily said in alarm, not wanting to believe what her mother had just uttered. "But...I don't want to live with anybody else. And what do you mean you can't see me anymore? This just isn't fair!"

"If we don't do as they say we could be excommunicated... and we'll all end up in hell!" Ruth's voice broke and burying her head in her arms, she sobbed uncontrollably.

Emily sat in stunned silence and disbelief as her mother's words slowly sunk in. *Could this be happening?* What had she done that had warranted such severe action? She felt confused and afraid; afraid that because she had dared to question, to argue, to show any sign of healthy independence, she had now lost her family and would be placed with complete strangers. Emily stared out of her window as anger began to rise within her. But what could she do? The church was her whole life, all she had ever known, and everyone she knew was a part of it. She could not risk excommunication. Besides, apart from her dad, she had no relatives outside of the church that she could run to and she was too young to live on her own. She was cornered. At fifteen years old she suddenly felt weighed down and controlled by the same church system she previously trusted. She felt disturbed that her mother had agreed to this course of action, especially without consulting Dad, but then her mum was just like her—this church had become all she knew, and how could she fight it? To disobey would mean their souls were in danger of hell, and her mum would do anything to avoid that! No—instinctively Emily knew she had no choice but to do as she was told. She hung her head in angry defeat as they slowly drove home in silence.

Elders Leonard McKenzie and Bob Everitt were waiting outside their house when they pulled into the driveway a few moments later. Leonard looked awkward and apologetic as he saw Ruth's tearstained face, but Bob seemed positively militant and impatient to get the job done. He glanced pointedly at his watch.

"They took their time. I haven't eaten yet, and the evening meeting starts in just under an hour," he mumbled to Leonard. But Leonard showed no sympathy.

"I think there are more important issues at hand here than your stomach, Bob," he whispered harshly.

Without saying a word to anyone, Emily climbed out of the car and went straight to her room, closing the door. She re-appeared a few moments later, quietly defiant but with rucksack in hand, and as Bob Everitt held the door of the black saloon open for her, she slumped into its back seat with head still bowed. Emily had been unable to look at her mother, much less embrace her, although she could hear her sniffling as she had walked past to the car. The fact was she had too much to process in her mind and hoped her mum would understand. Ruth felt the tears swell to her eyes again as she watched her daughter's defiant yet downcast manner. What had she done?

Seeing Ruth's distress, Leonard placed his hand tenderly on

her shoulder. "We'll look after her—I'm sure she'll be okay. Just give her some time," he said kindly, feeling her pain.

Bob Everitt, however, was not so sensitive. "We will let you know what family she has gone to in due course," he said gruffly. "Our instructions are that you are not to try and contact your daughter until further advised."

Leonard pulled him firmly by the elbow and drew him aside. "Is this really necessary, Bob?" he rebuked in a harsh whisper. Turning to Ruth he said reassuringly, "We'll be in touch. You take care now."

Ruth stood in the middle of their quiet little street and waved until the car had disappeared out of sight, although her daughter still did not respond. She felt heartbroken and dejected and ached deep within. Perhaps she should have done something—anything—to stop them from taking her away. But what could she do? An overriding fear had gripped her this whole day and had clouded her rational thinking. She could not fight against this system. She was terrified of going to hell and must do as the leadership bade her. Besides, she had obviously not been submissive enough or sufficiently obedient to have pleased her God, and this was surely her punishment. God had entrusted Emily into her hands and she had failed. Now he had taken her away. She had lost her daughter and was powerless to do anything about it, and it was all her own fault. For a fleeting moment she wondered if she should alert Social Services, or even the police, but just as quickly she pushed these thoughts away. This was yet another sign of her struggling against the church rules and that must be resisted. For the Bible clearly taught that all church matters should be dealt with by the leaders of the church alone and not by outsiders. Ruth sighed at the realisation of her pitiful lack of faith.

The evening was now fast approaching and, shivering, Ruth pulled her hand-knitted cardigan closer to her body. She dragged herself wearily back into the house and without turning on the lights fell to her knees in prayer, alone and discouraged. She had always believed the church and God were one, and she had trusted the leadership to act in a Godly manner. This had been their decision so it must be God's will, and therefore she must be obedient. She just couldn't understand why she felt so afraid; why it felt as though the heavens were made of brass; why God seemed so far away and uncaring.

But even as she knelt in the shadows of the darkened house grieving over the day's events, another thought was deeply troubling her. Her husband, Jack. He had left that morning on a business trip and would be gone for two weeks. But...how would she explain to her unbelieving husband that the church had taken away their daughter?

The flat was like an icebox when Zara returned home that Sunday evening, and throwing down her keys and coat, she quickly set about lighting the wood burner in the small lounge until its comforting heat began to radiate throughout the room. She had left Kate back at the church with Dan, bundled up in coat, scarf, and gloves and huddled on the steps of the car park—albeit at a respectable distance from each other, as Sunday evening was one of the few precious moments they had together. Zara did not envy them being out on such a cold night, but she knew they had little choice and once again she marvelled at the harshness of the church rules. Pouring herself a cup of hot coffee and placing it on the side table, she slipped her feet into a pair of soft sheepskin slippers and collapsed onto the sofa, revelling in the warmth of the fire.

It had been a long day: three services, two prayer meetings, and teaching Sunday school to a class full of lively four-year-olds who had the uncanny ability of spreading glue and paint from one end of the room to the other. Considering Sunday was to be a day of rest she felt completely exhausted, and sighing, she picked up a bridal magazine from a pile on the coffee table, randomly flicking through its pages with seeming disinterest. She and Kate had spent most of yesterday afternoon poring over these pictures, choosing outfits and flowers for the coming big day, while also planning for the up and coming engagement party in a few weeks time. They had diligently composed a list of the names of friends and family they would like to attend the party, and Kate had dutifully handed this list to a senior elder that very morning—as no gathering, large or small, could take place without first gaining the approval of Pastor Whitfield. He would examine the list and eventually get back to them, although Zara could think of no reason why he should disapprove and she had reassured Kate of this very fact, Kate being more than a little anxious about the whole ordeal.

Zara threw down the magazine and stared into the flickering flames of the fire, their reflections dancing on her face. She had always imagined a wedding to be a joyful occasion with great excitement and anticipation as the planning and preparations were made. But this was not the case with Kate, who instead seemed tense and worried as she desperately sought to avoid trouble, dutifully doing everything in her power to be obedient to the church rules. Anxiety was overshadowing her joy, and Zara suspected she knew the reason why.

Her eyes turned toward a silver photo frame sitting on the side cabinet in which sat a photo of Kate, herself, and their old flatmate—Bethany. They were arm and arm beside a lake, laughing in the sunshine of a bright summer's day, the sun catching the water behind them like diamonds spread over deep blue velvet. Zara reached up and, taking the frame, removed the photo from its holder, turning it over to read the inscription scribbled hastily on the back. It simply read:

Friends forever!
With all my love,
Bethany

Zara stared at the words, deep in thought. It had been two years ago that she had first met Bethany, although such had been their friendship, it seemed as if she had known her all her life. When Zara had first joined the church as a new Christian she had been placed together in this very flat with Kate and Bethany—"two sensible girls that could support and help her make a new start," she had been informed. During that first year she had quickly become best of friends with both of them and they had shared much laughter and happy times together.

But Bethany had a secret. Slightly older than Zara, she had already started work and had fallen in love with a colleague there—a Christian man—but from a Pentecostal church on the edge of town. As fellowshipping with anyone from outside the church of The Light was strictly forbidden, especially from *another* church, Zara and Kate had faithfully kept her secret, knowing that she would be in extreme trouble if it were ever to be exposed, especially as both her mother and father were church counsellors and expected to honour the ethos of the church. However, it was a year ago now that Beth's secret was discovered as she has been seen talking and laughing together with Tim outside their work place. One thing had led to another and soon the church leadership had forced her to make a decision. Either she was to cut off all association with this man, or be excommunicated from the church. Zara recalled the many painful nights that Beth had sat on her bed agonising over what she should do, knowing full well she was in danger of losing her family, her friends and even a place to live. But she was in love with Tim and, together with her strong sense of this being God's will, she made her decision. Under the watchful eye of two lemon-faced women sent from the church to supervise, she had packed all of her belongings and, tearfully hugging Kate and Zara, had said goodbye. They had not seen nor heard from her since—except for one solitary piece of mail.

Placing the photo down beside her, Zara stirred herself and walked across the room to an old writing desk where she pulled open a small drawer and carefully removed an intricately designed and delicate envelope. Gently lifting the flap, she withdrew its contents—an exquisite invitation to Beth and Tim's wedding; a wedding at which Zara and Kate should have been bridesmaids, but which both had been forbidden to attend. As Zara held the invitation in her hands she knew that this was the cause of Kate's anxiety. Kate feared Bethany's story would be her own if she failed to follow the rules explicitly and it was robbing her of her joy.

Zara returned to the sofa and once again picked up the photo, gazing longingly at the happy faces that stared back at her. The truth was she missed Bethany and longed to see her again. But how could she? Her thoughts reflected back to the pastor's words at the service that morning and something ached deep within her. *Avoid those who cause division and have no fellowship with them…for conviction has lifted…and they are on their way to hell.* Tears unexpectedly swelled to Zara's eyes and spilled over, trickling slowly down her cheeks. Was it really true her dear friend was doomed to eternal damnation for leaving The Light, and would Zara really never be able to see Beth again for fear of being poisoned by her new, yet supposedly false, doctrine? This did not seem possible, besides which, Beth did not seem the type of person who would want to persuade her friends toward anything harmful, unless of course as the pastor said, she was in deception.

Tired and confused, Zara rested her head on the arm of the sofa, watching the flames flickering before her, her eyelids growing heavy. Why was the Christian life so complicated with so many rules? But even before she could answer her own questions, the photo slipped slowly from her fingers and fell onto the floor as she drifted into a troubled sleep.

# Confused Loyalties

A heavy fog had descended over the town, cloaking the already darkened neighbourhood in a veil of white mist. Conscious of the hour, Leonard slowly made his way home through the winding streets, his progress restricted by the inclement weather. Guests were coming to their house for dinner that night, and Marjory had sent him out to the shops to fetch a few last-minute items such as cream and chocolates and a little something to drink with their meal. Leonard was rather partial to a glass of red wine with his dinner, but since any type of alcoholic beverage was frowned upon by the church of The Light, he and his guests would have to content themselves with the sparkling grape juice he'd bought, and of course, copious cups of coffee, which would go well with the Belgian truffles he'd discovered at the store.

Rounding a corner Leonard noticed a signpost that had come into view, pointing through the mist toward Maple Drive. Maple Drive was the street on which Ruth Henderson lived and Leonard shuddered involuntarily as he was reminded of the Sunday evening several weeks ago now when he had had the unenviable task of escorting Emily to her newly designated family. He could still see the pain on Ruth's face and the bewildered confusion on Emily's as they took her away, and he felt troubled and uneasy in his spirit. The phone call he had to make to Ruth several days later at the request of the pastor was awkward and unpleasant as Leonard had explained to Ruth where her daughter had gone and what the rules of this new arrangement were—simply that she could neither see nor talk to her daughter, nor could Emily contact her, least the disciplinary procedure be undermined. He groaned at such harshness and wondered if this was all really necessary—or indeed legal.

Leonard now turned into his driveway then, pulling his coat firmly around him and with groceries in hand, he headed wearily up the path toward the back door. In stark contrast to the icy night air outside, a blanket of warmth enveloped him as he stepped inside the cosy kitchen, and he was immediately greeted by the wonderful aroma of roast chicken and apple pie. Peering through into the dining room he saw that the table was laid in white linen with silver and crystal, and was adorned with bowls of delicate pink roses and softly glowing candles. Familiar, friendly voices talked and laughed in the sitting room and, as Leonard paused to listen for a moment, he felt cheered in his heart. Maybe this evening would be just what the doctor ordered.

"Leonard, honey, is that you?" Marjory's voice called brightly from the lounge. "Come and warm yourself by the fire. You must be freezing."

"I'll be right with you."

Leonard dutifully hung his coat and scarf up on the small wooden pegs beside the kitchen door and, replacing his boots with indoor shoes, joined Marjory and their guests in the front room.

"Yvonne. Paul. How are you both? Great to see you," he greeted warmly, shaking Paul's hand and kissing Yvonne softly on the cheek. "Sorry I was delayed. The fog is something else tonight, isn't it?" He sat down on the sofa next to Marjory, gently placing his arm around her shoulder. "You're both looking well."

"Thanks, Len," Paul smiled, seating himself back beside his wife again. "You're not looking too bad yourself."

Paul and Yvonne Pritchard were longstanding members of

the church of The Light and had been good friends of Leonard and Marjory's for many years now; although lately, due to one commitment or another, they had seen little of each other.

Yvonne looked across to the dining room admiringly. "Marjory, the table is looking lovely. Did you arrange the table centre yourself? The roses are divine," she gushed.

"Yes, our Marjory is a clever lady—and wait till you taste the apple pie. A new recipe, which I had the privilege of sampling earlier," Leonard winked.

Paul chuckled. "Yes, we know all about your sampling, Len. Still going on that diet then, are we?"

"Maybe I'll start tomorrow, eh, after dessert and chocolates. Anyway, tell me, Paul, how is the banking world these days? Any new investment opportunities I should know about?"

Marjory and Yvonne looked at each other across the room with raised eyebrows. If the men were talking business, this was their cue to excuse themselves.

"Would anyone like a cup of tea before dinner?" Marjory asked graciously, rising to her feet.

"That sounds wonderful, Marj. I'll give you a hand," Yvonne grinned, following her out to the kitchen.

As the two men settled into conversation about finances and world affairs, Yvonne and Marjory set about making the tea.

"It seems so long since we last had a good chat, Yvonne," Marjory sighed. "I really must phone you more often. So, tell me, what have you been up to lately?" Marjory stood waiting for the kettle to boil; her white curly hair complimented perfectly by her soft pink cashmere sweater and dove grey trousers.

"I know. The days seem to fly by, don't they? I've been busy being nanny to the grandchildren mostly," Yvonne replied, as she set out cups and saucers and reached for the sugar bowl. She too looked elegant in a floral blouse and pencil skirt with her greying hair swept up and pinned in a neat bun. "My daughter has been so tired with the new baby that I offered to have her older two children stay with us for a while. They were very good, bless them, but my goodness I'm exhausted. I really must be getting old."

Marjory smiled. "You're a wonderful grandmother! I'm sure you spoiled them rotten." She turned the kettle off and poured hot water into the china tea pot. "What about your son's boy, Rhys? He must be…eighteen? Do you see much of him these days?" she inquired.

At the mention of his name Yvonne paused, a fleeting look of pain and uncertainty crossing her face. Glancing at Marjory, she turned slowly and sat on a nearby stool, as though the weight of the world were on her shoulders.

"Yvonne, what is it?" Marjory asked with concern. "Is something wrong?" She, too, pulled out a stool and sat close to her friend, looking earnestly into her eyes.

After a few moments hesitation, Yvonne spoke. "Marj—you've been a good friend, and I know there are certain things about the church that we just don't talk about but…well…can I share something with you?"

Marjory placed a hand on her arm and coaxed her to go on. "You know you can talk to me about anything."

Yvonne sighed. "It's about Rhys. Yes—he is eighteen—and he's told his mum and dad that he's not going back to the church. About two weeks ago he packed his bags and moved out of their house into a flat with some friends from college. I hear they've been drinking and partying . . ." Yvonne stopped as her voice began to tremble, but quickly composing herself she went on. "Anyway, last weekend Elders Everitt and Henry arrived on my son, John's, doorstep, sent by Pastor Whitfield. It seems rumours of Rhys' behaviour had reached him—I've no idea how. They were demanding if these stories were true. John told them what had been happening, expecting their support and sympathy, but instead . . ." Yvonne's voice choked again and tears swelled to her eyes. "Do you know what they said?"

Marjory could guess. With Leonard as an elder, she was growing accustomed to the dealings of the church, but she tried to hide her contempt as she encouraged Yvonne to go on.

"Marj—they threatened John! They said that God's protective hand would be lifted off Rhys if he did not return to the church. And then they said his life would be in danger! They told him story after story of other teenagers who had left The Light and the horrible accidents or diseases that had befallen them. Do you remember the Carpenters' daughter who died of cancer last year? They said this was because she had left the fellowship. And Joe Bentley's son? Remember he died in an accident at work? Well, he too had left, and they said this was God's punishment!" Yvonne wiped a tear from her eye, anger rising in her voice. "When you think of all the pain those dear parents must have suffered at losing their children, and then being told it was because God was no longer protecting them—well...I know I shouldn't be questioning the leadership...but...it just can't be right, can it?"

Marjory put her arm around her friend's shoulder in an effort to comfort her, but what could she say? Inwardly she was struggling with her own anger and frustration. She was only thankful that this time the pastor had not called on Leonard to visit Yvonne's son, for how could she have faced her friend if this had been so? It was bad enough that Leonard had been made to deal with Ruth's daughter in the manner in which he had, causing the Hendersons so much pain. Marjory noted with cynical interest how the church had acted differently in both these cases. Emily was only fifteen and still able to be controlled, whereas Rhys was eighteen and the church could do nothing more than threaten his parents, attempting to control both he and his family by the use of fear. Why was it that the church needed to wield so much power? How could Pastor Whitfield be so seemingly callous and uncaring all in the name of God and for the sake of discipline...or perhaps more accurately, for the sake of control!

"Come on, Yvonne." Marjory stood to her feet in an effort to change the subject. "Let's take this tea tray into the lounge and then I'll serve dinner. I've got a humorous story to tell you about my recent visit to the old folk's home, and I think we could all do with a good laugh."

But as Marjory followed Yvonne into the sitting room she felt far from cheerful, and quietly she prayed that the negative words being spoken over their young people would have no effect. She prayed that Yvonne would be at peace and that Rhys would be kept safe—but deep in her heart she had a horrible sense of foreboding.

＊

When Zara entered the mall during her lunch break on Wednesday afternoon everything seemed exactly as it always had been. Relaxing music floated on the air, lulling shoppers into a sense of well being; a maze of escalators purred softly, while gently gliding toward multi-levels of shops; wonderful window displays showed enticing arrays of goods and wares; not to mention the majestic sky-lighted windows that stretched far above in a cathedral-like dome, allowing every ray of wintry sunshine to stream through onto the shoppers below. Yet today Zara sensed that something had changed. It had always been such an enjoyable experience visiting the mall, as though she were escaping into another world. But not today. No, it all felt different. *She* felt different. The truth was, it seemed the more time she spent at the church of The Light, the more she felt somehow alienated from the places she had once loved, as though she were now standing on the outside looking in. Perhaps it was because of the constant messages she was hearing of late, backed with strong persuasive quotes from Scripture like, "Although you are *in* the world, you are not *of* the world." "*Come out* from among them and be ye *separate*...touch *not* the unclean thing" (2 Corinthians 6:17, KJV). As a consequence Zara felt a confusing conflict of emotion within her as she stepped onto an escalator and headed toward what was usually her favourite shop. She wanted to enjoy her lunch break shopping but felt instead strangely guilty, somehow wrong for doing so. Maybe this was what her counselor referred to as the "old sinful nature" coveting the pleasures of the world. Zara sighed. Would she ever get it right?

Reaching the fourth floor, she stepped off onto the shiny marble tiles to be greeted by the heady scent of sweet perfumes. However, it was not the perfumery that she had come for, but rather the shop next door from which came the distinct aroma of new leather and boot polish. This was the best boutique in town for designer shoes, boots, and bags. Zara paused to gaze at the tempting window display of the latest shipment from Italy, knowing that her pay check would never stretch to such exorbitant prices. She also knew, however, she could never wear such worldly attire to church. No, plain and sensible would have to suffice today in keeping with being biblically modest, and with the air of one who had overcome temptation Zara headed toward the back of the shop where a more modest selection could be found. Her feeling of triumph disappeared, however, when she saw the dull range before her, and somewhat crestfallen she eyed the other customers enviously as they tried on and purchased the more exquisite boots and shoes.

"Do you have this style in a size six and perhaps in black?" a familiar voice inquired, not far from her.

Zara froze. She would recognise that voice anywhere. Quickly ducking down behind a display of fashionable leather bags, she peered out cautiously to see if her instincts were correct.

The tall, slim brunette was dressed in a smart two-piece trouser suit looking attractive yet professional, and although she had her back to Zara there was no denying who it was. It was her friend Bethany! Zara felt her heart quicken as she crouched down even lower so as not to be seen. What should she do? She knew it was against the church rules to approach Bethany or to engage in conversation, especially as Bethany had been excommunicated and both Kate and Zara had been given explicit instructions not to contact her. But she also knew she could not exit the shop without being seen, and in her heart she longed to speak to her old friend. Peering out curiously again she watched as Bethany tried on a pair of Italian shoes. How well and content she looked. *"Conviction has lifted,"* Pastor Whitfield's words echoed in her mind. *"They appear happy because they are no longer under God's discipline."* Zara shook her head as though to clear her mind, but was suddenly conscious that a woman nearby was looking at her strangely. Quickly she pretended to be tying a stray shoelace. This was ridiculous. What harm could really come from talking to Bethany? Besides, there was no one around from the church to see, and she was sure it would be safe. Standing resolutely to her feet and adjusting her skirt Zara walked quietly up behind her old friend.

"I hope you can afford those shoes," she whispered humorously.

Bethany turned in surprise and stared in wide-eyed delight as she realised who it was. "Zara? Oh my goodness! How are you?" she gasped, standing to her feet.

For the briefest of moments an awkwardness passed between them but stepping quickly forward, Zara placed her arms around Beth. "It's so good to see you…and I believe I should address you as Mrs. Blackman now?" she said, pulling back and lifting Beth's hand to admire her ring.

Bethany smiled as she wiped a tear from her eye; however, a sudden look of apprehension soon spread across her face. "I'm sorry, Zara, but I have to ask you this," she said, glancing around the shop uneasily. "Should you be talking to me? I would understand completely if you can't. I'm so used to being ignored by members of The Light. Won't you get into trouble?"

Zara tried to shrug off the comment. "I couldn't pass without saying hello to a good friend, could I?"

But Bethany placed a hand of warning on Zara's arm. "Please, be careful…I don't want to cause you any problems. It's why I haven't contacted you at all since...well, since I left. I didn't want to place you in a position of compromise. But I want you to know, Zara, that hardly a day has gone by when I haven't thought of both you and Kate."

Zara squeezed her hand. "We think of you too, Beth." Now it was her turn to wipe a tear away. It was so good to see Beth again. She hesitated as a daring thought entered her mind. "Listen—have you had lunch yet? How about we go to that little café on the top floor by the food court and grab something to eat? We've got so much to talk about...and I haven't seen anyone else from the church here this afternoon. Besides, they wouldn't see us amongst the crowds."

Bethany looked unsure, though pleased. "I'd love to...but do you think that's wise? Like I said, I don't want to cause any trouble."

"If no one sees us, they'll be none the wiser. Come on!"

Cautiously making their way through the crowds while constantly looking around them for signs of being spotted, the two girls located a secluded table at the café on the top floor, sitting strategically where all comings and goings could be easily surveyed. To their knowledge they had not been seen by anyone from The Light and after ordering a coffee and light lunch, they both began to visibly relax. They had much to catch up on and earnestly chatted back and forth, at times bursting into laughter. It felt just like old times. How hard it was to imagine that, as the pastor often preached, Beth might be devising in some way to poison Zara's mind by speaking against the church, even though she had every right to. Bethany had been through so much and must still be feeling the pain. Yet to her credit she said nothing, choosing instead to talk about married life, her job, and family.

"Are you still at Tim's church, Bethany?" Zara enquired. "What was it called...Grace Chapel?"

"Yes, we're still there and we're loving it." Beth's face lit up with delight at Zara's genuine interest. "It's just a small church—probably only about one hundred members, but they are so friendly and supportive and the teaching is great. We're both home group leaders now and hold meetings in our house each Wednesday. We've got one tonight in fact. We usually have about ten regulars attending, but it's a lot of fun."

The concept of home group was an unknown to Zara, as at The Light any group meeting within the home was forbidden. Seeing the blank look on Zara's face, Bethany nodded in understanding. She hesitated for a moment, then reaching into her bag pulled out two leaflets.

"Look, Zara. I know this is perhaps a bit bold...but I feel really strongly that I should give these to you. As I've said before, the last thing I want to do is to cause any trouble, but you might be interested in seeing what they have to say. I was going to lend them to a friend this afternoon, but then I didn't know I would be seeing you...I know she would understand." She pushed the leaflets across the table toward Zara.

Puzzled, Zara picked them up and silently read the titles: *"Spiritual Abuse"*...*"Recognising Religious Cults."* She looked up at Beth, confused.

"Listen, I don't mean to alarm you or cause *division* or anything," Beth continued. "I just want you to be informed and... well, careful. Believe me; I've given these pamphlets a lot of thought myself."

Zara tensed, feeling slightly uncomfortable. Could it be true? Had Bethany's mind really been indoctrinated by her new Pentecostal church so that she believed a lie? She had heard Pastor Whitfield say before that many of the charismatic churches in the area were jealous of the truth and enlightenment enjoyed at The Light and that persecution could be expected. Maybe he was right. Maybe *this* was the poison he spoke of, or the way division makers worked. A slight panic began to surface in her mind as she contemplated the situation. But pulling herself together, Zara pushed the thoughts away. Surely Beth was just showing concern as a friend, and it wasn't as though Zara didn't have her own secret doubts about The Light. Besides, the whole time they had been talking Zara had been closely observing Beth. She had been so calm and peaceful, and full of joy. There was definitely something different about her. She talked more freely about God and her relationship with him as though they were really close and intimate. She talked of healings and miracles and Zara couldn't help but feel...envious. No, although the suggestion that The Light could be involved in abusive or cultish practises was unthinkable, Zara *would* read the leaflets. She could at least do that for her friend.

"Okay, I'll see what I think," she simply replied.

Sensing her confusion, Bethany placed her hand on Zara's arm. "I'm sorry...I'd better not say any more. But if you ever want someone to talk to, my phone number is on the front of the pamphlet." She rose from the table. "I must get back to work. It has been lovely seeing you, Zara. Give my love to Kate, won't you?" She leaned over and hugged Zara tightly one last time. "I've really missed you," she whispered, choking back the tears. Then gathering her things, she quickly turned and disappeared down the stairs.

Zara sat for a moment, a mixture of emotions and thoughts racing through her mind. She felt an ache in her heart as she watched her friend disappear into the distance and wondered if she would ever see her again. But there was no time to dwell on her feelings. For, glancing at her watch, she realised her lunch break was almost up and, if she didn't hurry, she too would be late for work. Quickly composing herself, she slipped the pamphlets into her bag, then arose and headed for the escalators.

In a small florist shop adjacent to the food court and partly hidden from the café, a familiar face slowly appeared from behind a large display of yellow chrysanthemums. Unbeknown to the girls, two beady eyes had been watching them for some time with a look of superior self-righteousness, and the smile was of one who had cunningly discovered a great secret.

"Just wait until the church hears about this!" muttered Gladys Jones triumphantly.

# COSTLY SUBMISSION

Anxiously polishing the coffee table until it shone, Ruth placed a vase of red carnations in its centre, then stood back to survey the effect. She had been working feverishly all day in order that the house be perfect; her husband was due to arrive home any minute now from his two-week business trip, and she wanted everything to be just right. A leg of lamb was roasting in the oven, its pleasant aroma filling the house, and a freshly baked chocolate cake sat on the kitchen bench, waiting to be iced. Perhaps, if the atmosphere in the home was relaxed and welcoming enough, her husband would be in a lighter mood and might receive the news that Ruth must deliver to him tonight a little easier—at least she desperately hoped so. Jack had long been anti the church of The Light and its methods, protesting many times that it had come between him and Ruth and was ruining their marriage. He refused to go with her to any of the meetings and had only reluctantly gone along with its influence on his family to please Ruth, knowing how much it meant to her. He had been tolerant to a point, but how would he react to the news that the church had now removed his daughter from their home and placed her in the care of complete strangers? Ruth felt sick in her stomach as she nervously checked her hair and makeup in the mirror, contemplating his reaction. But she was determined her performance tonight would be pleasing to both God and Pastor Whitfield, and in preparation she had been reading and memorizing the many scriptures on submission and obedience. No matter what happened or how Jack reacted, she would submit herself to her husband as these scriptures commanded. Even if his reaction turned violent she would turn the other cheek and take it, for this is what The Light preached and she was determined to win back the approval of both the church and her God. Perhaps this way she could even earn back her daughter. Ruth sighed. She knew her husband loved her and would never willingly mistreat her, but his intolerance of the church had grown deep over the years, causing much bitterness and anger.

A taxi pulled up outside the house and Ruth could hear the mumble of voices as car doors opened and shut. Pulling the curtains gently aside she peered tentatively out of the window and into the night. Yes, it was Jack. She could only pray that he had not been drinking.

"Honey, I'm home!" he joked as he opened the front door and the two embraced. But Ruth stiffened. She smelt alcohol on his breath; not a lot, but she knew from past experience that under its influence his frame of mind could change from one of joking and congeniality to anger and contempt in a minute— something she could do without tonight. She would have to tread carefully. As he unpacked his things, Ruth hurriedly set the table and started to serve the dinner, wondering if he would notice that the table was only set for two. Perhaps he would assume Emily was out with her friends tonight and she could stall her explanation until tomorrow.

"Jack, dear. Dinner is ready," Ruth called, trying to sound calm and cheerful.

Moments later Jack appeared, rubbing his hands together with delight as he spied the cake and smelt the wonderful aroma of roast. He was famished. Before he took his place at the table he gave Ruth a peck of appreciation on the cheek. "So, you've missed me, then?" he chuckled.

Ruth placed several large plates of roast lamb and potatoes with assorted vegetables in the centre of the table. "Help yourself while everything is hot," she smiled. "Would you like gravy as well?"

"Yes, thanks. This looks great. I must say it is good to be home."

Setting a large jug of gravy down, Ruth seated herself at the table waiting patiently while trying to hide her uneasiness. "So how was the trip, Jack?"

Her husband was preoccupied with dishing large helpings of piping hot food onto his plate and did not look up. "Oh, you know—the usual. Budget hotels. Budget meals. I don't think I'll want to eat hamburger and chips again for some time to come. But I've made a few worthwhile contacts and shifted a bit of stock, so the boss will be pleased. Pass the salt, honey, will you?" Jack paused as he salted his food and poured on the gravy. "And what have you been up to while I've been away, Ruth?" he inquired as he passed her the meat. "Wait, don't tell me." He huffed to himself, his tone turning suddenly sarcastic and bitter. "Perhaps I should be asking how many prayer meetings you've been to or how many pews you've cleaned in my absence." Jack glanced up at Ruth almost apologetically, a small pang of guilt shooting through him. She'd gone to so much trouble; he should at least try to make an effort. "Sorry—you know how that place brings out the worst in me. Is that white wine still in the fridge?"

Sensing his agitation, Ruth quickly searched the refrigerator for something cold to drink, passing by the wine and choosing instead the lemonade. She *had* to change the subject.

"Well, actually I've been quite busy myself these past two weeks helping Dorothy next door with re-decorating." Ruth filled a glass with the lemonade and passed it to Jack. "She's wanted to redo her kitchen for about five years now, ever since her husband died, but has never had the money or anyone to help. But, now that she's working part-time and the boys are older, and of course with my assistance, we managed to get it done in just ten days. We've stripped the paint off the walls and cabinets and repainted them in cream. I even helped her sew yellow gingham curtains and cushions for the kitchen chairs. It was a lot of work, but the end result was worth it. It really does look lovely."

"Hmmm," smiled Jack. "I am impressed. Quite a handy woman. Perhaps you could start on our kitchen next."

He continued to eat in silence, deep in thought, as Ruth dished herself a small portion of food. She wasn't feeling hungry.

"Ruth?" Jack suddenly asked, stopping half-way between cutting a piece of lamb. "Dorothy doesn't attend the church of The Light, does she? Isn't it against the church's policy for you to befriend her then?" He stared at the ceiling. "No—wait a minute. That would only apply if she had once been a member and *left* the church, wouldn't it. *Unbelievers* you can mix with as long as there is the chance they might be converted, but *ex-members* you can not mix with as they are traitors and therefore the unforgiven. Correct?" He looked at Ruth cynically.

"Well—it...it's not quite that simple . . ."

"It is from where I'm sitting," he grunted. "Ruth, what are you playing at—this is not white wine, this is lemonade."

Jack rose from the table impatiently and finding the wine poured himself a large glassful. "By the way—where is Emily? Is she staying at Joanne's? I thought she would at least have stayed home tonight to welcome her old dad back, but then I guess I'm not as important to her as her friends these days. It's the school holidays, isn't it? So...what was she doing all the time you were so busy at Dorothy's? Don't tell me she helped too."

Ruth froze, watching him down the complete glass of wine and pour a second. Hastily she got up and grabbed the chocolate cake. "Dessert?" she asked weakly, cutting a generous slice of cake and handing it to him.

Taking the plate, Jack watched Ruth with interest, a puzzled expression on his face. He observed her slightly trembling hands and flustered appearance, and was curious as to their meaning.

"Ruth...is there something you're not telling me?" he asked as he took a dessert spoon. "And once again—*where* is Emily?" He glanced up again at his wife. "Have you given in and let her go to a school party after all? How sinful. What *will* the pastor say?" He placed a large mouthful of cake into his mouth. "I don't see what all the fuss is about," he muttered. "I mean what harm is there in going to a school party anyway." Jack washed his cake down with the remainder of his glass of wine. "Come now, my dear, tell me what's bothering you. I've been married to you for twenty years and I know when something is wrong." Jack leaned back in his chair and waited curiously for his wife to respond.

But Ruth turned her back to Jack pretending to make coffee, her mind in turmoil. Was this a good time to tell him? Her hands began to sweat and her head began to pound. Jack had already consumed two large glassfuls of wine and was beginning to make sarcastic comments about the church, but then that was normal. Otherwise he seemed in a fairly good mood, although that could change. The fact was she knew he would soon retire into the lounge with another bottle of alcoholic beverage and there would be no reasoning with him then. She had to tell him the truth sooner or later and it might as well be now. Drawing a deep breath, she silently prayed for strength and wisdom, then, gathering her courage, she turned again to face her husband.

"You're right, Jack—there is something I need to tell you."

⚘

Ruth's next door neighbour, Dorothy, stood at her kitchen sink up to her elbows in hot, soapy water, tackling the evening's dinner dishes. Her two teenage sons had had to leave the house in a hurry that night in order to catch the movies on time and she was left alone with the task of clearing up. But she didn't mind. She enjoyed working in her kitchen now that it had been freshly painted and decorated and she had her neighbour, Ruth

Henderson, to thank for that. What a pleasant lady she was, and how kind of her to give up so much of her time to help her redecorate while her daughter was away on holiday and her husband was on a business trip. Dorothy peered at the calendar on her wall. Actually, from what Ruth had been saying last week, it was *tonight* that her husband would be returning. Dorothy knew Ruth was planning a special dinner for her husband's return, and she hoped everything was going to plan, for Ruth was a lady who truly deserved to be happy. Dorothy glanced at the time on her microwave. In fact, she mused, they should be sitting down to dinner right about now. Wiping her hands on a tea towel, she gently pulled her yellow gingham curtains aside out of curiosity to view the Hendersons' house next door. From her window she could see one complete side of their little bungalow and could look easily into their kitchen, dining room, and lounge. As the house was well-lit against the dark of the night and the Hendersons' curtains were not yet fully drawn, Dorothy could see clearly into all the rooms and noted that Ruth and Jack were indeed talking together at the dining room table. She smiled to herself, remembering fondly the many happy years she herself had spent with her own husband before his demise. Replacing the curtain, she busied herself with the dishes again, lost in her own thoughts.

It was some moments later, however, that Dorothy suddenly stopped short, listening intently. Although very faint, she was sure she had heard the sound of smashing glass. Perhaps the cats had got into the dustbins. Pulling the curtains aside again, she peered into the darkness but found her eye was drawn immediately back to the Hendersons' dining room window where the two were seated just minutes before. She saw that Jack had risen to his feet, obviously greatly displeased about something. As she watched, he took several china plates, and in violent anger, began smashing them against the wall. Startled, Dorothy gasped, staring in horrified disbelief. What could possibly have caused such a sudden turn of events? Transfixed, she watched for a few minutes longer to see Ruth vainly trying to calm her husband, but he would not be pacified. Pushing her away he angrily hurled another plate, this time smashing into the window sending shards of splintered glass onto the lawn below. Deeply disturbed, Dorothy ran to the back door, throwing it open to ascertain what exactly was happening. Jack's livid voice could be heard vibrating through the night air, followed by Ruth's sobbing—then the frightening thud of a heavy object as though furniture were being uplifted from its place and thrown to the ground. There was more smashing of glass and the sound of Ruth pleading for her husband to listen. Hastening back to the window, Dorothy was just in time to witness Jack hurling his fist at Ruth's face as she collapsed onto the floor like a rag doll. Dorothy's heart began to pound faster as her mind raced in panic. Should she run next door and intervene? No—she had to get outside help—but who could she turn to? She knew from previous conversations with Ruth that her religion forbade her from seeking help from the police…perhaps she could call the church.

Quickly flipping through the phone book, Dorothy tried desperately to remember the name. What was the church called?! Was it The Lamp? The Torch? The Light? Yes—The Light. That was it! She scanned down the page to find an after-hours number and with trembling hands dialled.

The voice on the end of the phone was officious and distant, and resonant with religious superiority. "Hello…this is Mrs. Peggy Percival. How can I help?"

✣

As the sun rose slowly in the morning sky Ruth stirred from her sleep, the painful memories of the previous evening flooding her mind. She had spent the night on the sofa, which had been hard and unyielding, and stiffly sitting up she felt discomfort in her back and shoulders. Her jaw felt swollen and tender and her tongue searched the gap where two teeth had been knocked from their place. Jack had left for work earlier that morning, unable to look at or speak to her. Feeling emotionally drained, Ruth donned her dressing gown and shuffled wearily into the kitchen to make a cup of coffee. Her husband had lost his temper before, but never to this extent. Ruth looked sadly at the piles of broken china that had been swept into the corner of the room, a lump rising in her throat. Ironically, that particular dinner set had been a wedding present many years ago. Now she wondered if, symbolically, its shattered appearance represented their marriage. She had tried to explain everything to Jack last night, had tried to be meek and submissive as the church had taught, but the news of Emily's departure had not gone down well. Jack's anger had been directed largely at the church and Pastor Whitfield for his intolerable interference and suffocating control over his daughter and family. However, as the night had progressed and more alcohol had been consumed, Jack had turned his vengeance on Ruth, blaming her for her spineless character and inability to stand up for herself. He was furious she spent so much of her time at the church to the point of neglecting him and their marriage, and had even suggested she take her bed and sleep at the church to save time. Trembling, Ruth reached for a tissue as the tears began to flow down her cheeks. She felt shattered, weak and defeated. Who knows how much more damage she or the house would have sustained if it hadn't been for the unexpected visit of Leonard and Marjory McKenzie—alerted, it seems, from one of the neighbours, who had heard the noise and contacted the church. Leonard had been marvellous in taking Jack aside and calming him down, eventually settling him into bed in his somewhat drunken state. Marjory had helped sweep up the glass and straighten the furniture and her kindness and gentle words had been a comfort to Ruth. They had left in the early hours of the morning, but would never know just how much their help and encouragement had meant.

A loud banging on the front door suddenly startled Ruth from her thoughts, her nerves already raw. Apprehensively drawing her dressing gown closer to her, she wondered who it could be. Surely Jack had not returned! Her heart pounding, Ruth cautiously answered the door, alarmed to see that Elders Everitt and Henry stood in her porch. A large removal van was parked in the driveway and several workmen looked on impatiently.

"Sister Henderson," Brother Henry spoke gruffly ignoring her battered face and tearful eyes. "We've been given instructions to remove you, your furniture and belongings to a secret location."

"S...Sorry?" Ruth looked perplexed. Had she heard right?

"Your husband's actions of last night have reached our attention, and such behaviour cannot go unchecked. Pastor Whitfield has instructed us to remove you permanently from your husband and home and place you safely in an unknown location where your husband cannot find or contact you," Everitt explained impatiently. He glanced at her dressing gown, waving his hand in irritation. "You might want to get dressed quickly as the packers are here and waiting to get started. We'll be outside."

Ruth closed the door, her head spinning. Could this be happening to her? Surely this was all a bad dream from which she would awaken any minute. What should she do? Yes, last night had been traumatic—frightening—but she still desperately loved her husband and, despite all, knew deep in her heart that Jack loved her. Was such a sudden and drastic measure really necessary? She could understand a temporary separation while the church offered some counsel or discussion, some on-going support for both their needs, with an end to healing and reconciliation. But permanent separation? Ruth felt sick in her stomach, yet even as she contemplated this matter there was more banging on the door and angry voices telling her that the packers were growing impatient.

By four that afternoon the job was done. Ruth had stood by all day, watching helplessly as her things had been boxed and packed before her. She had numbly watched as the removal van had pulled away and had meekly followed Everitt and Henry to their car to be taken to her new destination. Tearfully she had looked out the car window to see her home and memories of many years slowly fade into the distance.

❦

Much later that night Jack put his key into the front door, pushing it open and flicking on the lights. He stood for a moment in stunned astonishment as he surveyed the scene before him. In desperation he ran from room to room, his steps echoing on the bare floor boards. His house was empty. His wife and belongings—gone!

# Dire Consequences

Feeling very pleased with herself, Zara strolled casually into the kitchen and switched the coffee maker on. For once she was completely ready for work with time to spare and might even indulge herself with a cooked breakfast. She wondered if Kate would like to join her, though she was running very late, waylaid in the hallway by a telephone call. Zara wondered who could be phoning so early in the morning. Perhaps it was Kate's mother with information about the lace that had been ordered for the wedding dress. She probably wanted to catch Kate before she left for work. Zara placed two English muffins into the toaster and contemplated what she should have with them. Maybe scrambled egg and bacon, she thought, as she heard Kate hang up the phone.

"Kate—how do you make that really creamy scrambled egg?" she called, flipping randomly through a well-worn recipe book without knowing quite where to look. "You know, the one with the parsley in it?"

Kate entered the room, a sniffle betraying her mood, and Zara looked up to find her in tears. "Are you all right?" she asked in alarm, snapping the recipe book shut.

Kate was still in her dressing gown and slippers, her wet hair wrapped up in a towel, having just emerged from the shower when the phone had rung. She slumped down at the kitchen table dejectedly, plucking several tissues from a nearby tissue box.

"That was Elder Everitt on the phone," she sniffed miserably, dabbing her face and nose.

"*Bob* Everitt? Why is he ringing you so early on a Tuesday morning? Is everything okay with your family?" Zara asked with concern, offering Kate a muffin. But Kate was not hungry.

"My family is fine...but...do you remember a couple of weeks back when you told me you had met with Bethany at the mall?" Kate inquired.

"Ye-es," Zara answered guardedly, sitting down at the table.

"You were convinced that no one from the church had seen you and apart from me you haven't told a soul, right?"

"That's right. Why? What's this all about?"

Kate shook her head. "The secret is out. It seems you *weren't* alone after all, Zara. *Gladys Jones* saw you having lunch with Beth and she's reported it back to the church!"

Zara stared at Kate in disbelief, feeling a mixture of anger at Gladys for being such a complete traitor, and alarm at the possible repercussions of being found out. Not only that, but why had Bob Everitt contacted Kate and not her?

"Okay—I'm confused—and *angry!* Gladys Jones is nothing but a self-righteous gossip." Zara stood up from her chair in annoyance. "How dare she go running to the church about me. Beth and I were doing no harm. This is all completely ridiculous. So what are they going to do about it—throw me out of the flat like they did with Bethany? Excommunicate me from the church? Make me lose my job at the office?" Zara was pacing the kitchen floor by now in agitated frustration. "And why did they phone *you* instead of me?" She stopped and looked at Kate, who had started to cry again. "Kate. What aren't you telling me?"

Kate looked up at Zara with fear in her watery eyes. "It's the engagement party," she almost whispered.

Zara felt her heart miss a beat. No—they wouldn't! Surely they wouldn't interfere with Kate and Dan's wedding to make their point.

"What about it, Kate?" she asked hesitantly, almost not wanting to know.

Kate dropped her eyes and stared at the table. "Well...Bob Everitt...he informed me this morning that because of your actions...well...you've been crossed off the list. Zara, you are the only one who has been forbidden by the leadership to attend my engagement party, even though you are my chief bridesmaid." Kate wiped her face with the edge of her dressing gown sleeve, looking up again. "You know what's happening, don't you Zara. You do get it. It's a warning!"

"Yes...but why not just warn *me*—why involve you and Dan?"

"Well...we all saw what happened to Beth. When she didn't obey the rules life got pretty difficult for her. Zara, you know the church has the power to stop our wedding or at least to make things very unpleasant for us all."

Zara huffed in annoyance. "They know I won't want another of my best friends to suffer and will toe the line as a result. That's emotional blackmail!" she cried in outrage.

"I don't know *what* it is—but...what are we going to do about it?" Kate looked desperate.

Zara stared thoughtfully out of the window as she watched powdery white clouds being swept across the sky by blustery, winter winds. "There's only one thing we can do," she sighed. "I'll just have to show the leadership how repentant, submissive, and obedient I can be. Don't worry. I won't be the cause of ruining your wedding."

Kate smiled weakly. "You? Submissive and obedient?" she sniffed. "Yeah, right—this is *really* going to work."

Back in her bedroom searching for her car keys, Zara's mind was in turmoil. She felt hurt and disappointed that she would not be celebrating her friend's engagement, but equally angry that the leadership were treating her this way. It wasn't fair—especially to involve Kate, who had done no wrong. What a start to the day, and now she had to go to work. *Great.* She was right in the thick of it there, working in the church office. No doubt Peggy Percival knew all about this latest development, for Gladys Jones would surely have filled her in on all of the details. *Real "birds of a feather," those two.* Zara sighed as she pulled open her top drawer, at last finding her elusive keys. As she reached for them, she noted that they rested on top of the two leaflets that Bethany had given to her at the mall. Zara had hastily placed the pamphlets in this drawer to be out of sight, meaning to look at them later, but as yet had not had the chance to do so. She pulled them out now from their hiding place, looking again at their titles with renewed interest. *"Spiritual Abuse" and "Recognising Religious Cults."*

"A religious cult. I wonder . . ." she mused, scanning quickly over the page. One section in particular caught her eye and she paused for a moment to read. Then, taking her work satchel, she slipped the pamphlets inside and headed out the door for the office.

⚜

Tuesday morning had always been shopping day for as long as Marjory could remember. Far enough away from the weekend to avoid the crowds, and early enough in the week for there still to be plenty of stock, it had always been the ideal day. Her mother had shopped on a Tuesday and so had her grandmother, and so Marjory had faithfully kept to the tradition, as well as carefully observing another—that being a morning tea or coffee after the shopping was done. Marjory always met with a friend at the little English replica tearooms across the road from the supermarket, and today was to be no exception. She was meeting Yvonne, for after enjoying dinner together at Marjory and Leonard's house just recently they both had agreed to keep more regular contact with each other by phoning or by outings such as this morning.

The day was not the most pleasant weather wise, with its

gusty breezes and patches of rain, and by the time Marjory had completed her shopping and placed all the bags in the back of her car, she was running more than a little late. Finally, however, she pushed open the little café door which rang with a small bell, noting that Yvonne was already seated in one of the booths.

The tearooms were quaintly decorated in old world style with collections of china teapots and bone china plates adorning the walls and ledges, and baskets of dried flowers hanging from exposed wooden beams. The atmosphere was of course completed by the wonderful aroma of coffee and cakes and the warmth that exuded from a crackling fire in the large stone fireplace. Just perfect for a wintry day.

"Yvonne, I'm so sorry to have kept you waiting," Marjory apologised as she removed her raincoat and scarf. "Do you know, my umbrella must have turned inside out at least four times while I was putting my groceries in the car." She sat down with a sigh. "So, how are you my dear?"

Yvonne's face looked pale and anxious as she sat rigidly on the edge of the padded wooden seat. "Well, to be completely honest—not the best, Marjory," she answered, her voice strained and small.

"Yvonne?" Marjory placed her hand across the table and gently touched her friend's arm in concern, but the waitress appeared beside their table before Yvonne had a chance to respond.

"Can I order anything for you?" she asked politely, holding her pad and pen in readiness.

Marjory was quick to answer, sensing the awkwardness of the moment. "Ah—I'll have a pot of tea with cream scones, thank you. Would you like the same, Yvonne? Yes? Okay, make that two tea and scones with both apricot and strawberry jam. Thank you."

The waitress disappeared and Marjory turned again to her friend, waiting patiently for Yvonne to explain.

"Do you remember the conversation we had at your place,

Marjory—the evening Paul and I came for dinner?" Yvonne started hesitantly. "We were sitting in your kitchen and I told you how my grandson, Rhys, had left the church and how Everitt and Henry had as good as threatened my family that dire things would befall Rhys if he didn't return?"

Yes, Marjory remembered this well. How could she forget? She had been diligently praying for Rhys and his family every day since.

She nodded, "Go on, Yvonne."

"Well, today as I was about to leave the house, I received a phone call. It was my son, John." Her voice began to tremble as she reached for her handkerchief. "He told me that Rhys had been on his way to work this morning when his motorbike had slipped on the greasy, wet roads. Marjory—he hit a power pole and the full weight of the bike fell back on his chest. He's been taken to hospital and is at this moment in intensive care." Her watery eyes were wide with fear.

"Oh, no!" Marjory gasped, as she placed her hand to her mouth. "Yvonne, that's terrible! Should you be up at the hospital now with your family?"

"No, that's just it. They don't want anyone there yet except his mum and dad until he is stabilized. I was going to cancel our outing this morning, Marj—I knew you'd understand—but then I realised I just couldn't stay at home on my own. I knew I'd go crazy. Marjory, what if something terrible happens to him? What if what the church is saying is true?"

This time it was Marjory's turn to wipe a tear from her eye. The God she knew did not deliberately strike down young people for not attending church. Sure, Rhys was not walking with God at this moment, but she strongly believed in the power of parents' prayers as a covering of protection over their children. How cruel of the church of The Light to have placed this heavy burden upon its people. To be honest, what effect were *their* negative words really having?

"I'm sure he'll be fine, Yvonne," Marjory encouraged, though not too convincingly. "Look—when we've finished here, we'll go back to my house and spend some time in prayer for Rhys. I'll be happy to give you a lift to the hospital, too, if you need it. You're right—you shouldn't be alone at this time."

"Thanks, Marjory. I appreciate your support. It's just a pity that that same support is not coming from the rest of the leadership at the church," she said bitterly.

The waitress appeared again, tray in hand. "Two tea and scones?"

# THE LIGHT IN DARKNESS

Zara placed the last bundle of envelopes into the box and closed the lid with relief, thankful that the job was finally finished. She'd been folding leaflets and addressing envelopes all morning; something that was undertaken on a regular basis at the office to invite outsiders in the neighbouring districts to the church meetings—advertising, if you will—but it was not a job that Zara enjoyed and she was always glad when it was done. At least the afternoon should be quieter. Two of the ladies she worked with were part-time and had already gone home, and Peggy Percival was out for the afternoon and not expected to return until 4:00 p.m. With Pastor Whitfield on an all-day fishing trip, Zara would in fact be alone in the office for several hours, and she was glad. Although nothing had been said directly to her, Peggy's self-righteous, judgemental attitude had said it all, and Zara was tired of it. Obviously her personal life was an open book for all to gossip about and if it hadn't been for her promise to Kate to "behave" herself, she knew she would have snapped and said something she would have regretted. Perhaps it was just as well that Peggy and the pastor were out this afternoon.

Looking at her watch, she saw that it was time for lunch and picking up her satchel Zara headed down the hallway toward the staff room for a well-earned break. She sat down wearily at one of the tables, rummaging through her bag as she searched for a sachet of soup she was sure she'd left there yesterday. She seemed to have everything else, from makeup to old shopping receipts...even pamphlets. That's right. The pamphlets she had slipped in there that morning. Pulling them out, Zara now placed them on the table in front of her. Why had Bethany been so keen for her to read these? She had said something about "being careful as well as informed." Zara scanned the front page. She knew she was alone, but just looking at this material made her feel guilty, as though these pamphlets were somehow condemning her very surroundings. Grabbing an apple from a nearby fruit bowl and propping her feet up on a wooden stool Zara turned again to the section in one of the leaflets that had caught her eye earlier that morning and began to read.

KEY POINTS TO RECOGNISING A RELIGIOUS CULT

In identifying a cult, several aspects should be looked at:

• Leadership
*What is the structure of the Leadership within the organisation?*
Is there one, supreme leader at the top to whom all must be obedient, with no Board of Governors to answer to—no checks and balances? Is this leader in turn supported by a smaller, subservient group of "yes men" who do his/her bidding?

• Membership
*How controlled is the membership?*
Ask yourself, "How are the members brought into the group, how are they kept there, and how easy is it to leave?" Then ask, "How are those who *do* manage to leave treated?"

• Doctrine
*What is being taught?*
Does this organisation teach that they have the "whole truth" and are the only true, enlightened

ones—and is there a feeling of superiority or pride in that teaching? Is there a "them and us" mentality? Do you have a sense of being out-of-touch with the rest of the world?

- The Individual

Does the will of the group have precedence over the will of the individual and is independent thought encouraged or crushed? Is a good performance demanded above the needs of the individual and is there a sense of being punished for bad performance? In fact, is the individual/group manipulated through fear and guilt?

Zara took another bite of her apple. The church of The Light certainly seemed to have issues on all of these points. She read on:

Further to the above, a religious cult that is truly destructive in nature can be identified as one that is using what is termed as "mind control techniques." In other words, a damaging cult is one that seeks to affect a person's will by the use of mind control to such an extent that they can gain control over that person's mind, will, feelings, and emotions, thus causing them to conform to the organisation, losing their own identity—not necessarily desirable by the person, but necessary for their survival within the cult. Often the individual may not even be aware of the extent of this change of identity until they have come out from the cult, though friends and family outside the cult may have often noticed these changes for some time. Mind control can be a very subtle thing, and is often administered in the form of many repeated suggestions going into the subconscious mind. These suggestions are received in a type of hypnotic state where the individual or group have had to forcibly listen to lectures or indoctrination for many hours, days, or years on end where the message has been repeated over and over. These messages are administered in a very controlled environment where the leader professes he has "divine" access and knowledge and therefore must be listened to and obeyed. The individual is made to feel unworthy, guilty, and shameful, and is pressed to work hard at being "holy" or "pure," although the many rules and regulations to gain such a state of purity are not clearly explained, rather are expected to be accepted without question. Doctrine takes precedence over the individual and is, of course, the absolute truth. Those who don't believe so are from the "devil" or some other equally dubious source.

Zara let out a long, low whistle. "Mind control. Now that's getting pretty heavy. But I wonder . . ." She turned the page.

Many may be disturbed to realise that there are some churches that fall under the banner of "damaging cults." Sincere people join these churches because they genuinely want to know God and follow him—yet are deceived and manipulated to believe and act in ways that are far from his will. Many of God's children are labouring under manmade burdens, oblivious to his grace, and have lost the joy of their salvation. Such leaders are truly accountable to God for their actions. God himself has said, "But if anyone causes one of these little ones who believe in me to sin, it would be better for him to have a large millstone hung around his neck and to be drowned in the depths of the sea" (Matthew 18:6, NIV).

Zara shook her head, feeling somewhat disturbed. "Oh my goodness," she whispered. She went back and reread several paragraphs again, letting the words sink in. This indeed sounded like the church of The Light and could in fact have been written expressly about them. She would never have called this place a "religious cult," yet it certainly presented all of the danger signs. She had always suspected that something was not quite right here, as recent events were proving, but hadn't been able to put her finger on it. Religious cult or not, how could she have not seen this? Zara's mind began to race. Was it possible then that there were other things happening at this church that both she and the general congregation had no knowledge of? Were other members of the church being dealt with harshly too, unable to say anything for fear of the system? Zara put down the pamphlet and her half-eaten apple and sat for a moment deep in thought. There was a way she could find out. Her heart raced as an idea began to formulate in her mind. The office would be empty for at least another three hours. Was this not the perfect opportunity to search for proof to substantiate her claims? She had to uncover what was going on here. She owed it to herself, to Beth—and to Kate!

Quickly putting the leaflets back into her bag, Zara slipped into the hallway and quietly crept toward the pastor's office. She stood for a moment outside the door to once again ascertain that no one else was around, but apart from the loud thumping of her heart and the rain that gently pattered against the window-panes, the buildings were deathly quiet. A shiver ran up and down her spine as she contemplated what she was about to do and the possible repercussions should she be found out. But there was no turning back. Silently she opened the office door and entered.

The room was dark and dismal, reflecting the rainy winter's afternoon outside its windows, and having been unoccupied all day felt damp through lack of heating. Zara waited for a moment as her eyes adjusted to the dark, afraid to turn the lights on for fear of being seen from the carpark below. Peering through the shadows she saw a large silver filing cabinet sitting against the windows on the far side of the room from which Peggy often worked. Perhaps this would be a good place to start her search. Creeping across the room she carefully pulled open the heavy top drawer and found herself looking at a myriad of files, diligently divided into sections and categories. A divider marked "Property" caught her eye and pulling the file out, she flipped through its many pages. She had not realised how much property the church actually owned—whole blocks of the surrounding district, plus large areas of countryside *and* land overseas. It also seemed the church was bidding to take over many of the shops in the nearby town. *What could they possibly want with such a large property portfolio? To gain more control maybe?* She pulled out a second folder marked "Finances" and quickly ascertained how they could afford such properties. The church was sitting on large amounts of money, although, interestingly enough, she discovered that the "Missionary" folder was very thin and showed little activity.

Closing the top drawer, Zara pulled open the second. "Security." *This could be interesting.* As expected the folder was full of paperwork for the state-of-the-art security systems that had been installed in and around the church buildings and grounds; nothing unusual there. However, as Zara turned to the back of the folder she saw something that was of much more interest. A bunch of leaflets held together with a rubber band had been placed in a plastic wallet and as Zara removed them she saw that they advertised a series of European products—for *bugging* devices. Could this be real? Bugs for telephones; for rooms; bugs to be placed in clothing and shoes. Were these people the Secret Service or a church? One particular leaflet stood out and opening it Zara read its contents with interest. It seemed this was an advertisement for an instrument that could be used for listening in on conversations some considerable distance away. The user could sit in a car, for example, and clearly hear what was being said in a nearby house. Alternatively, one could sit in any given room and listen in on the conversations of all adjoining rooms. But perhaps most disturbing of all was the fact that a receipt had been stapled to this particular pamphlet showing the amount paid and the date of purchase. Did this mean they were actually using such a device? Zara shuddered. *Was this even legal?*

She glanced at her watch. Time was passing quickly and she must be careful. Closing the cabinet she walked quietly across the room to the pastor's desk, hesitating for a moment, a wave of guilt and uncertainty flooding over her. Should she really look any further? Was this going a little too far? The picture in her mind of Kate's tearstained face that morning at the realisation her wedding could be destroyed, and the urgency she'd seen in Bethany's eyes as she'd handed Zara the pamphlets, caused her to press on. Moving behind the desk she pulled open the top drawer: pens, pencils, staplers—nothing there. The second drawer: envelopes, letterheads, a bag of mints. The third: tapes. Rows of tapes—all named and dated. Zara recognised most of them as being names of people in the congregation. Could these be taped conversations? She looked a little closer at the dates and saw the most recent had been a conversation between Pastor Whitfield and Ruth Henderson. She also noticed a notepad had been placed beside the tapes and quickly flicking through its pages noted the writing was that of Peggy Percival and seemed to be a handwritten recording of various conversations. Very curious indeed.

Closing the drawer, Zara quickly scanned the bookshelves behind the pastor's desk, checking each folder's title. She stopped at one marked "Confidential," carefully pulling it down in order to search through its contents. Page after page of names had been entered of those whom it was suspected were questioning the leadership and scribbled beside each one the names of either elders Everitt or Henry—supposedly the minions who were to keep an eye on these individuals and report back on any new developments. Zara shook her head in disgust. This was unbelievable and added new meaning to the often quoted Scripture, "Obey them that have the rule over you and submit yourselves: for they watch for your souls, as they that must give account" (Hebrews 13:17, KJV). She had seen enough.

About to close the folder, however, Zara suddenly noticed a section that had been placed at the back. It was devoted to children who had been removed from their homes for disobedience and rebelliousness to their parents and/or to the church rules. Addresses and phone numbers had been entered of the new families they were sent to within the church. Now Zara felt sick in her stomach and she wondered what Social Services would have to say about all this. She noted that the latest entry was Emily Henderson who had been placed in the care of the Scofields. She wondered what it was that poor Emily had done and how she must be feeling, not to mention her parents. Zara had only seen Ruth Henderson from a distance, but she had always seemed such a sweet, gentle lady—what could possibly have gone so wrong?

It was then that Zara had a sudden thought. Quickly she turned back to the section marked "Those to be watched," searching its entries. There it was—*Zara Williams*. Her heart missed a beat. Her name had been entered, and Bob Everitt had been assigned the task of watching her! Zara's blood began to boil. This was all so wrong. The only question remaining was—what was she going to do about it?

# A Bruised Reed

As Ruth looked dejectedly out of the bus window at the houses and shops that whisked quickly by, she noted that the first signs of spring were starting to appear. Daffodils could be seen here and there in gardens and on lawns, their cheery yellow a welcome sight against the winter weary backdrop. But unlike the flowers, Ruth did not look nor feel cheerful. Since the break up of her marriage and the loss of her daughter, a heaviness had settled over her that she could not shake, and she had lost all sense of joy. Besides which, the bills had been steadily mounting and the small benefit she was to receive each month would not be sufficient to cover them all. It was out of necessity, therefore, that she was on her way to the city to apply for a job in a large department store as a shop assistant, selling women's clothing and accessories. It had been many years since Ruth had had to look for work, as her husband had been an adequate provider, and she could not help but feel out of touch and lacking in confidence. Indeed she wondered how she would cope. The truth was, she had not been coping very well of late. Her doctor had been concerned she was developing an anxiety disorder and had insisted she take anti-depressants. But the mere mention of this medication had caused her dismay as the church had long preached that such medication was of the devil, and to take such pills would mean complete lack of faith in God. It was only after some convincing that she had agreed instead to let the doctor prescribe her sleeping tablets, although she would never tell the church this. Yet, once at home, she could not bring herself to take even these, lest she be displeasing to God. She had, instead, endured many sleepless nights, and stifling a yawn Ruth now turned her attention from the window to the couple sitting opposite her. They sat hand in hand and were engaged in happy conversation. Ruth watched them for several minutes, but their happiness and contentment only served as a painful reminder of her own loneliness, and Ruth's eyes suddenly filled with tears as she quickly looked away again. Not a day had gone by when she had not thought of her own husband. She wondered how he must have felt to find his house empty, his wife and daughter gone. Was he still angry at her or did he realise this was again the actions of the church? Either way, she did know this about her husband. Once he had calmed down he would be beside himself with worry and guilt, wondering where both of them were. She'd heard from Emily's teacher that Jack had been to the school office asking for contact addresses and phone numbers for his wife and daughter, but being unsure of the circumstances, the school had withheld the information. Ruth had longed to phone him herself but she feared the church's reaction should they find out. She couldn't see how they would find out, yet uncannily they always seemed to know everything that took place. The fact was, they had placed her in a small cottage on the other side of town and had forbidden her to make contact with Jack, just as they had forbidden her to make contact with Emily, and she was too fearful to disobey their orders.

The bus had slowed down now, pulling into a small bay to collect more passengers, and as Ruth dabbed her eyes with her handkerchief, she watched as several people boarded. One was a well-built man in his mid twenties, his arms completely covered in tattoos, his hair gelled in spikes and his body bedecked in black leather, body piercings, and chains. Ruth felt herself stiffen in alarm. Pastor Whitfield had preached about such men of the world, saying they were murderers and rapists, and now one such possible man was on her bus! The man glanced around, searching for a place to sit and seeing the empty seat at Ruth's side headed straight toward her. Ruth froze in horror. What should she do? Her heart began to pound, her hands shaking and sweating.

"All right then, love?" the young man asked pleasantly in a British accent as he seated himself beside her.

But Ruth could not answer. Petrified, she stared out of the window, her eyes wide with fear, her breath short. Desperately she quoted scriptures to herself and did not relax until he had exited the bus several streets later. By that time they had entered the city and were thankfully nearing her own stop.

Finally on the pavement Ruth breathed a sigh of relief, glad to see the bus move on. She'd not had to catch a bus for years and had found the experience harrowing. But now an even more daunting task was before her: the task of finding the department store for her interview. How often she had heard sermons on the state of the world in these last days and, despite her present issues with the church, she hated to venture beyond the safety and familiarity of its walls and its people, no matter how harsh the rules. The city was heaving with traffic and noise, and warily Ruth started up the street amid car horns honking, choking pollution, and pushing crowds. Rounding a corner she passed a group of drunkards squatting in the doorway of a building with leering, bloodshot eyes and foul mouths. Terrified she held her purse closer to her and with head down shuffled quickly on. Surely the store must be near. Approaching a cinema Ruth glanced up at the movies now showing, shocked by their evil titles. The pastor's words rung in her head, *The devil reaches people through music and film—never enter a cinema for the devil's presence abounds within.* Silently she muttered a prayer of protection as she quickly passed its doors. It was several streets on before she finally spotted her destination. Bromley's Department store was a popular family shop and she would be working on the second floor in the women's section. On entering the front door, however, the loud pop music that greeted her seemed anything but family friendly. By the time Ruth entered the elevator, her head was spinning and her stomach nauseous. This was the music of anti-Christ and non-believers. How could she work in an atmosphere such as this? As the doors opened into the women's department, Ruth knew she was about to vomit with anxiety and, seeing her distress, a shop assistant rushed to her side.

"Are you okay, ma'am?" she asked, guiding her to a chair. "Can I do anything for you?"

Ruth could take no more. She knew she could never work in such a place as this. She had failed again. "Please," she said weakly. "Could you order me a taxi? I need to go home."

It was late in the afternoon when Ruth finally stumbled up the shabby wooden stairs of the little cottage to her front door and, safely inside, she dropped wearily onto the sofa, holding her head in her hands. She felt dizzy and stressed, and worried about money. But how could she ever get a job? The world had become an unsafe place and she felt desperately uncomfortable in it. As her husband had bitterly pointed out many times before, the church had become all-consuming and had become her whole life, causing her to close out the "world" and everyone in it. Yet as she reflected on the recent events of her life at The Light she began to wonder—did she really feel any more comfortable in the church? The fact was she was terrified of the world, yet just as fearful of the church. The truth dawned painfully upon her. She didn't fit anywhere. Leaning back in her chair she gazed in confusion around the small room, cluttered with unopened boxes from the shift. She had been unable, or perhaps unwilling, to unpack these boxes in the hope that she would soon be reunited with her husband. Feeling hot tears sting her eyes once again she stirred herself. She seemed to spend so much time these days crying—but she mustn't sit here in self-pity—she must get herself up and into bed. If she could just sleep then maybe she would think of a solution.

Surely things would look brighter in the morning—if only she could sleep.

Dragging herself into the bedroom Ruth glanced at her reflection in the mirror. She looked pale and drawn and a familiar rash of anxiety covered her neck. Ruth's eyes moved to read a small scripture card that had been stuck to the side of the mirror which read, "I am come that they might have life, and that they might have it more abundantly" (John 10:10, KJV). Feeling an ache deep within her, she hurriedly plucked the card from its place, concealing it in the top drawer. "Lord," she cried. "How can this be the abundant life?"

As evening fell, Ruth finally climbed between the clean white sheets of her bed, hugging a hot water bottle for both comfort and warmth and puffing up her pillows to support her aching shoulders. The wind outside had picked up and as Ruth lay in the dark she listened as the house creaked and groaned with every gust. A sudden noise at her window startled her and clutching the blankets under her chin, she tensely listened in fear, imagining fingernails scratching at the pane. In time she realised it was only a branch scraping against the glass in the wind, and weary from the day's events she eventually fell into a troubled and restless sleep.

It was around midnight when Ruth was suddenly awakened. Had she heard a noise outside or was her imagination playing games again? How many more nights must she endure these awakenings? Turning on her side she attempted to go back to sleep, but a rustling at the front of the house startled her. She lay still in her bed, straining to hear every little sound; her eyes wide open in the darkness. Yes! There it was again—coming from the front porch. Ruth sat upright in bed, her heart pounding. Was that someone tapping on the front door? Quickly slipping into her dressing gown and slippers she crept into the hallway and gasped. A shadowy silhouette could be seen through the glass against the dim street lamp outside. Someone was trying to get in! Ruth's legs began to tremble beneath her, and falling to her knees she cried out in prayer. "Oh, Jesus—protect me. Please protect me!"

It was then the shadowy figure stopped short and moments later she heard a strained whisper through the door. "Mum—is that you? Mum—it's me, Emily! Open up!"

Ruth froze for a minute before a wave of relief flooded over her and quickly getting to her feet she ran to unlock the door, allowing her daughter to stumble in. "Emily—what on earth…?"

But Emily was quick to silence her, looking nervously over her shoulder as though afraid she had been followed. "Shh, Mum—don't turn on the light—I mustn't be seen!" she whispered in fear, her voice thick with emotion. "Quick. Take me to the back of the house."

Holding Emily's hand tightly, Ruth carefully led her through the darkened house toward the kitchen. Closing the door behind them she reached for the light, anxious to speak to her daughter, for she was afraid that all was not well. The light had no sooner flooded the room than Ruth's worse fears were suddenly realised. Crying out, she gazed in horror at the blood that trickled down her daughter's cheek from a deep gash on her forehead; one eye was bruised and almost swollen shut. Her knees suddenly weak again, Ruth reached for a chair before collapsing into it.

"Dear Lord!" she gasped, her hand over her mouth. "What has happened to you, Emily?"

But Emily could not speak, and holding her head in her hands she let out a deep and painful sob. Devastated, Ruth arose and held her close, the small body trembling in her arms. Ruth's own inward pain was immeasurable and her own tears mingled with her daughter's. What could have happened? Had she fallen? Had she been attacked? And where had she come from? After several minutes she released Emily from her grip and quickly gathered warm water and towels to cleanse her wounds.

"Are you ready to tell me what's going on?" she whispered softly as she lifted Emily's chin and began dabbing at the gash.

"I…I've run away from the Scofields—the people I'm meant to be staying with," she managed feebly. "Mum, I can't go back. Please don't let them make me go back!" she pleaded with fear in her eyes.

Feeling alarmed, Ruth pulled up a kitchen stool and sitting down looked intently into Emily's eyes. "Emily…I need to know what is going on. I need you to tell me the truth. How did you get this gash and bruising on your face?"

Ruth waited patiently as Emily drew a deep breath and tried to steady herself. She appeared afraid and uncertain as though she could trust no one and, despite her efforts to calm herself, her body continued to shake. Ruth reached out and took her hand reassuringly. "You can tell me," she coaxed gently, though her own heart pounded heavily in her chest.

Emily wiped the tears from her cheeks with the sleeve of her shirt and stared at the floor as she hesitantly began. "Mr. Scofield locked me in the basement…they're always locking me in the basement. Often I have nothing to eat, and only the concrete floor to sleep on," she sniffed. "At times when I've been desperate I've rummaged through the freezer they keep down there so I can at least eat frozen, raw sausages or anything else I can find. I don't mind the hunger so much—it's the dark and the cold I'm afraid of." Emily shuddered. "But tonight I discovered that one of the basement window latches was loose. All the other windows had been locked, but this one I could pry open. So I squeezed my way through and ran all the way here. I knew where your house was because I overheard the Scofields talking…but I didn't realise how long it would take to get here by foot. Mum, I was so scared!"

The Scofields' house was a good four miles away and the hour was late. Ruth rose anxiously to look out of the small kitchen window into the night, shuddering at the evils that lurked deep in the shadows. Anything could have happened to

Emily as she trudged the distance to her cottage and she was not sure whether to rebuke Emily for her actions or be relieved that she was safe. The latter seemed more important. Still, to be locked in a cold and dark basement with no food—no wonder she had been compelled to escape, and Ruth was appalled to hear of such treatment. What could Emily have done to warrant such harshness? And this still did not explain the wounds to her face. Sensing there was more to this story, she turned again to Emily.

"*Why?* Why would anyone be so cruel?" She sat down again beside her daughter "You must tell me *why* they have been punishing you like this."

"To...to discipline me, Mum—when they think I'm lying. Just as they make me swallow hot chilli powder when they feel I haven't submitted to their rules."

"Chilli powder?" Ruth cried, her stomach turning in disgust. "Emily—what is it they think you've been lying about? And what rules are you not submitting to?"

There was a long silence as Emily's cheeks began to redden. Unable to look her mother in the eye, she turned toward the wall, a deep sob welling up within her as she covered her face in shame. Once again her pain was tangible, and her small body trembled in distress. Ruth could feel her own anxiety levels rising as her head began to pound.

Finally Emily muttered, "I refused to go to the neighbour's house."

Ruth was perplexed. "The neighbours? *Why* Emily? *Who* are the neighbours?" She was determined to know the truth.

Emily stood to her feet and began pacing the floor anxiously. "Mr. Lealman," she almost yelled. "Mr. Lealman is their neighbour."

This conversation was making no sense. John Lealman was a prominent member of the church of The Light, respected by everyone. A single man in his mid-thirties, he ran youth programmes on Saturdays and was well known for his work with troubled teens. Why would Emily refuse to see him?

"I...I don't understand," she said puzzled. "Why were the Scofields insisting you visit Mr. Lealman at his house, and why did you refuse?"

"I *didn't* refuse at first. They wanted me to see him for some counseling, especially as he was just next door, and to start with he was really cool—until . . ." Emily picked up a tea towel and began twisting it in obvious agitation.

"Until what...?" Ruth urged.

Emily could take it no more. Throwing the towel down and wringing her hands she looked pleadingly at her mother. "Until he started touching me, Mum. You know—*touching* me." It was as though saying the words had released a dam within her and falling to her knees, she wept and wept.

The colour drained from Ruth's face as she realised what her daughter had been trying to say. She stared at Emily's quivering body in stunned disbelief, a flood of nausea overwhelming her and rushing for the kitchen sink she leant over, retching. How much more could she take? How much more could her *daughter* take? In silent prayer she asked for the strength that she so desperately needed; the strength that she no longer had. Somehow she must sustain both herself and her daughter in her time of need. Holding a towel to her mouth and shaking, Ruth helped Emily to a seat and sat beside her.

"Did...Lealman . . ." she could hardly utter his name. "Did *he* do this to your face?" She was not sure she wanted the answer, but Emily slowly shook her head.

"I finally found the courage to tell Mr. Scofield what was happening at Mr. Lealman's house...but they wouldn't believe me, and locked me in the basement until I told the truth. They insisted I keep visiting him...and it kept happening."

Ruth interrupted. "You were being *sexually abused* and they insisted you keep seeing the man?" she cried in angry disbelief.

Emily nodded. "Finally tonight…after it happened again…I told them I would call the police if they wouldn't listen to me. We started to argue…and that's when…when Mr. Scofield hit me."

Ruth's eyes grew wide with horror as she felt the urge to retch once more. "Mr. Scofield did *this* to you!" she cried, holding her stomach in pain. "After everything you've been through? Oh, my precious child." In deep despair, Ruth held Emily tightly in her arms. Why her? Why was this happening to *her* family?

Tears were streaming down Emily's cheeks once again as she looked up at her mother. "Mum—what am I going to do? What will happen when the church finds out?" Emily's voice was fearful.

Ruth stroked her daughter's hair reassuringly, though she was seething with anger. "I don't know. But we can't do anything about it tonight. I'll make up the spare bed and you'll stay with me here until this is sorted. Don't worry, Emily. We'll get through this." Ruth wiped the tears away from her daughter's cheek, before dabbing her own. "Somehow…we'll get through this."

⚜

Marjory placed two cups of steaming hot tea onto a wooden tray along with a plate of homemade shortbreads, and carefully made her way out into the garden. After a somewhat blustery evening the night before, it had turned into a lovely spring day and Leonard had been planting vegetables all morning, ready for the summer. Setting the tray down on a white wrought iron table, Marjory surveyed his work.

"Lettuces, tomatoes, beans, carrots…how wonderful! We'll be able to feed a small army this summer!"

"Oh well, my dear. If we can't eat them all, there will always be someone else in need we can give them to. Thanks for the tea—just what I feel like."

Marjory and Leonard sat down together contentedly sipping their drinks and listening to the birds singing in the branches above them. The garden was beginning to come alive, with clumps of spring buds appearing everywhere in corners and under trees and it wouldn't be long before the garden would be ablaze with colour.

Marjory broke the silence. "I was on the phone with Yvonne this morning," she said, placing her cup down on the tray.

"Oh, yes. How is Rhys coming along—any improvement?" Leonard asked with concern.

But Marjory shook her head. "He's still in intensive care and still in a critical condition. I'm really worried for him, Leonard. Yvonne was so upset this morning. There is a very real concern Rhys may have septicaemia and they are carrying out more tests this afternoon. She is asking everyone to pray."

"Yes—of course we'll pray. What a distressing time for them."

They both fell into reflective silence again. Next it was Leonard who spoke.

"I can't get Jack and Ruth Henderson off my mind. After everything Ruth went through with losing Emily, and now being moved away from her husband—dreadful. You'd think Pastor Whitfield would consider counseling first or some attempt at reconciliation before charging in."

"Counseling is not his style, my dear," Marjory commented cynically. "Have you heard how Emily is getting on with the Scofields?"

"No, but I can't imagine she's enjoying it there. Max Scofield has a reputation for being arrogant and legalistic, which might impress the pastor, but not those who live with him. One look at his timid wife and children will show you that. I do hope she's okay."

"Yes, so do I. Perhaps I'll give Ruth a call. I was going to ask her if she'd like a lift to the meeting next Saturday anyway."

"Meeting? Oh, yes, of course. The country prayer meeting."

Marjory suddenly looked up, listening intently. "Is that the phone, Leonard? Yes...I believe it is. Wait here. I'll get it."

She disappeared quickly into the house and was gone for some minutes before eventually reappearing, looking concerned and anxious.

"Leonard, you wouldn't believe it. After just talking about her, that was Ruth Henderson on the phone and your predictions were correct. It seems that Emily ran away from the Scofields last night after an argument. Ruth mentioned something about physical abuse! She was very upset. The problem is, Pastor Whitfield has heard about it and is sending Everitt and Henry over as we speak to deal with the situation. Ruth is very worried and wondered it we'd mind going over to her house to support her."

She didn't have to ask twice. Leonard was on his feet immediately, walking determinedly toward the house to get his keys. He knew how Everitt and Henry "handled" things and he would not stand by and allow the church to damage this family any further.

"Quick, Marjory. We've not a second to lose. I'll meet you in the car!"

# ABIDE WITH ME

Nervously pacing the floor, her stomach in knots, Ruth glanced anxiously at her daughter slumped quietly on a chair in the corner of the room. Her face was expressionless, her eyes dull, and Emily's whole demeanour was that of a lamb about to be led to the slaughter. For one so young she had lost the wonderful zest for life that everyone had so loved and admired in her and instead she stared lifelessly at the floor. One eye had completely swollen shut, surrounded by black and blue bruising, and the gash on her forehead looked angry and red. Hot tears stung Ruth's eyes. Every time she looked at her daughter, she felt anger and fear rise within her. She couldn't tolerate seeing her in this state, yet felt so out of control, so helpless—as though everything around her was being manipulated and ordered without her ever having a say. She had mentioned to Marjory about the physical abuse from Max Scofield, but had not been able to bring herself to say anything about the sexual abuse from John Lealman. It somehow was unmentionable. Every time she thought about him she wanted to vomit. It was enough that the church gossips already knew much of their business. She couldn't stand for this to be idly talked about to all and sundry as well. Besides, such knowledge would only black mark Emily, for they would never believe that John Lealman was capable of such a thing, and there could be no hope of any real counsel or support for her daughter. No—for the meantime at least, this would be hers and Emily's secret.

A tap at the door startled Ruth but peering through the windows she was relieved to see that it was only Leonard and Marjory. How glad she was that they had arrived first, before the others. Somehow she knew that they would be supportive at least, and would surely not judge her daughter.

"Thank you for coming so quickly," she said gratefully as she led them both into the lounge, which she had temporarily cleared of boxes for this morning's meeting.

Marjory gasped involuntarily as she saw Emily's face and quickly moved to put her arm around her. "Max Scofield did this?" she asked in amazement.

"This has gone too far!" Leonard muttered in disgust. "Does Pastor Whitfield know all the details?"

Ruth shrugged her shoulders uncertainly. "I tried to explain to Bob Everitt earlier this morning on the phone, but he wouldn't listen. He said there were always two sides to every story."

"Then he should have listened to *yours*. I don't believe it," Leonard shook his head, appalled.

A heavy knock at the front door signalled the arrival of elders Henry and Everitt, and seeing the look of alarm on Ruth's face, Leonard was quick to reassure her. "Listen—don't worry, Ruth. Let me handle this."

Stepping into the hallway Leonard was quick to answer the door and directed the men to where the women were waiting. Meanwhile Marjory beckoned to Ruth to sit between her and Emily as the men filed solemnly into the lounge and took their seats. Ruth noticed that Emily had tensed at the sight of the elders, and gently she took her hand.

"Well, I must say we didn't expect the pleasure of the McKenzies here this morning," Bob commented sarcastically as he looked questioningly at Leonard with raised eyebrows. "But I'm sure we can still proceed nonetheless."

Henry seated himself on a wooden stool, a grim expression on his face, but Bob Everitt chose to stand. He was as militant and impatient as ever, refusing to look at Emily and choosing instead to direct his words toward the frightened Ruth, who seemed dwarfed by the tall and intimidating figure.

"I'll get straight to the point, Sister Henderson," Bob folded his arms menacingly. "As you know Max Scofield has spoken to us this morning, reporting the incident of last night. He suspected Emily would have come here; a fact that we are obviously most displeased with, seeing as Pastor Whitfield gave explicit orders that she was not to contact her mother. However …" he turned and looked disdainfully at the teenager, whose head was bowed and shoulders slumped, "…disobedience and rebellion are two characteristics we have come to recognise in Emily." He looked around the room before he continued. "She will obviously *not* be staying here and due to her tendencies to argue, lie, and disobey the Scofields, she will not be returning to their house either."

Indignant at this last statement, Ruth tried in vain to protest. "You…you don't understand. That's not how it was at all and . . ."

But Bob held up his hand. "*Instead,*" he continued irritably, glaring at Ruth, "we have arranged for her to be taken to another family—the Van Der Deckens—who will be expecting her this afternoon."

Emily looked pleadingly at her mum to do something—anything—but Ruth felt powerless to intervene. Not in the face of such unyielding opposition. Even if she tried to argue their case, these two would not believe her and would only twist the whole story around. Besides, she had not the strength to stand up to the leadership. All night she had been pondering her own inadequacies and the truth was—she had failed. She could not protect her family, nor be there for them. She was but a weak and sinful Christian who could not even be trusted to look after her own daughter.

"There is one other thing I should mention," Bob added as he waited for all eyes to be turned on him again. "Because of Emily's actions last night, there are to be some *further* changes." He glanced smugly at Emily. "Pastor Whitfield feels it is necessary to withdraw Emily from her school, effective immediately."

Emily gasped in disbelief. Withdrawn from school and all her friends? Why? She had done nothing! *She* was the victim in all of this. But Bob ignored her reaction as he continued.

"Mrs. Van Der Decken is a retired teacher and will be happy to provide her with any necessary schooling until she turns sixteen." He looked at Ruth triumphantly. "After which, we will be placing Emily in a *factory* to earn her living. It's a factory that cleans car parts and is a little on the *dirty* and *dingy* side, but it will teach her discipline and humility, which she is so obviously desperately in need of."

Tears of disappointment and resentment began to stream down Emily's face. She had always dreamed of doing something with the arts—to act; to paint; possibly to dance, if the church allowed it. How could she ever endure working in a factory? This was too much for her to bear.

Feeling her pain, Marjory attempted to say something. "Come now, Bob. This all seems a little harsh, doesn't it?"

But disinterested, Everitt shrugged his shoulders unmoved. "Pastor's orders."

In desperation Ruth looked across at Leonard, who had been silently watching and listening to the proceedings, his anger growing. He now stood up and walked across to Emily, crouching down beside her. "Have you *seen* her face, Bob? I mean, actually taken the time to look at it and question what really happened?" he exclaimed angrily. "This amounts to *child abuse*. Don't you think she has suffered enough?"

Brother Henry looked slightly shocked at Leonard's reaction, but then narrowed his eyes cynically. For the first time that morning he spoke up. "We have it on good authority, Leonard, that Emily was rebellious and argumentative to Brother Scofield and in need of discipline."

"What?" Leonard almost shouted. "And by discipline you

mean a grown man's fist in a young girl's face! Max Scofield is known for his legalistic approach and is too handy with his fists. Surely it is *he* who should be brought to account!"

"That depends on your perspective," Henry smiled smugly.

"Well, from where I'm sitting I think the evidence is pretty clear!" Leonard stood angrily to his feet. "Perhaps we'll see what the police have to say about the matter!"

There was a stunned silence as everyone in the room turned to stare at Leonard in disbelief.

"I'm sure you know, Brother, that that is completely unscriptural. A higher law governs us all," Bob Everitt oozed Pharisaically. "As an elder of the church I thought you would be aware of this. Tell me, Leonard. Whose side are you on? You wouldn't want to go against the pastor's and therefore *God's* wishes now, would you?"

But Leonard was resolute. "I believe Brother Moss is an Inspector in the Force. Let's see what Pastor Whitfield has to say about me contacting him then, shall we?" he challenged. "Ruth, can I use your phone?"

An awkward silence followed as Leonard left the room to make the call, with Everitt and Henry looking uncomfortable and slightly disarmed at this unexpected turn of events. Ruth handed Emily a box of tissues to dry her tearstained face, praying desperately that the situation would soon be resolved. How she wished she had never gone to the leadership for advice in the first place and had instead kept her problems to herself. Her family would then still be intact, spared of all this trauma and destruction. Again she blamed herself.

In the kitchen Leonard's muffled, but angry voice could be heard as he spoke to the pastor down the phone. It was some ten minutes later before Leonard reappeared again, his face flushed but satisfied. "It's settled," he announced. "Emily will come to live with Marjory and I—and as for being withdrawn from school, this will *not* be happening. If Emily behaves herself, as

I'm sure she will, she can remain at school until she has passed her exams, at which point the situation will be reviewed."

Marjory looked quickly at Ruth, anxious for her approval, and receiving her nod, she turned to Emily with a smile. "Are you okay with coming to live with us for a while?" she asked kindly.

Emily nodded weakly. "Thank you," she whispered.

But Everitt and Henry were not pleased. They had been embarrassed and humiliated in front of the others and their authority, and thus the authority of Pastor Whitfield, had been openly challenged. With menacing scowls they rose to leave.

"An interesting shift of loyalty displayed here today, Brother," Bob muttered harshly as he and Henry were escorted by Leonard to the door. "I would watch my step from now on if I were you, Leonard. You may wish you had been more discreet."

"Is that a threat, Bob?" Leonard questioned, unmoved. "Because if it is, I'm sure Inspector Moss would like to know about that too!"

In disgust Henry and Everitt left the house, their car soon disappearing down the road and out of sight, but Leonard lingered for some minutes on the porch, his thoughts disturbed, and his spirit deeply troubled. The sun was high in the pale blue sky now, though a cold wind reminded Leonard it was still only early spring, and the clumps of yellow daffodils that had been planted along the cobbled pathway swayed peacefully in the breeze. But how far from peaceful he felt.

"It's wrong, Lord," he whispered in troubled prayer. "It's all *very* wrong."

⚡

The house was deathly quiet and unbearably empty now that Emily, for the second time in recent weeks, had been taken away. Leonard and Marjory had stayed on for some time, sipping tea and reassuring Ruth, before taking Emily home with them, and

Ruth was thankful once again for their help. Somehow she had known that Leonard and Marjory would understand and would deal more kindly with them than other members of the leadership. In contrast, how harshly Henry and Everitt had wished to treat them. Ruth shuddered as she considered how differently the outcome of this day might have been had Leonard not intervened. Yet the fact still remained that Emily had gone again and she had been powerless to do anything about it. Ruth stared blankly out of her window. She could not remember a time when she had felt so low; so discouraged; so desperately lonely. How she wanted her daughter back with her, well and happy; how she wanted her husband by her side, no matter what his faults; how she wanted her family back together again as they had been before all this had happened. Emotionally exhausted, Ruth took her head in her hands and let out a deep sob.

The trauma and anxiety of recent events had taken every ounce of energy from Ruth. Wearily stumbling into the bedroom she sat dejectedly on the edge of her bed, dabbing her eyes with a tissue, unsure what to do with herself. The shadows of the low afternoon sun through the barren trees outside her window had begun creeping up the walls, making strange and contorted shapes and as Ruth considered them she could not help but compare these to the mental images of her mind—deep, contorted, indescribable images of pain. Her doctor had said these were stress-related images, which were a type of hallucination; a sign that the brain was overloaded and sending out distress signals. Ruth had not told him the extent of her condition. She feared he would force her to take a drug that the church disapproved of, so she had withheld the complete truth. The fact was, however, there had been other things—things that were not only images. Ruth had been aware of something else that would not stop nagging deep within her head; something that sounded like...voices. Voices echoing in her mind, tormenting and giving her no peace. She could hear these voices now and with trembling hands Ruth held her head again in distress. What was happening to her? Was she losing her mind?

*You're pathetic*, she could hear. *Why didn't you stop them taking your daughter away? You know you'll never see her again. Curse God and die!* Ruth sat up in alarm. She would never curse God. How terrible. She knew she was a lot of things, but she would *never* blaspheme God's name. This was a new thought to her and one that disturbed her greatly. "Oh God!" Ruth cried out in fear. "Where are you?"

But the higher her anxiety rose, the louder the voices grew. *Don't pray to God—he isn't listening. He is not going to help you—he is angry with you. Can you not see his face? It is a face of terrible anger. You have failed as a mother, as a wife, and as a Christian. God has turned his back! Look at you, you are pathetic.* Pathetic! *Curse God; curse God;* curse God—*your life is worthless! Face it, Ruth Henderson—you have nothing to live for.*

Ruth covered her ears in desperation, beginning to quote any scripture that would come into her tormented mind. Stumbling toward her stereo, she frantically began searching through her CDs for something soothing, some reassuring Christian music. Perhaps she could drown the voices out with song. Hastily selecting an album of hymns, she placed the disc into its holder then turned the volume up as loud as she could bear before returning to collapse onto her bed.

> Abide with me, fast falls the even tide;
> The darkness deepens, Lord with me abide.
> When other helpers fail and comforts flee,
> Help of the helpless, O abide with me.

*It's a lie. God doesn't abide with you. He's abandoned you. He doesn't even love you*, the voices hissed. *How is he helping you now? Own up to the facts—your life is a mess. There is no reason to live!*

With tears flowing down her cheeks Ruth sat up, opening her top drawer in desperate search for her Bible. It couldn't be true. God would not abandon her. Surely he would speak to her through his word. But even as she grasped her treasured Bible, the bottle of sleeping pills prescribed to her by her doctor fell into sight. Ruth froze, struggling with her thoughts. She hesitantly picked the bottle up, staring at them in her trembling hand.

> Swift to its close ebbs out life's little day:
> Earth's joys grow dim; its glories pass away;
> Change and decay in all around I see;
> O Thou who changest not, abide with me.

*Take the pills*, the voices insisted. *You need to sleep...to sleep...to sleep.* Ruth shook her head, feeling pain pounding against her temples. Maybe just one pill would do the job—or maybe two. Maybe, if she could just sleep, she would find a little peace. Maybe the voices in her head would finally stop. As though in a trance, Ruth slowly removed two of the tablets from the jar and placed them hesitantly on her tongue.

*Why sleep for one night only?* a voice sneered. *Why not sleep forever!*

"Oh God, I can't take this any more," Ruth cried out in despair. "I give up. I can't be all you want me to be. I can't be all the church wants me to be. I have failed you and everyone that I love. I am worth nothing."

With tears streaming down her face and overwhelmed with hopelessness, pain, guilt and fear, Ruth emptied half the jar into her hand. Then, in deep anguish, she slipped the pills into her mouth and with one quick sip of water she swallowed. The pills were gone.

"Forgive me, God. Forgive me," she whispered as she lay back on the bed.

> Hold thou thy cross before my closing eyes;
> Shine through the gloom and point me to the skies.

Heaven's morning breaks, and earth's vain shadows
flee;
In life, in death, O Lord, abide with me.

Struggling to keep her eyelids open, Ruth drifted into a strange and tormented sleep. The bottle of pills that she had been holding slipped to the floor with a small thud, its remaining contents spilling out across the carpet—but Ruth did not notice. Her hand instead dangled helplessly beside the bed, limp and lifeless...

In life, in death, O Lord, abide with me.

# CONTROLLING THE ELECT

As gentle spring rains lightly watered the gardens and dampened the patio flower pots, Zebedee the cat meowed impatiently at the back door for his breakfast. Unlike the flowerpots, he did not appreciate getting his soft fur dampened, nor did he like to be kept waiting for his food and indignantly he shook his paws and whiskers in protest. But Gladys Jones was too busy to notice either the weather or her beloved cat, for the phone had been ringing off the hook all morning and she had much to keep her occupied.

It seemed that Emily Henderson was the centre of all the commotion, having climbed out of a basement window and run away from the Scofields in the middle of the night. Rumour had it that she had caused an argument with her foster family where there had been some sort of a scuffle and as a result poor Mr. Scofield had injured his hand. Apparently Emily had then turned up at her mother's house, despite warnings that she was not to contact her mother, for it was said that Ruth Henderson was far too soft on her daughter and would only interfere with the disciplinary procedures. And it appeared these sayings were correct, for when Elders Everitt and Henry kindly offered to place Emily with another family (the Van Der Deckens) Ruth had apparently flatly refused and instead insisted poor Elder McKenzie and his wife, Marjory, take her daughter on. What would *they* know about raising a teenage girl? They'd had no children of their own.

It was all most curious, but by no means the end of it. For the latest telephone call had revealed that Ruth Henderson herself had now been rushed to hospital in an ambulance, having been found by a neighbour in the early hours of the morning. It seemed the neighbour had noticed Ruth's lights had not been turned off, though the hour was late, and—much out of character for Mrs. Henderson—loud music could be heard pulsating from her bedroom. Growing suspicious, the neighbour had peered into Ruth's window, as numerous telephone calls had gone unanswered, and there she had seen Ruth unconscious and splayed upon her bed. It was later discovered she'd taken an overdose of sleeping pills (*well*, pastor always said such medication was of the devil!) They had pumped her stomach at the hospital and she had pulled through, narrowly escaping death, and it had all been *quite* a drama. What a to-do! Yet there could be no doubt as to Ruth's intentions (and Gladys certainly had her own opinion on the matter; one which she shared freely with all who had phoned her that morning with the news). Gladys could not help but feel that this was all a desperate bid by Ruth to gain attention, having just recently been abandoned by her husband (so she'd heard). And what with all this business over Emily—well—she *must* be feeling put out. No woman would want to admit that they were a failure as a wife *and* a mother, not to mention as a Christian (for a *true* Christian woman would know her place in the home). No, this latest desperate attempt to take her life was surely pure attention-seeking to gain some measure of sympathy, but it would get her nowhere. At least it was painfully obvious now that the leadership was correct in removing Emily. Ruth Henderson was clearly unstable and an unfit parent and, as usual, the church in its wisdom had been accurate in their dealings all along.

Finally moving away from the telephone, Gladys opened the back door to allow a disgruntled and somewhat wet Zebedee in, the former apologising profusely. "Well it's not every day that we have so much news to indulge in, now is it, my dear?" she

crooned as she reached for a tin of cat food and began opening its lid. Zebedee rubbed against her legs, purring with joyful anticipation, but his joy was short-lived, for the phone had
begun ringing again.

"Hello...this is Gladys Jones."

In a huff Zebedee turned his back and stared out of the window, watching impatiently as droplets of rain drizzled down the
glass, while flicking his tail in annoyance. Would this woman
*ever* stop talking?

"Hello, Cynthia, how are you? What's that...? *More* news...?
This has been quite some day!" She listened intently for a few
minutes before thanking Cynthia and hanging up the phone.

"Oh come now, Zebedee, stop sulking," she said, finding her
cat on the windowsill. She gently stroked his fur. "I've just had
some very interesting news. Ruth Henderson has been placed
in the same critical care unit as the young Rhys—you know,
Yvonne Pritchard's grandson. It seems he is in a critical condition with confirmed septicaemia and not expected to live. Now
*there* is a story, Zebedee. Rhys left our church, you know, and our
good pastor warned him that God's hand of protection would be
lifted if he didn't come back. Well, now it seems he was right.
The problem is, my friend, if he *should* die—where would they
hold the funeral? For it cannot be held at the church seeing as
he had left it, regardless of the fact that he spent most of his life
there. It's such a shame that the young people of today will just
not listen."

Gladys finished opening the cat food, placing a healthy dol-
lop into Zebedee's own special bowl as she continued talking.

"I know one thing is for sure. I won't be doing any flowers for
the funeral. Oh, no. It just wouldn't be right. Here you are, my
dear. Your breakfast."

Seeing his food and a warm plate of milk, Zebedee meowed
in delighted gratitude. Just as long as he was dry and warm and
had a bowl of good food to eat, then all previous grievances were

forgiven, and quite frankly, she could now talk as much as she pleased.

Gladys put the kettle on to make herself a cup of tea. Of course, in all this excitement there had been one piece of gossip that had been overlooked. Zara Williams. Gladys gazed out of the window at the rain as it gently pattered against her pane, reflecting on the situation. It was because of her eyewitness account of seeing Zara lunching with an ex-church member that Zara had been banned from Kate and Dan Marshall's engagement party to take place that very night. Gladys smirked self-righteously as she looked down at her cat, purring contentedly as he ate his food.

"Now *there* is a story, my dear," she whispered. "There is a story!"

☙

Zara had chosen not to tell Kate about her findings at the church office, though the matter had been weighing heavily on her mind. Kate had had enough to worry about of late and tonight was her engagement party. But should Zara tell someone what she had found, or was she really just overreacting? After all, she had no actual proof that any of what she had seen was actually happening, and maybe she was just jumping to all the wrong conclusions. Sure, she had seen a receipt suggesting a bugging device had been purchased, but there could be many explanations for this. She had no evidence one was actually being used or that it was being used illegally. So she had seen her name on a list paired up with Bob Everitt. But had she ever seen Bob shadowing her like the Secret Service? No—her imagination had got the better of her. Certainly this church was strict, as tonight's exclusion from the party had proved, but maybe they were just acting out of a genuine desire to maintain a high standard of godliness. Maybe they weren't so much a cult as just slightly old fashioned and legalistic. Yet even as she thought this, she felt a nagging uncertainty deep within. Why had they acted so harshly with Beth, and why was it that Zara knew if she stepped out of line too far, she too would lose everything? It just didn't make sense. Zara shook her head in confusion. She needed to clear her mind. Perhaps Kate needed a hand getting ready for her party tonight. As she headed toward Kate's room, the doorbell rang. The lounge had been filling steadily with presents for Kate's engagement and Zara had rarely witnessed such generosity. It seemed everyone in the church had given something to mark the occasion, even if just a potted plant.

"Kate!" Zara called as she closed the front door. "Another gift has arrived. I'll put it with the others."

Instead of an answer, however, a cry of dismay sounded from the bedroom and Zara ran quickly to see what was amiss. She found a beautiful but nervous Kate staring in the mirror with dismay at a small damp patch on the front of her dress.

"I've spilled my coffee!" she wailed.

You can hardly see it," Zara reassured her calmly. "I'll sponge it off for you and we can use the hair dryer to dry it. It'll be fine. By the way, you're looking gorgeous!"

Kate looked gratefully at her friend. "I'm feeling so nervous. How am I going to get through tonight without my best friend with me? It's so unfair. I wish you were coming."

"Well we both know why I'm *not*. Don't worry. You'll have Dan beside you—and your mum. You'll have a wonderful night, you'll see," smiled Zara, sounding more cheerful than she felt. She wanted to be a part of the celebrations as well, but it was not to be so. Carefully she dabbed at the spot with a damp cloth before blowing it dry with the cool air of a hair dryer. "So...are you ready for the 'ring giving,' Kate?" she asked teasingly, trying to lighten the mood.

But Kate rolled her eyes looking suddenly flushed. "Ooh— I'm terrified!" she giggled nervously.

The practise of "ring giving" had become somewhat of a tradition at the church of The Light. As any form of physical contact had been strictly disallowed during the courtship and all meetings had been supervised or chaperoned, this was, in fact, the couple's first moment to be completely alone together. It was a time in which the engagement ring was presented, followed by the couple's first kiss, and was considered to be very special, although often nerve racking. The couple were usually allowed ten to twenty minutes alone in a closed room to perform this ritual, at which time the bride's mother would ring a small bell and open the door. Then the celebrations would begin. In Kate's case they would be going to a restaurant first with friends and family, before returning to Kate's family home to open gifts and have coffee.

The dress now sorted, Kate stood back waiting for her friend's approval. "Well, what do you think?" she asked uncertainly.

"Let me see," Zara said in mock severity. "Testimony hem line…check. Modest amount of makeup…check. No earrings… check. You look perfect!" grinned Zara. "That Dan Marshall is a lucky man; that is as long as his sideburns are trimmed and his hair is the testimony length for the church's approval."

"Stop it!" giggled Kate, as she affectionately threw a stuffed teddy bear in Zara's direction.

The next half hour was spent carefully carrying the many presents into Kate's car, piling them high into her boot and back seat. She was taking them around to her mother's house to be opened later that night, and Zara was again amazed at the number of them. If these were the engagement gifts, what would her wedding be like? Finally, however, Kate was ready to go and the two girls embraced each other, holding back tears.

"Careful—you don't want to ruin that testimony makeup as well as your dress," Zara teased. "You have a lovely time and I'll be thinking of you."

But Kate could not answer. Blinking away her tears, she quickly climbed into the driver's seat and with a friendly wave was gone. Zara watched as her car disappeared down the street feeling the sting of disappointment. With a reluctant sigh she turned and went back indoors.

The flat now quiet, Zara was left alone with her thoughts. She had not yet wrapped her own gift to Kate, not wanting to place it with all the others—it didn't seem appropriate somehow. Instead she would place it on Kate's bed for her to discover when she came home much later that night. Zara held the gift in her hand—a silver photo frame with a picture of her and Kate, and just like Beth, Zara had signed it with the words:

Best friends forever

Staring at the words she now wondered if they could be an omen of prophetic significance. Perhaps, just as Beth had been separated from Zara and Kate after penning her words, so she too may be separated from Kate and the church. Zara looked up at the photo of Beth perched on top of the cabinet. How she had enjoyed catching up with her friend again recently, yet the meeting had been bittersweet. As a result Zara would now be spending tonight alone instead of celebrating with Kate at her engagement. It was all so bizarre, especially as Beth had been so keen *not* to cause any trouble. She had even been reluctant to give Zara the pamphlets, though she had obviously wanted to warn her of something. Zara considered this for a moment. In all fairness she should spend more time reading the material Beth had so earnestly given her to discover in full what that warning was. She had been considering the ideas presented in the first pamphlet on "Religious Cults," but what did the second have to say? Zara slipped her hand into her bag and searched for the pamphlets again. Perhaps now, while she was all alone, she could safely continue reading and maybe find some answers to her nagging questions.

Making herself a coffee, she settled herself down into a comfortable chair, this time picking up the leaflet entitled "Spiritual

Abuse," and in the quiet of the twilight evening began to study the information with interest:

### What is Spiritual Abuse?

The word of God is rich with scriptures that describe for us what the Christian life should be like. Words such as: *good news, abundant life, freedom, light burdens, joy, healing,* etc. God's word also describes the type of spiritual authority or leadership that should be set up over us, whose job it is to guide God's people into this freedom of living, much as a shepherd guides and cares for his sheep.

What happens, however, when this same spiritual leadership, who should be building and equipping God's people, begins instead to control and manipulate them for their own purposes? The results are devastating. Freedom becomes control, light burdens become heavy burdens, the abundant life a set of rules riddled with guilt and condemnation, and the believer's relationship with God is confused and damaged.

Whenever spiritual authorities begin to manipulate and control those in their care for their own purposes or to make themselves look good, thus harming or crippling another's faith, this, in essence, is Spiritual Abuse.

To identify Spiritual Abuse then, look for the following:

### The Warning Signs

- Control

Abusive systems control. There is little room for independence or freedom of thought or opinion. Instead the leader controls everything—his/her words are the final say. To doubt or criticise his/her actions is to be black marked or disapproved of. An unspoken feeling of fear often prevails and an understanding that one must obey or suffer the consequences.

• Rules

The list of rules (mainly "Do Not") is endless. Many of these rules are not strictly scriptural, but rather a twisting of Scripture to meet the demands of the leader. To break the rules is to be punished or to be looked down upon.

• Perfectionism

There is a strong emphasis on the "outward" looking good—whether this be the appearance of the church building itself, or its people (who all look and act the same). Often this is more important than the inward state, and many people find they are weary and in desperate need of inner healing. However, they must keep smiling, looking good, and never talk about their real problems. They must keep striving for the often impossible standards of the leadership and therefore God.

• Performance

The message is quickly received that to keep the leadership happy and God happy one must perform, perform, perform. Be a "good testimony" to those watching, attend meetings, get involved in the church, don't make mistakes, strive for God's approval, be obedient to his will and word. All have the feeling of being driven by a whip and are constantly accompanied by feelings of guilt, of never quite being good enough.

• Elitism

It is preached that you are the elite, that your church alone has the whole truth or the "light," unlike any other organisation. You are encouraged to stay within the four walls of the church and not to mingle with "outsiders." All marriages are among and within the church members only and inter-family relationships become a strong bond, often making it difficult to leave. You begin to feel "cut-off" from the outside world.

- Secrets

Often what is presented to the outside world and new converts is not the same as what is really going on within the church, and is often not discovered until a member is firmly ensconced in the system. There is an unspoken knowing that many things should not be spoken of nor disagreed with. Secretiveness often overshadows such subjects as finances or the ways different members are being "dealt with."

- Leaving the system

Leaving the group is difficult and you are often made to feel fearful. It is implied that you will be "out of God's will," taking second best, or worse, that some accident or misfortune will befall you. Once you do leave, you are cut off from all members and snubbed or ignored from that point on. Your name is often used in sermons as examples of those to be avoided, and should you seek to make contact with any existing member, you are accused of being a division maker.

Zara folded the leaflet up slowly and sat in silence for some time, strangely calm. Somehow, deep within her, she knew this was a picture of the organisation she had become involved with, for these words were very familiar. It was as though someone had handed her the missing piece of a jigsaw puzzle, and the picture had become suddenly clear. Her nagging doubts about the church were now quieted within her for they had been justified, she felt, with the truth. But how she wished there was someone she could talk to. Someone who could tell her what she should do. Did the pamphlet include contact phone numbers or addresses? Turning to the back page Zara found the name of the organisation who had written the material, but they were based overseas and it would be impractical for her to phone. Perhaps she would write to them later. About to replace the pamphlets in her bag, however, Zara noted that Beth had written her own telephone number very faintly on the top corner of the front page. She recalled Beth's words to her last time they had spoken, *"Zara, if ever you want someone to talk to, my number is on the pamphlet."* Zara wondered. Should she? Dare she make contact with Beth again and share her heart? In all truth, Beth might just be the only person she knew right now who would actually understand what she was going through. By phoning no one would see her, and there was certainly no one in the flat who could hear her. This was the perfect opportunity.

Zara went into the hall and picked up the phone, hesitantly holding it in her hand. Was she doing the right thing? She had promised Kate she would avoid trouble for the sake of the wedding, yet who would know she had called Beth? Besides, her discoveries tonight demanded answers. Quickly, before she changed her mind, she dialled the number and waited.

"Hi, this is Beth speaking," a pleasant voice answered.

"Beth? This is Zara. Zara Williams."

"Zara?" Beth cried with delight. "How great to hear your voice! I didn't know if I would hear from you again, but I was hoping you'd call me. How are you?"

"Well...I've been better." Zara was quick to fill her in on the recent developments of being excluded from Kate's engagement party after being seen lunching with her at the mall. Beth's delight soon changed to concern as she heard of Zara's predicament.

"I was afraid something like this might happen," she muttered. "I knew we were taking a risk. Zara, they'll be on to you now, watching you like a hawk. You'll have to be really careful."

"Well—they'd be more worried if they knew what I'd done since then." Zara went on to explain her findings in the church office.

Beth was uneasy. "Zara, you know this is quite serious. With findings like this the church could go sky high. Have you told anyone else?"

"Who else could I tell? I don't want to worry Kate—somehow I don't think she'd understand anyway...and I certainly can't go to anyone else at the church. So that's why I've rung you. I figured you would be the only one who had any idea what I was talking about. I've been reading the pamphlets you gave me and I'm beginning to see what you were trying to warn me about. The church of The Light has some real issues, but the thing is—what should I do about it?"

A sudden crackling noise on the phone interrupted their conversation and for a moment they were silent before Beth continued.

"Have you paid your telephone bills?" she teased. "This line is bad. Listen, Zara. It sounds like you need some confirmation just as I did before I had to make some difficult decisions...and I have an idea. This Sunday night at the Town Hall in the city centre a well-known South African preacher will be speaking. I know you would enjoy listening to him. Look—this may sound crazy, especially in the light of recent events...and I know it is forbidden by The Light, but why don't you come along to the meeting and I'll meet you there. It might help put things into perspective for you a little more by seeing for yourself how other Christians are getting along. I know it may be difficult for you to come without your absence being noticed, but it seems as though carrying on the way you have been with so many doubts is also going to be hard. You have to make your mind up one way or another. So...will you come?"

The phone crackled again. Zara felt a thrill of excitement at the prospect of Beth's suggestion, but she also felt nervous. "I'd love to...but I'll have to think carefully about it first," she replied as the phone crackled for the third time, accompanied by a strange clicking sound. "Did you hear that?" Zara asked—then suddenly she froze. "Beth! Don't say another word—just hold onto the phone for a minute."

Quickly placing her receiver down onto the hall table, Zara rushed to the lounge window and cautiously peered through the blinds to the road outside. She gasped! A familiar black saloon could be seen parked right outside her house. A small aerial protruded through its window and inside the car an accompanying small red light could be seen flashing through the darkness. Although in partial shadow, the light from a nearby street lamp illuminated the face of...Bob Everitt!

Zara hurried back to pick up the phone again. "Beth? I...I've got to go. I'll explain later." She hung up quickly, her heart racing. So it was true. They *were* using technology for tapping into telephone conversations. Her case against The Light was growing stronger by the minute. Yet one fear remained. How much of the conversation between Beth and herself had Bob Everitt heard?

# WAITING FOR THE PROMISE

As Kate's car bumped along the open country roads, Zara held tightly to her seat, trying to appear calm and relaxed. The countryside was green and lush at this time of the year and Zara would normally be enjoying the scenery if it weren't for the many pot holes encountered along the way, and Kate's unique talent for driving into each one. Zara was beginning to feel a little ill and would be glad to reach their destination.

"Are we nearly there?" she groaned, rubbing her head as it knocked against the car roof on the rebound from yet another pothole.

"Almost. Why? Not enjoying the ride?" Kate glanced across at her friend with a grin.

It was early Saturday morning and Kate and Zara were on their way to one of the bi-annual "country prayer meetings" held by the church of The Light at a hired campsite hall in the countryside. Not that either of them were looking forward to it; for it was well known that such meetings were long and drawn out, and although no one would actually say, it was attended by most out of religious duty and pressure from the pastor rather than by choice. It didn't help that the sky was deep blue and cloudless, and that the sun streamed warmly through the car windows. Zara could think of many other things she would rather be doing in the countryside than sitting indoors all day at such a meeting, even though the pastor would say this was the "flesh" speaking and wholly unspiritual. She had so much on her mind from recent events and still had not decided whether to risk meeting with Beth tomorrow night at the Town Hall. She was desperate to, but didn't want to cause any more trouble. How could she endure today's meeting when her mind was in such turmoil? How could she act as though everything was normal when it clearly wasn't?

Kate had slowed the car now to allow a herd of sheep to cross the road before them into a nearby pasture. Zara watched them with interest as they huddled together compliantly following each other. They reminded her of the members of The Light who compliantly followed the leadership's orders without outward question or complaint. Yet she wondered how many, like her, were inwardly struggling and questioning the system. Take today's meeting, for example. Zara was the first to confess her knowledge of the Bible was somewhat limited, yet even she wondered if these prayer meetings were completely scriptural. The idea was based on the scripture in Acts 1:4, 5 which read:

> And, being assembled together with them, commanded them that they should not depart from Jerusalem, but wait for the promise of the Father, which, saith he, ye have heard of me. For John truly baptized with water; but ye shall be baptized with the Holy Ghost not many days hence.
>
> Acts 1:4,5(KJV)

As with many other scriptures, Pastor Whitfield had his own unique and literal interpretation of these verses. He believed that in order for the Holy Spirit to be received into one's life, a complete day needed to be dedicated twice a year when all the church members assembled in the countryside and waited until the Holy Spirit's presence fell and filled them. This special service was therefore aptly called the "country prayer meeting" and the location was of necessity in the countryside to be far away from the hustle and bustle of everyday life, where one and all could tarry in peace and tranquillity. As "speaking in tongues" was the obvious outward evidence that one had been filled with the Holy Ghost, and therefore an enviable gift to possess, great pressure was applied by the pastor on the congregation to perform, and the hall was divided into the "those who could speak in tongues" and "those who could not." Zara was the in latter group and once again cringed at the thought of having to walk up to the front seats once more to receive special prayer. The atmosphere of pride and looks of religious superiority from the "those who could" section was almost tangible and she hated it. Besides which, Pastor Whitfield seemed to think each person who did speak in tongues was a personal victory for him; a feather in his cap, as though this was his showcase to the world that he was on the cutting edge of Christianity. Zara wondered if this was really what the book of Acts intended.

At last, Kate turned her car into the little dusty lane that led to the old wooden community hall where today's meeting would be held. The grass fields surrounding it were already filling up with cars, and gratefully Zara opened her door to drink in the fresh country air before following Kate toward the building.

The hall was already half full as Kate and Zara entered, making their way awkwardly down the centre isle toward the front and seating themselves on the hard wooden chairs. Zara could almost feel the eyes of self-righteousness piercing into the back of her head. It was going to be a long day. Thankfully she had not had to endure as many of these prayer meetings as Kate, who had been attending them ever since she was thirteen; although she still had not received the gift of tongues. Zara wondered why it all was so difficult, for didn't the Bible say to simply ask of the Father and he would gladly give this good gift? She sighed, wondering if today might be that day for both herself and Kate.

Exactly on the hour the meeting got underway with Pastor Whitfield giving his usual short but condemnatory sermon about the need for complete holiness and surrender, and a yielding of all sin before the Holy Ghost would come. Zara always felt uneasy listening to this message, for it seemed to suggest the reason she had not received was due to some consistent and gross sin, which she could never quite put her finger on. She was trying to do things right, but would she *ever* be pure enough to be acceptable to God? Would he ever bless her with his presence?

The pastor then asked that all heads be bowed and all eyes closed in order that the first song be sung in an atmosphere of reverence and meditation. The pianist led with an introduction that sounded somewhat morbid, and the song was dutifully sung then repeated twice more. But by the fourth time round Zara began to shift uncomfortably in her seat. Would God be tempted to manifest himself in such a funereal atmosphere? Yet another two verses and several more songs were to be endured before the "praise and worship" began. Zara had always been puzzled at this part of the service. In her heart she wanted to praise her God and worship him for who he was, but the feeling here today was very different. She couldn't help but feel an overwhelming pressure to perform, as though an invisible whip were being applied to her and in reality this "praise and worship" time had become a gruelling two hours of repeating phrases monotonously, of chanting, of praising, of doing and saying anything that was appropriate to keep your lips moving in order to maintain the "atmosphere." Hour after hour of united mumbling and muttering resounded around the room, broken occasionally by outbursts of wailing and weeping and the consequent rushing to their side of an elder who would then proclaim that this one had received or that one had been filled. Zara's head began to spin. For hours she praised, thanked, asked, and pleaded as the pastor suggested, but all to no avail. She had received nothing more than a headache and was thankful when at last a bell sounded announcing lunch.

Kate and Zara chose to eat on a grassy bank overlooking the river that was partially shaded by the branches of an old willow tree. They spread out their picnic rug and proceeded to unpack a modest lunch before leaning back to enjoy the peaceful gurgling of the brook and early spring sunshine. Kate's new engagement ring sparkled in the sunlight as she sipped her coffee from the cup of a thermos flask. Dan sat some distance from them, for although they were now engaged, they still could not be seen together, especially at a prayer meeting. This would be a distraction that was wholly unspiritual and not appropriate on such a day. To be engaged should be one of the happiest times in a young woman's life, yet as Zara quietly studied her friend's face, she was not convinced that all was well.

"Kate—is everything okay?" she inquired as she propped herself up on her elbows to pour herself another cup of hot coffee. "You were really quiet on the drive down here and you seem a little preoccupied now and...well, almost sad. I know you've told me everything went well at the engagement party last week, but ever since that night you have seemed somehow different."

Kate dropped her eyes as she stared intensely at her ring twisting it nervously between her fingers. Her faced looked flushed, her manner agitated. Eventually she looked up, gazing uncertainly in Dan's direction as he sat with a group of friends not far from them.

"I...I'm not sure if Dan is the one," she said shakily, now choking back the tears.

Zara was not prepared for this. "You're not *serious?*" she exclaimed, as she sat upright, staring at her friend. "But...I don't understand. You were so sure, so radiant last week. What has changed?"

"I don't know, Zara." Kate shrugged, gazing down at her ring again. "I just feel so confused. I said the party went well last week but to tell the truth...well, it all started when he gave me the ring. I was alone for the first time with this man and I suddenly realised I hardly knew him. I was so nervous and we only kissed. Zara, what will I be like on the honeymoon? I really panicked. Then all night it was like something had come between us. I just didn't feel close to him—and he hardly said a word to me. I mean…he said he was happy; he actually even stayed on at the house until the early hours of the morning helping to clean up—but he just doesn't talk a lot or laugh. What if I'm making a huge mistake?"

Zara looked at her friend, feeling anger rising within her. She couldn't help but feel this was all the direct result of such archaic and regimental dating proceedings. No wonder Kate was terrified. She'd had such an unnatural courtship with Dan that they were practically strangers; a point she had raised on several occasions, though to reiterate that now would be unfair.

"Kate, you have to talk to Dan about this. You must be honest with each other. You've often said you believe marrying Dan was God's will. Do you still feel this is true?"

Kate began to weep softly, but nodded her head.

"Then that's what you have to hold on to. Maybe you're just going to have to work extra hard at getting to know each other—write each other letters or something, and really share your heart. I'm sure you're going to make it."

Kate smiled tearfully. "Do you really think so?"

"Of *course* I do!"

"Zara, if only you'd been there at the engagement. I would have had someone to share this with."

"Yes, well, I've been dutifully punished and am humbly repentant, so let's hope that's the end of it," she said lightly.

But Kate looked pleadingly into Zara's eyes. "*Please* don't do anything else that will place you in trouble. I couldn't bear it if you weren't at my wedding."

"Oh—so there *is* going to be a wedding then, is there?" Zara teased, avoiding Kate's statement. For how could she tell Kate of her recent telephone conversation with Beth; her possible plans to meet her tomorrow night; and her suspicions the call had been bugged?

"Good afternoon, girls," a gruff voice sounded behind them.

Startled, they turned to see Bob Everitt standing over them.

"I hope Zara's conversation today is in keeping with the church's doctrine and that she is not leading you astray," he smiled sinisterly. "The meeting will begin again in ten minutes."

The girls thanked him and laughed nervously as Bob turned and walked away. But when he was out of sight Kate turned to Zara in alarm.

"What did he mean? Do you know what he was talking about?"

Zara shrugged nonchalantly beginning to pack the picnic basket away. "I'm sure he was only joking. It's just his dry sense of humour," she commented casually to allay Kate's fears, but as she rose to return to the meeting, she knew she wasn't so sure.

The afternoon wore on much the same as the morning with more singing and repetitive praising, but Zara could no longer concentrate. She was worried as to how much Bob Everitt knew and how this could affect her already fragile friend's wedding. She knew she had promised Kate once before to stay out of trouble, and she really desired to do so, yet she could not so quickly drop her growing concerns and knew she needed answers. The meeting at the Town Hall was tomorrow night, but should she risk going?

As the hours ticked slowly by Zara sat quietly, her mind churning over and over. She thoughtfully watched the scene around her, observing the straining and the striving of the people who were working so hard for God's approval. She listened as they sung and praised God, begging him to presence himself among them, desperate for his touch. They looked wearied and burdened and for so many their joy had all but gone. She reflected on the meaning of "Spiritual Abuse" that she had so recently read about in the material Beth had given her, feeling that she was witnessing such abuse first hand. She considered the meaning of a religious cult and couldn't help but compare this to that which was before her. She contemplated her findings in the church office, her telephone conversation that had been bugged, and the overwhelming control of Pastor Whitfield. Finally she reflected on the way Beth had been dealt with, Kate had been dealt with, *she* had been dealt with—and with sudden clarity Zara knew what she had to do. Despite the possibility that Bob Everitt could be monitoring her every move, she needed to go to the Town Hall meeting tomorrow night—she'd think of a way to get there unnoticed. The fact was she *had* to see how other Christians were living their lives. She had to know if there truly was life outside of this church. And if there was…she would consider leaving. Not straight away of course, for she would bide her time until Kate was married. She would put on a good show at the church of The Light and ask no more questions. She'd get involved to keep the peace. But as soon as Kate was safely married, she would attempt to sever her ties with this church. It would pain her to be parted from her friend—but then, perhaps she could persuade Kate and Dan to join her? It was at least her plan.

Little did Zara know, however, how soon her plans would be thwarted.

⚡

The sun was disappearing behind the distant hills in a blaze of oranges and reds when Marjory, Leonard, and Emily finally walked through the door after an exhausting day at the country prayer meeting. Leonard collapsed wearily onto a kitchen chair, throwing his keys and paper down onto the table in frustration. He was deeply troubled at the outcome of the meeting, for many people still had not received their heavenly language, despite eight hours of praying and interceding. Marjory had patiently listened to him as he had let off steam all the way home and now she endeavoured to calm him down.

"Why don't you go upstairs and get changed into something a little more comfortable, and when you come back down read the paper for awhile? I'll put the kettle on for a cup of tea and maybe I could whisk up some of your favourite cheese muffins. I think we still have some homemade tomato soup in the freezer that you like as well. We'll just have a nice relaxing evening, and put the frustrations of the day aside for a while. How does that sound?" she asked kindly, rubbing Leonard's weary shoulders.

"Hmm, that sounds like a good plan." Leonard closed his eyes for a moment, enjoying the back massage. "You'd really make me some of your famous cheese muffins?" he said, looking up at her almost boyishly. His Marjory always knew how to ease his worries.

Moments later, Leonard plodded obediently up the stairs to change his attire while Marjory took her apron from its peg behind the kitchen door and prepared to make the dinner. Emily had been searching through the mail in the hallway as though eagerly anticipating a certain piece of correspondence, but finding nothing, dejectedly walked past Marjory toward her bedroom. Marjory stood for a moment, watching her as the door quietly closed, sending a clear message that she wanted to be left alone. Emily had hardly spoken a word on the journey home and instead had stared dolefully out of the window. Marjory had glanced at her several times in the car mirror, feeling very concerned and had decided that after they had eaten she would have a little chat with her. She knew that Emily was deeply worried about her mother, who was still in hospital, and realised how difficult it must be for her to be living in a stranger's house when her family was experiencing such desperate times. She knew Emily was also missing her dad, having not heard from him in some time, and would be longing to make contact with him. It was only natural that she would want to let him know that her mum was in hospital and besides, she would benefit from his fatherly arms of comfort at this time. Yet the church had made it clear that while Emily was being disciplined, all such contact was forbidden, and it seemed to Marjory that this had only served in pushing Emily to the edge of isolation and loneliness.

She had her friends at church, but as they were all part of strong Christian families Marjory suspected Emily felt they wouldn't understand, and had therefore kept much of her troubles to herself. It was clear Emily was not coping and Marjory's heart went out to her. For one so young she had been through so much, yet it certainly wasn't over. They had been to the hospital to visit her mum every evening since the overdose, despite the church's orders for non-contact. Marjory was appalled that Pastor Whitfield could appear so inhumane at a time like this when, of course, Emily must be with her mum, and had chosen, on this point, not to inform the church of her actions. However, what would happen when Ruth was released from the hospital? Marjory was troubled at the thought of Ruth returning to her lonely little house where Emily would be forbidden to visit and she would be isolated once more. She was worried that the stresses of life would all too soon surround Ruth, causing her to break, and to be honest she feared Ruth might try something again but with more fatal results. If *she* had worked this out, Emily must surely have done the same and she only hoped Emily did not blame herself for any of this. Marjory sighed as she busied herself measuring flour and milk and grating cheese into a bowl. Teenage years were difficult at the best of times, but there seemed to be so many more deeply hidden hurts in this young girl's life. She desperately needed healing and counsel, and Marjory hoped that one day Emily would trust her enough to open up her heart and share some of her pain. Having finished mixing the muffins, Marjory spooned the mixture carefully into the muffin tins, popping them into the oven and standing back for a moment in thought. Perhaps she could make another batch to take with them when they visited Ruth tomorrow.

Leonard had appeared again with slippers in hand. "There now, all I need is my pipe—if I had one that is," he grinned, dropping the slippers to the floor and slipping his feet into them. "Sorry for getting so upset before, Marj," he apologised. "I just get so frustrated with it all. I mean, in the New Testament the gift of speaking in tongues flowed so easily. It was a natural out-flowing of being filled with the presence of God's Holy Spirit. But today's meeting . . ." he shook his head, "...it was nothing more than striving and hard work."

"Well," said Marjory wisely, handing him a cup of steaming hot tea, "you can be sure the problem is not at God's end."

"Pastor Whitfield then?" Leonard said, raising his eyebrows as he settled himself with his cup of tea at the kitchen table while removing the sports pages from his paper.

Marjory nodded. "He has filled the people with so much fear and condemnation; I don't think any of them believe they are good enough for God's love, grace, and forgiveness—let alone his gifts. If the songs had been any drearier today, I would have guessed we were at a funeral service."

Leonard sighed, nodding in agreement. "Did you notice the way . . ."

But his sentence was suddenly interrupted by a heavy and sickening thud from the bedroom, followed by smashing glass, as though something had been knocked from the dressing table. Startled, Leonard and Marjory looked up at each other in alarm. Emily? Marjory hastily washed her hands under the tap, as Leonard rose quickly from the table, about to head in the direction of her room. But just as suddenly the phone began to ring, its shrill tone abruptly demanding to be answered.

"Leonard!" Marjory cried. "You take the call—I'll check Emily."

Hastily walking toward Emily's bedroom while drying her hands on her apron, Marjory paused outside her closed door, listening intently for any further sounds. Nothing could be heard. She knocked tentatively. "Emily—are you all right?" she called, but hearing no response, she firmly grasped the handle and pushed the door open.

The room was in complete darkness from the heavy curtains that were drawn against the twilight night, and Marjory stood for some moments as her eyes adjusted to the dark. Seeing a figure beside the bed she called softly again. "Emily—is that you? Are you okay?"

But there was no response. Searching with her hand against the wall, Marjory flicked on the switch and waited as the room flooded with light. But no sooner had the darkness dissipated than Marjory stepped backwards in horror with her hand across her mouth, her eyes taking in what her mind could not comprehend. Emily lay unconscious on the carpet with a pool of blood surrounding her wrists and a razor blade abandoned not far from her hand. A bedside lamp lay shattered where it had fallen, knocked by her body as it had collapsed onto the floor, and the normally soft pink bed linen was soaked in the deepest of red as blood had been splattered across it. Letting out a cry of dismay, Marjory rushed forward and fell to her knees. Quickly she picked up a nearby scarf and bound it around Emily's wrists to reduce any further bleeding. "Oh my child—what have you done?" she whispered in despair as she held her limp body close to her own. She could hear Leonard hanging up the phone, his soft footsteps rapidly approaching her down the hallway.

"Marjory! That was Yvonne Pritchard on the phone. Rhys' condition has worsened and they don't think he'll make it through the night. They've asked if we'll come to the hospital straight away and pray . . ." Leonard stopped short in his tracks, staring in shock at the scene before him.

"He's not the only one who'll need our prayers tonight," Marjory turned to him with fear in her eyes, her face drained of colour and her body shaking. "Quick, Leonard. Call an ambulance!"

# A Glimmer of Hope

The hospital drapes flapped gently in the spring breeze as it blew softly through a half-open window, giving the occupants welcome relief from the stuffiness of the centrally-heated ward. Weary and subdued, Ruth lay on her bed with her cubicle curtains drawn around her, enjoying the coolness of the breeze, while listening to the early morning sounds of the hospital as it gradually began to wake up. The cleaning staff had already set to work with the swish of mops and hum of vacuum cleaners echoing up and down the narrow corridors, and nurses' footwear could be heard squeaking and squelching against the highly-polished floors as they set about their morning chores. The smell of breakfast wafted on the air, accompanied by the rattle of dishes and stainless steel cutlery, and the yawns and groans of the other five people in her ward signified that they, too, were finally stirring. But Ruth had been awake for hours, her mind churning over the events of the past few days, refusing to grant her sleep.

She reflected lugubriously on her own desperate attempt to end her life and now, perhaps more painfully, the attempt of her own precious daughter to end hers. The old, familiar feelings of failure and fear had returned, seemingly unaffected by her near-fatal attempts to eradicate them, and in fact, felt more intense. God now seemed so far away that she could not even find it within herself to utter the smallest prayer, and her head spun with the tormenting voices that had driven her to such despair. Her life was a mess, and she felt ashamed to call herself a Christian. What would the church say when they heard of these recent events? No doubt they would be angry at her for her sinful actions, and blame her for Emily's self-harming. Distressed, she pulled the thin, green hospital blankets up around her chin to comfort herself. How could she ever look the leadership in the eye again? To add to her sorrow, news had reached her that Yvonne Pritchard's eldest grandson, Rhys, had passed away in the night, finally succumbing to septicaemia and serious chest wounds that were the result of a motorcycle accident. Ruth turned over in her bed and gazed at the whitewashed ceiling above her, her face damp. Why was it that this young man's life had been taken and hers spared when all she could see stretched out before her was a path full of loneliness and hopelessness?

"Good morning, Ruth," the cheery voice of Nurse Symons startled her as she drew back the cubicle curtains and proceeded to plump up her pillows. "How are you feeling today? Are you ready for some breakfast?"

Taking her beaker to the nearby sink, the nurse filled it with fresh water as Ruth discreetly attempted to wipe her tear stained face with her sleeve. Then, smiling weakly, Ruth struggled into position ready, to receive her tray. Ruth wasn't feeling particularly hungry, but Nurse Symons was a force not to be reckoned with, and she dared not disobey. Ruth glanced nervously across at the woman in the bed beside her—Deborah—who was also being encouraged to sit up by the nurse, whether she felt inclined to do so or not. Deborah was in her mid-forties and had recently undergone a hysterectomy, which had been, by all accounts, quite complicated. Yet, despite her obvious pain, she was friendly and polite to everyone. Though Ruth had not felt particularly chatty of late, she had engaged in some small conversation with Deborah over the past few days, discovering that she was, in fact, a Christian who attended a small Pentecostal church called Grace Chapel. Ruth had mixed feelings about this, given her own state of mind at the present, but to Deborah's credit she had instinctively avoided any prying questions of Ruth, instead keeping the conversation light and impersonal. However, her immediate kindness and acceptance had shown that she understood enough to know that Ruth needed a friend more than a judge at this time in her life, and for this Ruth had been grateful. Despite herself, she had been observing Deborah with both interest and curiosity, knowing that the church of The Light was completely anti-Grace Chapel or those of the Pentecostal persuasion. What she had seen in Deborah had quietly impressed her. For as she had prayed, read her Bible, or effortlessly chatted to those around her, Deborah possessed such a peace, such an obvious joy, that Ruth had, in fact, felt quite envious. How she longed for that peace and assurance herself; that joy she had once known when first she had met Christ but now seemed to have lost.

"Well, here goes," Deborah winked at Ruth as she looked at her tray. "I wonder what culinary delights we'll discover under here this morning," she grinned as she lifted off the lid that covered her breakfast plate. Ruth had the same—pale and watery scrambled eggs on soggy white toast.

"Well P.T.L. it's not runny porridge again!" Deborah exclaimed.

"P.T.L.?" Ruth questioned quietly as she picked up her knife and fork, preparing to chase the egg around her plate.

"P.T.L.—Praise the Lord." Deborah turned and studied Ruth's face for a few minutes, her gentle blue eyes seeming to look right through her. "Did you have a difficult night again last night?" she asked softly. "Is there anything I can help you with?"

Ruth looked down at her tray abruptly, taken off guard by her unexpected interest. She knew better than to get too close or friendly with members of other churches, and felt fearful that, if she accepted Deborah's offer of help, she might be tempted to listen to the false Pentecostal doctrine that Pastor Whitfield had so often negatively preached about. Yet an overwhelming ache within her longed to be appeased, and she felt inexplicably drawn to Deborah's gentle and godly manner. The truth was she was desperate to share her burden, and maybe it would be good to talk to someone outside the church who would be unbiased in their opinion. Slowly she nodded in response to Deborah's question.

Deborah continued to look at Ruth with concern, almost hesitating to say what was obviously on her mind. "Can I share something with you?" she asked gently. "I know we don't know each other very well yet, but from what I can tell we do know the same God, right?" she smiled. "I have a feeling you don't need a sermon right now, and the last thing I want to do is give you advice which you haven't asked for. But I do feel the Lord wants you to know something. No matter how great the problem, our God is greater. His *grace* is sufficient for you, Ruth; his *strength* is made perfect in your weakness. His love, acceptance, and understanding toward you and your family are deeper than you'll ever know."

Ruth looked up, astonished, feeling tears dampen her eyes once again. Deborah's simple words had struck to the very depths of her heart like a single droplet of water on dry and parched land. She couldn't remember the last time someone had spoken to her like this, with such assurance and confidence in their God, and something stirred within Ruth. Something that she had not felt in a very long time, for it felt like...hope. "Thank you," she whispered softly.

As the nurses busied themselves with their rounds, clearing trays, straightening beds, and distributing medication, Ruth sat quietly on her chair, watching the proceedings. Deborah was absorbed in a book and Ruth noticed she had a pile more beside her on her bedside cabinet. Keen to continue conversation, she cleared her throat.

"Do...do you like to read?" she asked hesitatingly, afraid she might be disturbing her reverie.

Deborah looked up and laughed. "Looks impressive, doesn't it? Just making the most of being bedridden. Would you like to look at a few of them?" She handed several books across to Ruth, who took them uncertainly and quietly read their titles. "*Spiritual Warfare, Deliverance from Demons and Inner Healing, Prophecies and Intercession.* Goodness, that's quite heavy reading."

"No, just very necessary reading," Deborah responded, once again studying Ruth's face over the rim of her reading glasses. She placed her book down. "Sometimes the things we are battling against in our own lives and in our families are not just purely physical, nor just the circumstances and people we see around us. Instead they are more often than not spiritual. As Christians we need to know how our enemy works, learning well the strategies to fight him. We also need to learn how to walk with the Holy Spirit, listening to his instructions and exercising the many gifts that he has given us." Ruth laughed. "There, I've given you a sermon after all when I promised I wouldn't. I just can't help myself."

But Ruth was fascinated and, despite her fears, was not offended. She'd been a Christian for many years but had never heard this message before—not in the way that Deborah presented it. Ruth knew the devil existed and that his temptations of sin were to be resisted. She had heard often enough from the pulpit that if she failed in her Christian endeavours, the horrors of hell would certainly be awaiting her; these messages were all too familiar. But she'd never heard the term "spiritual warfare," nor "inner healing"—and what was "deliverance"? As for the gifts of the Holy Spirit, were these not just for the leadership? At The Light it was the elders only who were entrusted with the task of praying for healing, though she had seen little evidence of it. Come to think of it, what other gifts were there? Perhaps Deborah referred to the gift of tongues?

Seeing Ruth's puzzled expression, Deborah smiled. "Listen—I'm going to shuffle along to the showers now with all my tubes and bits 'n' pieces, but you're welcome to borrow any of the books that take your interest. If you have any questions at all, or just want to chat, I'd be glad to help."

"I...I'm not sure that I should, Deborah . . ." managed Ruth uncertainly, although her heart was saying something different than her head.

"Oh, call me Deb. Everyone else does," she grinned cheerily. "Look, the books will be here as long as I am. If you change your mind, just help yourself."

Arming herself with towels and toiletries, Deb prepared to shuffle off in the direction of the bathrooms. This was no easy task as she was still attached to drips and bladder bags (which Deborah affectionately called her "Gucci bags") and her steps were still a little shaky and uncertain. Nevertheless, before she left, she made her way over to where Ruth was seated and, leaning down, she gently placed a hand on Ruth's shoulder. "Don't be afraid. You're in God's hands...and I've got a feeling you and I are going to be good friends," she whispered.

Ruth was taken aback, and for the second time that day felt touched by her unexpected words of kindness. Feeling strangely warm, she watched thoughtfully as Deb exited the room.

Visiting hours were between 2:00 p.m. and 4:00 p.m. that day, and Leonard and Marjory had promised to bring Ruth news of Emily's progress. Emily's ward was in another wing of the hospital, making visiting impossible for Ruth, and she had to therefore content herself with second-hand information. How she longed to be near her daughter. It had been nearly two days since the incident, and Ruth was desperate to talk to her. She needed to reassure and comfort her. How wretched Ruth felt as she considered her own actions may have been partly responsible for her daughter's self-harming. Nevertheless, although her heart was heavy, she could do nothing but wait.

In the meantime, between doctor's visits to her bed and hospital routines, Ruth had given some thought to Deborah's books and had plucked up the courage to borrow one. She'd decided she could always put the book down if it was contrary to her beliefs and so had chosen the one entitled *Spiritual Warfare*. Merely holding the book in her hands had made her, at first, feel rebellious and in danger of being indoctrinated. But as she had started to read, she felt such a hunger to learn, such a drawing to the words that she soon found she could not put it down. Somewhat embarrassed, she had been peppering Deborah on and off all day with her many questions, although Deborah (or Deb, as she liked to be called) had been patient and helpful with her explanations. Ruth was amazed at the depth of understanding she seemed to have, and the lack of knowledge she herself seemed to possess. She was also amazed at the amount of material and seminars available on these subjects, as Deb quickly filled her in on her many travels and visits to conferences around the country and even occasionally overseas. Why was it that for a church who proclaimed to have "the whole truth" the church of The Light had never taught on these subjects before, when it was obviously such common knowledge to so many other Christians? Why was it that when she listened to Deb talk she felt life and strength slowly flowing back into her, and a sense of hope and victory in her God beginning to grow? Indeed she felt like a dry sponge soaking up all that Deb, and the book, had to say.

As 2:00 p.m. arrived and visitors began to wander in, the nurses closed off the cubicle curtains to allow each patient the privacy they needed to talk with friends and family. The cotton fabric, however, provided somewhat of a false security, for it did not block out the sound and one could still hear the conversations that went on around the room. Trying not to listen, Ruth curled up on her bed and opened her book again. Leonard and Marjory would be arriving around 3:00 p.m., so she had time to relax and was eager to continue reading. As she turned to her place, however, she heard that Deb had joyfully greeted two of her own friends in the cubicle next to hers and was thanking them for the beautiful flowers they had obviously brought her.

They quickly engaged in happy conversation and Ruth found that, despite her efforts to concentrate on her book, she soon was smiling at the laughter and jokes that could be heard through the flimsy curtains that separated them. Ruth placed her book down beside her and gazed thoughtfully out of the window. It had been many years since she had laughed and joked with friends of her own, and in fact she realised she had never really been close to anyone, except her family. Oh, she was *friendly* to a lot of people at The Light, but somehow these friendships seemed so superficial and unreal and did not feel meaningful. How she longed for the relationships that Deb so obviously enjoyed.

The laughter soon died down, however, and serious conversation followed, so that instinctively Ruth turned back to her book again, not wanting to pry. After some time all grew very quiet in the adjacent cubicle and, intrigued, Ruth wondered if Deb's guests had actually left. But she heard the mumbling of low voices and saw the curtains move as though her friends were gathering around the bed and soon realised that they were, in fact, preparing to pray. The male voice began to speak, lifting up Deb to his God and asking for her healing and blessing. Fascinated, Ruth found herself listening intently to his every word, for he did not pray like the elders at her church. Instead he prayed with such authority, as though he knew his God and was partnering with him. What a wonderful thought, and much to her surprise Ruth found her heart stirring with excitement.

"Ruth?" Deborah's voice suddenly called unexpectedly to her from her cubicle. "Ruth, are you free for a minute? I'd like you to meet my friends."

Taken by surprise, Ruth quickly sat up, adjusting her hair and pulling the blankets discreetly around her. "Ah—sure," Ruth called back hesitantly, clearing her throat. "Come on in."

The curtains soon pulled back and in stepped a couple in their early fifties. The man was tall and thin with greying hair and casually dressed, but with a smile on his face and a twinkle in his eyes that immediately betrayed a great sense of humour.

He was followed closely by his wife who, though dressed more elegantly, had a kind smile and friendly manner.

Deb was quick to make the introductions. "Ruth, this is Brian and Lynn Somerville, whom I have known for many years…and this is my new friend, Ruth Henderson."

Brian held out his hand, grasping Ruth's warmly. "Delighted," he said genuinely.

Lynn too placed a hand on Ruth's shoulder. "So pleased to meet you," she said kindly.

There was a moment's pause as Brian and Lynn studied Ruth's face, their expression mellowing to one of compassion and concern. "Deb has told us you are a Christian. Would you mind if we prayed for you, Ruth?" Brian asked, his eyes looking straight into hers.

Ruth felt a small moment of panic. Would Pastor Whitfield be happy with this? She was already in so much trouble. But her memories of the prayer she had heard moments before and a longing deep within her quickly pushed all doubts aside. "Yes… okay. I'd like that," she said, before she had time to change her mind.

Brian and Lynn gathered around her while Deb closed her eyes and reached out her hand toward Ruth from her own bed. Ruth bowed her head, feeling her heart pounding within her chest.

"Father in heaven," Brian began, as he lifted his face upwards, "we thank you for Ruth. How we thank you that you have a plan and a purpose for her life and that your love surrounds her at this moment."

He gently laid his hand on top of her head and immediately Ruth began to tingle. She felt an intense warmth flood through her body, as though she had suddenly been enveloped in purest sunshine. Her thumping heart began to calm and she felt peace; wonderful, deep, inexplicable peace that brought tears of joy to her eyes. Brian paused for a moment as he quietly whispered praise to God, as did Lynn and Deb. Not strained, not striving—just genuine praise to a mighty God that flowed from the heart. Then Brian started speaking again, but this time his tone took on the authority she had previously heard, and a grace that seemed to come from the very throne of God himself:

"The Lord would say to you this day, my daughter, 'Fear not, for I am with you. Be not dismayed for I *am* your God. I will strengthen you, yes I will help you, yes I will uphold you with the right hand of my righteousness. For have not I declared in my word, says the Lord, to go from faith to faith and as one door closes so another opens. And I would have you know, my daughter, that I would take you even from faith to faith through an open door. I would have you move even in a new dimension, into a new realm of service. For there are areas that you have not yet comprehended, nor understood in the spiritual realm. Yes, there are dimensions that are yet to come to your understanding that will come to you by revelation. And I would have you to have an eye that is open in faith to see beyond circumstances and the present around you and the physical dimension, and I would have you to understand that which is in the spirit realm. For you will begin to understand and know the reasons why certain things exist the way they are, and you will see with the eye of the Spirit and will look beyond the present to see that which I am doing in the unseen world. Let your vision be fixed and steadfast and know that I have purposed for you the fulfilling of my word in your life. For I am causing you to be uprooted from one place, yes, even to be transplanted into another. Do not fear, my daughter, for I will cause your roots to go down even into this new place, and you shall build relationships, and you shall build even into the lives of men and women around you, and they shall invest in you and cause you to flourish in a way that you have not done until now. Therefore know that you go forth in my purposes, says the Lord. For I open a door effectually before you that no man can close.'"

Lynn now stepped forward and placed her arm around Ruth's shoulders.

"Yes, the Lord would say to you this day, 'My daughter, come.' Just as he spoke to Peter in the boat and said 'Come,' and Peter stepped out upon the water—so the Lord would say to you also, 'Come.' Because even in the moving out of the old situation and into the new, surely there shall be a sure platform under your feet and even as the water became a solid foundation for Peter to walk upon, I say to you as you do respond and move into that realm that God has given to you without fear or doubting, surely there shall be a solid form and a solid way under your feet. Surely the way that seemed before to be so unstable will become solid for you. And as the Lord says 'Come' to you, surely his word will release you afresh even this day. And he would also say to you 'Remember not the former things. For I am a God who comes to restore and even heal the wounds of yesterday. My seal of love is upon you for surely, my daughter, it is a new day. Arise,' says your Lord, 'in the confidence and strength that is in your God.'"

Once more Brian joined in, placing his hand on her shoulder. "Father, we pray today in the name of Jesus Christ that you would break off Ruth that fear of man which has been upon her. In the name of Jesus, *fear*—be gone! Father, we just ask you for your anointing to flow right now; a pouring out of your love in her heart in a tremendous and new dimension of understanding of how much you love her, Lord, and how much you love her family. We pray and thank you for these things in the wonderful name of Jesus...Amen."

Ruth sat for a moment with her head bowed, tears of joy flowing down her cheeks. She felt as if a huge weight had been lifted off her shoulders and an inexplicable urge to laugh bubbled from deep within. Overwhelmed and choked with emotion, she found she was unable to speak, but instinctively she reached up to embrace both Brian and Lynn in thanks; a couple who were but a few moments ago complete strangers and yet now felt like dear friends.

When eventually they both left, Ruth finally had the chance

to turn to Deb and ask her where it was that she had met Brian and Lynn. She found that Deb looked at her with a twinkle in her eye.

"Well, actually...they are my pastor and his wife," she confessed.

Ruth immediately tensed. "Your pastor!" she gasped in disbelief. Her experiences with religious leaders had left their mark. "B...but you called him Brian."

Deb chuckled. "Yep—no form or ceremony with him, just likes to be called plain Brian, thank you very much. He's a great advocate of pure truth and down-to-earth reality. Gives a fabulous sermon as well. You should come along some time and hear him preach—when you're ready, that is," she winked.

Late that evening when all visitors had gone, all meals had been eaten, and all goodnights had finally been said, Ruth sat in her chair beside the bed gazing out at the moonlit darkness and star speckled sky. The lingering sensation of warmth and peace from Brian and Lynn's prayers still remained with her, and a deep feeling of contentment permeated her being. She had so much to process, so much to comprehend, and the quiet darkness surrounding her felt comforting as she reflected on the day's events. As promised, Leonard and Marjory had visited her later in the afternoon after first calling on Emily. They had reported that her daughter was disturbingly depressed and would not be released until in a more stable condition. They had then also prayed with Ruth and she had appreciated deeply their kindness, yet their prayers had lacked something. They had lacked power and authority and couldn't compare to the prayers of Brian and Lynn. For when *they* prayed, for the first time in her life she had *felt* the presence of God in such a real and tangible way. She had heard God speak to *her* personally and tenderly, and had heard him call her "my *daughter*." She had had a glimpse of hope and victory...and the truth was, she wanted more. She *longed* for more! She was tired of feeling afraid and lonely; weary of the unkind dealings of a legalistic leadership whose cruel words seemed only to put her down. She wanted healing for herself and her daughter. She wanted her husband back. But most of all she wanted her *God* back! Ruth reflected again on the words Brian and Lynn had spoken over her that day. They had talked of an open door leading to a new place. *A new place. What could this mean?*

From the cubicle beside her, she heard the rustle of the crisp white hospital sheets and a stifled cough as Deb moved uneasily in her bed.

"Deb!" Ruth whispered. "Are you awake? Can I get you anything?"

"No, no, my dear...I just can't seem to sleep. But you're still up. Is everything okay?"

Ruth moved quietly beside her new friend's bed.

"Deb...I need your help."

# REVELATIONS

Zara's heart raced with both anxiety and excited anticipation as she strategically parked her VW on the roadside outside the church of The Light, its bright canary
yellow deliberately visible to all entering the main gates for
tonight's Sunday evening service. Turning the engine off, she
sat for a moment in the darkness, plotting in her mind her next
steps. After her tapped telephone conversation of last week,
there was every likelihood her movements were being moni-
tored and so she must be careful. She intended to meet Beth
tonight at the Town Hall, but planned to make an appearance
here at the church first to allay any suspicions. She would seat
herself near the back of the auditorium, awaiting the moment
all fell into darkness at the start of the customary Sunday evening gospel film, at which time she would quietly slip out and
make her way to the Town Hall meeting, hopefully unnoticed.

Pulling open the heavy glass doors of the church building,
Zara stepped into the crowded foyer and quickly wove her
way around the chatting groups toward the chapel entrance.
Although she smiled and greeted several people as she passed,
there was really only one person who needed to know she was
here—Bob Everitt. Bob usually stood at the main doors, with
arms folded, silently surveying all comings and goings from the
auditorium and tonight was no exception. His hawk-like eyes
did not miss a thing and this would be to Zara's advantage.

"Good evening, Brother Everitt," Zara smiled cheerily as she passed him by, stopping to pick up a hymnal.

On seeing Zara, Bob looked suddenly surprised, and with a puzzled expression, he glanced at his watch. Then, with eyes narrowing in suspicion, he watched as she took her seat. Zara smiled to herself. *Yes, Bob Everitt. You thought I'd be on my way to the Town Hall by now, didn't you? Well, two can play at this game!*

Sitting in silence, waiting for the service to begin, Zara quietly observed the now nearly full sanctuary. No one moved or talked and all heads looked straight ahead. To an outsider, the congregation in all likelihood appeared reverential and religiously disciplined, but Zara was beginning to see the truth. In reality she suspected the people sat in fear: fear of imperfection; fear of angering God and the leadership; fear of making a mistake. Zara glanced at her watch, knowing all too well that feeling of fear. Would she be able to leave this place tonight without being seen? She noticed that Bob Everitt had taken his seat a few rows in front of her own, which was good. Hopefully she would be out of his sight when she made her exit.

At last the service began, with the organist dolefully sounding out the introduction to the first hymn as everybody arose. But Zara groaned as she looked at her hymnal. The song was eight verses long. This would take an act of endurance. She was obviously not the only one who felt this way, for as verse followed verse, people shuffled uncomfortably from foot to foot, gazing distractedly around the room or at the ceiling as they sung. Zara found she had become fascinated with the hat in front of her and wondered where it had been purchased. Finally, however, the hymn was over and everyone gratefully took their seats again as the collection and notices were mechanically undertaken and the lights dimmed for the start of the film. Zara waited impatiently in the darkness as the title and credits were being displayed; noting that the film was at least twenty years old and much out of date. Sister Pelling, who was seated beside her, had already begun to nod off and Zara would not be surprised if many others soon followed her example. In any case, glancing around she decided now would be a good time to make her move.

Slipping discreetly out the back doors and into the deserted foyer, Zara prepared to duck into the ladies' bathroom should she be followed. But as the moments passed and the coast still remained clear, she silently stepped out into the night air. Once outside, her heart pounding, she crept along a stretch of grass and through a side gate that led into a narrow and darkened alleyway where, as prearranged, a taxi was waiting. By taking a cab, her unmistakeable yellow VW could remain parked outside the church for all to see—especially Bob. It was the perfect plan. As the taxi pulled out into the busy main street, Zara looked behind her at the church of The Light slowly fading into the distance, feeling a thrill of excitement. She was on her way!

Fifteen minutes later, a familiar voice squealed with joy as Zara stepped out onto the pavement. "Zara, you made it!" Beth threw her arms around her friend's shoulders with a warm embrace. "Follow me," she said excitedly. "The meeting has already begun, but Tim has saved us some seats."

Zara followed Beth through the marble-arched entrance way and into the richly carpeted reception area. The meeting was taking place in the grand central hall behind the closed doors in front of them and while some singing could be heard from the foyer, nothing could have prepared Zara for the impact of sound that hit her as she stepped through into the auditorium.

The atmosphere in the hall was electric. Several thousand people were on their feet singing and praising God, clapping or raising their hands at will. The seats were tiered around a central stage where a panel of young people led the singing, accompanied by a full orchestra. Joy and excitement radiated from their faces and life vibrated throughout the building as everyone sang.

Shout to the Lord all the earth let us sing

> Power and majesty praise to the King
> Mountains bow down
> And the seas will roar
> At the sound of Your name
> I sing for joy at the work of Your hands
> Forever I'll love You, forever I'll stand
> Nothing compares to the
> Promise I have in You

As Beth beckoned to her to take her seat beside Tim, Zara was completely overwhelmed, convinced the roof would lift with the sound. The exultant singing flowed effortlessly on for another half hour, but she did not want it to stop. Life was beginning to pulsate through her and a joy sprung from deep within. She had never seen such freedom, such uninhibited praise displayed by both old and young alike, yet combined with an awesome sense of respect and wonder for a majestic and mighty God!

Eventually, however, the guest speaker stepped onto the stage and everyone settled down in their seats in preparation for the message. Initially there was a slight technical problem with the microphone and Zara caught herself tensing. Surely someone would be severely reprimanded for this mistake. Yet everyone around her seemed relaxed and smiling, and the speaker immediately made a joke that caused the audience to laugh heartily. How different this was from The Light, in truth how refreshing, and soon Zara found that she, too, began to relax as she listened intently to every word being spoken. For the next hour she heard of the miracles of healing, provision, and deliverance occurring throughout the world. God was manifesting himself in amazing ways in meetings, homes, and even in remote jungles, and Zara found that she was hungry to hear more, as though spiritually starving for good news. She had never heard of such happenings, and was suddenly aware of how isolated she felt from the larger body of Christ.

Finally an altar call was made, giving the opportunity for prayer, healing, or salvation. Zara watched aghast as more than one hundred people surged forward. She was also fascinated to see that as they were prayed for, many gently fell to the ground, although no one had actually touched them, and they remained there for some time. When they eventually stood, they were crying, speaking in tongues or declaring they had been healed! The whole time the congregation continued softly singing in the background while praising God. It was an awesome sight, and one Zara knew she would never forget.

But the time was marching quickly on, and she had yet to return to the church of The Light before her presence was missed. Hugging Beth and promising to stay in touch, Zara left the building and regretfully climbed into the back of the cab. She felt close to tears as she watched the hall disappear and wanted desperately to go back. But it was not to be. All too soon she arrived at The Light in time for the closing hymn and appeal for salvation. Zara slipped quietly into her seat where she noticed Sister Pelling was still asleep and joined in the singing on the second verse.

> Just as I am, though tossed about
> With many a conflict, many a doubt,
> Fightings and fears within, without,
> O Lamb of God, I come.

The pace of the song was unbearably slow, and most people looked weary and ready for bed, but the next four verses were faithfully sung as the congregation waited patiently for somebody—anybody—to respond to the altar call. Finally one elderly gentleman struggled to the front, to the relief of all, and the meeting was called to a close.

Zara sat for a while as everyone filed solemnly out of the church, making eye contact with Bob Everitt as he passed by her pew. Yet somehow she didn't care anymore. The contrast between the two meetings she had attended that night and the country prayer meeting of yesterday had been poignant, and she knew which one she preferred. She watched as the elderly man who had gone forward was given a booklet explaining the steps of salvation, and couldn't help but compare this to the hundreds of people who had surged forward excitedly at the Town Hall, receiving prayer and healing. She had only been away for two hours, yet she felt she had received more life in those few moments than in her entire time at the church of The Light—and she wanted more!

As the lights slowly began to dim, and the last of the hymnal books were collected, Zara slowly arose and made her way back to her car. She knew she could do nothing until her dear friend Kate's wedding. But how could she wait that long? How could she now endure this place, knowing what lay beyond?

⚥

Leonard listened as the lounge mantelpiece clock chimed out its melancholy tones, sounding eerie through the stillness of the night. The hour was late, but Leonard could not sleep. He had come to his study so as not to awaken Marjory who had gone upstairs to bed some time ago, weary from the past day's events. That same weariness rested heavily on his shoulders.

Drawing the maroon velvet curtains together and switching on a large cream table lamp, Leonard stood thoughtfully for a moment in the soft ambience of its light. The night air was still cool, and wrapping his navy blue dressing gown tightly around him, he adjusted the heating before sitting down at his oak desk and reaching for his much-loved Bible. The word of God had been a source of deep comfort and strength to him over the years and had been an anchor through many troubled times. Taking his glasses he turned to Matthew 11:28–30 and read:

> Come to me, all you who are weary and burdened, and
> I will give you rest. Take my yoke upon you and learn
> from me, for I am gentle and humble in heart, and you

will find rest for your souls. For my yoke is easy and my
burden is light.
Matthew 11:28–30 (NIV)

"My burden is light..." Leonard whispered. "...and you will
find rest for your souls." He held his weary head in his hands.
"Lord, I come to you...for I feel so burdened, so troubled," he
groaned in prayer. "I see the needs of your people all around me
and yet feel so helpless. Please help me; *please* guide me."

Lifting his head Leonard thought for a moment before reaching for his pen and journal. He would note down his prayer concerns that he might pray for each more effectually. Hesitantly
he began to write:

Ruth Henderson:

Leonard paused as he reflected on Ruth's situation. It could
all be summed up by saying, "attempted suicide due to the pressure and harsh dealings of the church." He jotted this down,
and then continued.

Emily    Henderson:    attempted    suicide    due    to
despondency, physical abuse, and the harsh dealings of
the church.
Yvonne Pritchard: grief due to grandson dying, but also
from the unkind and threatening words of the church.
Country Prayer Meeting: striving of the people; lack
of receiving God's promised gifts, due to the heavy
expectations of performance placed on them by the
church.
Poor response to Sunday evening appeals: due to the
rigidity of meetings; lack of life; lack of freedom.
Heavy condemnatory sermons: due to a lack of grace;
many manmade rules and traditions.

Leonard laid down his pen, staring sadly at the journal

before him. "Lord, what is wrong with our church?" he uttered in despair.

Glancing across again at his opened Bible, Leonard's eyes fell upon a portion of commentary below Matthew 11 that he felt prompted to read. It was regarding the religious leaders of the time, the Pharisees, with a further reference to Matthew 23:

> One of the reasons a person may be carrying a heavy burden is because of the excessive demands of religious leaders. Jesus frees people from these burdens. The "rest" that Jesus promised is love, healing, and peace with God, not the end of all labour. A relationship with God changes meaningless, wearisome toil into spiritual productivity and purpose. The Pharisees were so concerned about religious rituals that they missed the whole purpose of the temple—to bring people to God. If we become more concerned with the means to worship than with the One we worship, we will miss God even as we think we are worshipping him. Jesus made it clear how ridiculous and petty the Pharisees' rules were. God is a God of people, not rules.
> The Pharisees' traditions and their interpretations and applications of the laws had become as important to them as God's law itself. The problems arose when the religious leaders: a) took man-made rules as seriously as God's laws; b) told the people to obey these rules but did not do so themselves; c) obeyed the rules, not to honour God, but to make themselves look good.
> People desire positions of leadership not only in business, but also in the church, but it is dangerous when love for the position grows stronger than loyalty to God. Jesus made stinging accusations toward the Pharisees because the leaders' hunger for more power, money, and status had made them lose sight of God, and their blindness was spreading. A religion of deeds puts

pressure on people to surpass others in what they know and do. Thus a hypocritical teacher was likely to have students who were even more hypocritical. We must make sure we are not creating Pharisees by emphasising outward obedience at the expense of inner renewal.

Jesus mentioned seven ways to guarantee God's anger— often called the "seven woes":

- Not letting others enter the Kingdom of heaven and not entering yourselves.
- Converting people away from God to be like yourselves.
- Blindly leading God's people to follow manmade traditions instead of God's words.
- Involving yourself in every last detail and ignoring what is really important: justice, mercy and faith.
- Keeping up appearances while your private world is corrupt.
- Acting spiritual to cover up sin.
- Pretending to have learned from past history, but your present behaviour shows you have learned nothing.

These seven statements about the religious leaders must have been spoken with a mixed tone of judgement and sorrow. They were strong and unforgettable. They are still applicable any time we become so involved in perfecting the practice of religion that we forget that God is also concerned with mercy, real love, and forgiveness.

(NIV Life Application Bible Commentary)

Leonard slowly closed his Bible, the verse in Matthew 23:4 still in his mind: *"They tie up heavy loads and put them on men's shoulders, but they themselves are not willing to lift a finger to move them"* (NIV).

In silence he hung his head.

"Lord," he whispered. "What do you want me to do?"

# The Truth Will Set You Free

Laying her gardening gloves on the kitchen bench along with the freshly picked bunch of sweet-smelling flowers, Ruth filled the kettle and switched it on for a cup of tea. She'd been working in the garden since early that morning and her cheeks were pink and tingling from the crisp morning breeze. Humming to herself, she arranged the flowers in a vase, the sun warming her back as it streamed in through the window. How happy and content she felt.

It had been several weeks since she'd returned home from the hospital and she had been feeling both physically and emotionally stronger by the day. This had been largely due to the fact that Deb had kept regular contact with her and had been a great help and support. Ruth knew that her friendship with Deb would never be condoned by The Light and that there would be more trouble to pay if ever this were discovered, but she was prepared to take the risk; her experience while in hospital had deeply touched her, and for the first time in many years she had felt the love and peace of her God. Having been so desperate, so deeply troubled, she could now at last see light at the end of the tunnel and she would not let go of it easily. She so looked forward to Deb's phone calls and found she could talk more freely and honestly with her than she had ever been able to do with her associates at The Light. And Ruth had needed a friend to talk to. Emily had also returned from the hospital to Leonard and Marjory's home and, although her outward wounds were healing well, it would take much longer to heal the inner, emotional pain. Ruth longed for Emily to find healing from the torment of abuse she had suffered, and was desperate for her to experience the presence of God as she had in the hospital. So much so that she planned to do something about it.

Sitting down at the small kitchen table with her cup of tea, Ruth admired the flowers she had placed on the windowsill while serenely thinking through her present situation and the course of action that she intended to take. One particular conversation she had had with Deb in the hospital before she had left was uppermost in her mind. It had been late at night when Ruth had sought Deb's help and advice, sharing tearfully with her the details of her situation, and as a consequence they had talked well into the early hours of the morning. Deb had listened in genuine compassion, being deeply concerned over what she termed as "spiritual abuse," and had been adamant that Ruth take action; although she had wisely suggested Ruth do nothing until her strength had fully returned. Until that time they had agreed together that Ruth should continue attending all of The Light's meetings as usual to carefully maintain appearances of normalcy—and Ruth had done just that. But how hard it had been to sit through the meetings hearing the endless preaching of condemnation and guilt; listening to the lifeless prayers and singing; knowing that people were gossiping about her and her daughter. She had been acutely aware of the sideways glances and whisperings around her, but had held her head high, knowing this must only be endured for a short time longer. How hungry she was for genuine friends and deeper spiritual food. How desperate she was to leave this place—for that is exactly what she and Deb had planned. When Ruth felt well enough, she would take Emily with her and leave the church of The Light with its painful memories and legalistic control, and they would instead attend Grace Chapel. Ruth had seen this clearly in the hospital, as though God had opened her eyes to see the truth, and she knew it was what she must do. She had, of course, been worried about her accommodation, knowing that she would lose her house by leaving The Light, but Deb had kindly offered Ruth her empty two-bedroom basement flat, even agreeing to help her move. Deb had also suggested Ruth slowly start attending some of the midweek morning meetings at Grace Chapel where Brian Somerville would be preaching. This would help her to get a feel for the place and she would also meet some of the people before eventually becoming a member.

Ruth glanced at her watch, feeling both a sudden thrill of excitement and equal apprehension. Today would be the first time she would be attending one such meeting and Deb would be picking her up at 10:00 a.m. Ruth placed her cup in the sink. She'd better get moving if she wanted to be ready on time. But as she busied herself with running hot, steamy water into a bath, and looking desperately through her cupboard contemplating what she should wear, a familiar anxiety began to grow in the pit of her stomach. Would it be discovered that she was attending meetings at a Pentecostal church? Would someone see her getting into the car with Deb and question what she was doing? Would she really be able to go through with all her plans? Although feeling stronger, she was still so emotionally fragile, and although "excommunication" from The Light would be convenient for her, she knew she could not physically tolerate any more trouble. Feeling suddenly overwhelmed, she bowed her head in prayer. "Lord," she whispered. "Don't let me give into fear. Help me to be strong. Please continue to confirm to me that it is your will I leave The Light and begin fellowshipping at Grace Chapel. You know I am hungry for more of you and I really want to do this. But in my own strength I am so weak. Please help me."

A sudden tap at the front door startled her, disturbing her thoughts. She had not been expecting guests and it was too early to be Deb. Looking out her bedroom window Ruth did not recognise the car that was parked outside her house, but when she peered through the front door peephole she groaned as she saw that it was Gladys Jones. Interestingly enough, the leadership had made no effort to contact her for counseling, or offered any kind words of understanding; rather they had only treated her with disapproval and disdain. However, they had asked several church members to drop off the odd meal, or perhaps some baking, and no doubt Gladys was doing just that—although Ruth suspected her motives were probably less charitable. If there was gossip to be had, she would find it, and Ruth hoped she did not plan to stay long. Deb would be here in just under an hour and of all the people in the church, Gladys Jones was the *last* person she wanted to discover her secret.

"Gladys—what a surprise," Ruth said as she opened the door, trying to sound pleased. "How are you today?"

"Well, *I* am fine of course. Never been better. But the question is—how are *you?*" Gladys strained her neck to look behind Ruth and into the house, as though searching for something, but Ruth moved strategically to block her view. She had nothing to hide but objected to meddlesome prying.

"What do you have there, Gladys?" Ruth asked, looking at the covered plate she carried in an effort to distract her attention.

"Oh…I've made you some oatmeal cookies. Shall I put them on the kitchen table?" Gladys stepped forward but Ruth quickly took the plate from her, standing in her way.

"Thank you, Gladys, that is very kind of you," she said hastily. "I'm actually a little busy right now, but I will certainly enjoy them later."

Gladys' eyes narrowed slightly. "Busy? Well, what are you doing? Is there anything I can help you with?"

"No, actually I was just about to relax in a hot bath before doing some shopping. But thanks for asking." This was not completely untrue, for after the morning meeting she did have a few things to pick up from the shops. However, Gladys stood her ground, unwilling to move. She seemed determined to gain *some* news before leaving to make her trip worthwhile and Ruth knew she would have to think fast.

"Actually Gladys...there *is* something you could do for me," Ruth said suddenly, "if you'll just wait there."

Ruth reappeared a few minutes later and handed Gladys an empty medicine jar. "I actually am due a repeat prescription of these sleeping pills and wondered if you could drop into the pharmacist to pick them up for me."

Gladys' mouth dropped open in horror as she stared at the empty jar.

"I...I certainly will not. It...well, it just wouldn't be right and...I've just remembered I have something else to do. I'll pick up my plate later. Goodbye, Ruth." And with that Gladys turned on her heels and walked quickly back to her car.

Ruth closed the door, smiling to herself at the horrified look on Gladys' face. Of course after what had happened, Ruth had no intention of ever taking sleeping pills again, or in fact, of ever having them in her house, but she could imagine what Gladys Jones would say. *Did you know that Ruth Henderson asked me to get her more of those evil pills? I believe she is planning to do something silly again in an attempt to gain even more attention.* In reality it was all very sad. No one from The Light, except maybe Leonard and Marjory, had sought to find out the correct story, and had instead been gossiping over hearsay. They had no idea of the true pain she had suffered or of the harsh manner in which her family had been dealt with by the leadership, and what's more, no one seemed to care. Or maybe it was not so much that they didn't care but that they were afraid to think independently for themselves, choosing instead to blindly receive what was fed to them. She had to admit she had been trapped in this mindset for many years herself, but not anymore. With God's help she would change. With renewed resolve Ruth readied herself for the meeting at Grace, feeling calmer and more reassured by the minute at her decision to leave, and quietly she thanked the Lord for his answer to prayer.

Grace Chapel was a modern building on the edge of town that had once been a warehouse but was now converted into a church. Several floor-to-ceiling windows had been inserted into one wall to allow as much light as possible to flood in onto the tasteful decor of soothing greens and creams and rows of padded chairs faced a raised platform that was complete with lectern and musical instruments. A large kitchen was built into the back of the building around which wooden tables and chairs were scattered, and when Deb and Ruth entered that morning, several groups of people were already sitting casually chatting and laughing while pouring themselves tea and coffee. The atmosphere struck Ruth as being friendly and inviting and despite her apprehensions, she felt an immediate warmth.

"Right, Ruth, my dear," Deb said, linking arms and coaxing her in the direction of one particular group. "Let me introduce you to some folks."

Brian Somerville spotted Ruth and, jumping up immediately, came over to greet her. Still holding Ruth's arm, Deb sensed that she had tensed at the sight of a church leader and reassuringly she whispered to her. "It's okay, my friend. Remember, there's no form or ceremony with Brian. You can just be yourself."

"Ruth! I'm so glad you could make it. Deb said you might be coming this morning." Brian put his arm around Ruth's shoulder and squeezed it. "Have you met everybody yet?"

"Well...no. Deb was just about to make some introductions." Ruth blushed a little. Relaxing with a pastor was going to take some time.

Brian stepped into the middle of the room. "Listen up, folks. We have someone new with us today who I would like to introduce you to." He turned to look at Ruth. "This is Ruth Henderson, a friend of Deb's. Why don't you make yourself known to her and make her feel welcome?"

For the next half hour Ruth chatted effortlessly to genuinely friendly and interested people, knowing that she would never remember everyone's names but also that she would never forget how accepted and loved she felt. It was as though she had known these people all her life, and by the time the service began she felt quite relaxed and at home.

The meeting was an informal affair with everyone sitting casually in their seats, some even dressed in jeans, and Ruth had to admit she felt somewhat strange without the customary wearing of a hat. But Brian's message was captivating. Hungry for spiritual food, Ruth found she hung on his every word. He spoke of the Kingdom of Heaven being here and now, not some far-off, long-awaited place in the sky; and he taught on the authority believers should exercise *now* on the earth as its citizens. He affectionately referred to the present-day pleasures of the Kingdom of Heaven as "steak on your plate while you wait, rather than pie in the sky when you die" and he showed how in Jesus' name Christians could heal the sick, cast out demons, prophesy, and extend God's Kingdom. It was a concept she had never considered before and she was fascinated.

As he continued teaching, however, Ruth noticed that more than once he glanced in her direction, pausing as though listening to something or someone before resuming his message again. He did this several times until eventually he stopped talking altogether, making Ruth feel more than a little uncomfortable. Had she done something wrong? But glancing around the room she saw that no one else seemed perturbed, in fact everyone waited patiently to know what was on his mind, obviously familiar with his style.

Brian closed his notebook and started flipping through his Bible until he came to the verse he was searching for. "Before we go any further, I feel the Lord wants me to share something with you and I need to be obedient to his voice. I didn't plan to talk about this with you today, but the Holy Spirit has impressed upon me that someone in our midst needs to hear this message, and so let's go with the flow! It is, in fact, something that is a very important concept for us all to grasp and I may even continue studying this at the Sunday morning service." Leaving his planned notes on the lectern, Brian stepped off the platform and sat casually on its edge with Bible in hand. "I feel the Lord wants us to talk about 'grace' versus 'the law,' or if you like, 'faith' versus 'works.' So first up…can anyone tell me what the Ten Commandments are?" He looked out across the audience as everyone turned to each other and began mumbling those they could remember. Finally a hand went up. "Yes, Pete—what have you got?" Pete recited as many as he could, being helped by those around him and amidst much kind laughter eventually made it to the tenth. "Okay, great. Next question. Why do you think we were given the Ten Commandments?"

*Finally,* Ruth thought to herself. *Something that I know. The Commandments were given to us as a model or a moral set of standards for us to live our lives by.* However, she was too shy to put her hand up and instead sat back as the woman in front put up hers.

"Yes, Barbara?"

"We were given the Ten Commandments to show us that our performance was falling way short of God's standards; helping us realise we can *never* live up to them by ourselves and therefore need his help."

*That's not quite right,* thought Ruth.

"That's *correct,* thanks Barbara." Brian grinned. "The sad thing is many people think that the Ten Commandments are a set of rules or standards by which they must run their lives, and they exhaust themselves trying to live up to them. They convince themselves that by accomplishing the commandments— which is actually impossible to do—that this will please God and assure their entrance into heaven. Unfortunately it doesn't work that way and there are going to be a lot of surprised people on Judgement Day. We need to consider two verses of scripture to clear this one up. Let's all turn to Ephesians 2:8, 9. Who would like to read that one out for us?"

Deb volunteered. "For by grace are ye saved through faith; and that not of yourselves: it is the gift of God. Not of works, lest any man should boast" (KJV).

"Amen—thank you, Lord. Now let's look at Matthew 7:13, 14. Have we got another volunteer to read this one? Thanks, Joyce."

"Enter ye in at the straight gate: for wide is the gate, and broad is the way, that leadeth to destruction, and many there be which go in thereat: Because straight is the gate, and narrow is the way, which leadeth unto life, and few there be that find it" (KJV).

"Okay, thanks. Now—what are these verses saying? Firstly, that we are saved...by God's *grace*, through our *faith* in Jesus Christ, and it is a *gift* of God. In other words our salvation is something we don't have to work for. We can simply have peace and right standing with God by *believing* in his son Jesus Christ and entering into a relationship with him. That relationship is based on *his grace* and *our resting* in Jesus' performance on the cross, not on our own performance. And in this relationship we *have* God's full approval. Then, as his Holy Spirit abides within us, we learn to walk as Christians—not by striving and trying harder to live up to a set of spiritual rules, but by simply walking, resting, listening, learning from his Spirit and enjoying the automatic bearing of his fruit in our lives because of his presence, such as love, peace, and joy. Now that we are living by faith and grace we are no longer under the Old Testament Law. Are you following me so far?"

Everyone nodded and some muttered, "Amen." Ruth found she was spellbound.

"Okay. So what happens when you meet a group of Christians, perhaps even a church or a pastor, who insists that you follow a set of rules or standards to better your performance, making you feel guilt and condemnation for not doing so? You soon realise that you are becoming weary, weighed down, and have lost the sense of joy you once had. In essence what has happened is that you have been placed back under the Law again from which Christ died to set you free! Jesus himself came across this problem with the religious leaders of his time—the Scribes and

Pharisees. He said they were people who 'tied up heavy burdens and placed them on men's shoulders,' and he also said they were folk who would 'strain out a gnat, yet swallow a camel.' In other words they were so picky about the small insignificant details of the Law that they overlooked the larger picture. They were more concerned with outward appearances, self-righteous works and legalistic performance than with the real issues of the heart and Jesus warned us not to follow their example. Which brings us to the second verse of Scripture we all read together in Matthew 7. This verse talks about two gates: the straight gate, and the wide gate. And guess what, folks? The meaning of this is quite simple. To get through the straight gate, one had to enter just as they were, with no baggage. The wide gate on the other hand was big enough to accommodate all baggage, all burdens, any and everything that you could carry. And the message was clear. Those who entered the straight gate brought nothing with them; no good deeds or self-righteous works or the burdens of manmade rules and regulations. Just them, Jesus, and life everlasting. Those who entered the wide gate, however, went in with all their baggage of good works, legalistic rules, and tiresome burdens, and they found a life full of destruction. What the Lord wants us to hear this morning is this. Be careful of being pressured into performing a set of legalistic rules and manmade standards as a means of gaining God's approval and salvation. It will only end in exhaustion and sadness. Take heed to his word when Paul says in Galatians, 'It is for freedom that Christ has set us free. Stand firm, then, and do not let yourselves be burdened again by a yoke of slavery' (Galatians 5:1, NIV). Trying harder and striving fretfully for perfection is the wrong approach to the Christian life. We need to walk with Jesus, being led by the Holy Spirit, while resting in the finished work of the cross. Jesus said, 'Come to me, all you who are weary and burdened, and I will give you rest. Take my yoke upon you, and learn from me, for I am gentle and humble in heart, and you will find rest for your souls. For my yoke is easy and my burden is light' (Matthew 11:28–30, NIV). Praise God for his grace and forgiveness; his gentle mentoring and teaching; and his never-ending love and compassion toward us. Mike, why don't you grab your guitar, and let's all sing a song together in thanks."

An hour of teaching had flown by and Ruth found that she was disappointed when Brian finally closed with a word of prayer after their jubilant singing. She wanted him to go on, eager to know more, and as everyone eventually rose to leave she sat for a few minutes deep in thought. She reflected on the church of The Light with its many rules and regulations. She considered the harsh rebuke and actions of the leadership toward her, Emily, and her husband for not living up to these rules, and worse yet for questioning their existence. She thought of the fear, the pain, and the torment that such legalism had caused and her heart ached as she realised how wrong it all had been. The Pharisees of The Light had placed her and her family under the harsh rules of the Law—and she wanted to be free!

Deb had been chatting to the lady next to her but now picked up her bag and Bible and stood to her feet. "Are you ready to go then, my dear?" she said cheerfully, turning to Ruth.

But Ruth continued to sit, staring at the platform before her. "Deb…I can't go back," she whispered quietly.

"You mean…to your house? Is something wrong?" Deb sat down again, looking anxiously at Ruth.

"No—I mean…I can't go back to the church of The Light." She turned and looked determinedly into Deb's eyes. "I'm ready to leave—today!"

# CONFLICTS OF EMOTION

How Zara longed to share her experience at the Town Hall with her best friend. How hard it was to conceal the newfound excitement that had began to bubble deep within her and the eager anticipation she felt of new things to come. Yet instinctively she knew she must not burden Kate. As it was, Kate was over-anxious about the wedding, expressing to Zara repeatedly her concerns that something was going to go wrong, or that somehow the leadership would find something to stop their plans from going ahead, and Zara grieved for her friend. Kate was too uptight and worried to be happy about her big day and instead longed for the wedding to be over, that all might be safely put behind them.

Over the following weeks Zara kept in touch with Bethany—albeit from the safety of a public telephone booth—and they talked excitedly about the possibility of Zara joining Tim and Beth for other up and coming events. As no one had seemed to notice Zara's absence and attendance at the Town Hall meeting, she felt confident she could achieve another secret rendezvous, and so when Beth asked her to a "Healing and Deliverance" meeting at the city Performance Hall, Zara agreed to go. As an extra precaution, Beth and Tim suggested picking her up from a meeting place well away from prying eyes, and so times and dates were set. It would mean skipping one of the mid-week meetings at the church of The Light, but Zara hoped her absence would once again be overlooked. Anyway, Kate always left for the meetings well before Zara, liking to get there early in case she glimpsed Dan in the distance or, even better, exchanged a few words with him in the foyer. And, Zara reasoned, if she was back in good time, she could slip into the flat before Kate returned home and be safely in bed to avoid any questions. As for Bob Everitt, Zara had heard it rumoured that he had been unwell for several weeks, which must be true as she had not seen him around. Still, just to be on the safe side, she had been discreet in her conversations lest he or anyone else be listening, and had generally kept her head down in case she was being watched. Perhaps they had lost interest in Zara and gone on to observe other poor souls at The Light who had put a foot out of place. In any case, Zara was convinced that she would be safe.

When the night arrived, therefore, Zara was feeling quietly confident. Beth had suggested she meet Zara at the house of Tim's parents, who lived in a new development outside of town. His folks were away on holiday for the week and the garage was standing empty. Zara could safely park her vehicle there, hidden from sight of the street, and together they would make their way in Tim and Beth's car into the city to the Performance Hall.

Tim pulled the garage door shut and locked it. "There you go—all safe and sound, Zara. Wouldn't even know your VW was there. Our car is parked around the back." He pointed into the shadows where a silver hatchback was discreetly hidden against the house.

Beth was already seated in the front as Zara slipped into the back seat. "You know, this is kind of exciting," Beth giggled in hushed tones. "Real cloak and dagger stuff."

"I know," grinned Zara. "Exciting until you get caught—but let's hope that isn't going to happen tonight. I'm pretty sure Everitt is laid up with the flu at the moment, so the coast should be clear."

Tim started the car and pulled out onto the road.

"So tell me, Beth. What is this meeting about tonight?"

Zara asked with interest. "I couldn't talk long last time I called you as I was running out of coins! You mentioned 'Healing and Deliverance'? I'm not familiar with the term 'Deliverance.'"

Beth turned around in her seat to talk to Zara. "It's one of the real keys we've learned about to help you live a victorious Christian life." She hesitated for a moment, glancing at Tim before going on. "I don't want to run The Light down, Zara— but it's not a subject you are likely to ever hear about there."

Zara nodded in agreement. "The only time I've heard the word used is in the Lord's Prayer when Jesus prays, 'Deliver us from evil.' Is it something to do with that?" she asked thoughtfully.

Beth smiled. "Something like that, Zara. Do you know the scripture in Ephesians 6 that says, 'For we wrestle not against flesh and blood, but against principalities, against powers, against the rulers of the darkness of this world, against spiritual wickedness in high places' (Ephesians 6:12, KJV)?"

"Well, yeah. That's sort of the devil's temptations that we have to resist, isn't it?"

"Yes—but it goes a lot deeper than that. Would you agree that we as human beings are made up of body, soul, and spirit? The soul being our mind, our will, and our emotions?"

"Sure."

"Okay...well, when we became Christians—you know, 'born again'—our *spirits* were made alive to God. Before we were Christians, because of sin, our spirits were dead and dull to God. The Bible says, 'The natural man *cannot* receive the things of God, they are foolishness to him, being spiritually discerned' (1 Corinthians 2:14, KJV). We didn't understand a lot about God or spiritual things. In fact we thought they were foolish. But by asking God's son, Jesus, to be the Lord of our life; by believing Jesus died on the cross as a sacrifice to remove our sins; and by repenting of those sins, God has recreated or 'turned the light on' in our darkened spirits, so they are brand new and alive to God. We are able now to talk to God and hear him talk to us, and understand his Bible, and receive his help to be who we were truly created to be. What we once thought to be foolish now becomes truth and life."

"Okay, that bit I understand—although I've never heard it explained that way. So, go on," Zara encouraged.

"Well, our spirits are now spiritually alive, but what about our *soul* and *body?* Obviously our physical bodies are still much the same as they were...I mean we still age and eventually die—although as born-again Christians, we now can look forward to eternal life with God after we die, right? So that leaves our soul. Our mind, our will, and our emotions aren't always immediately changed either, are they? We still have wrong desires and temptations and want to do things our own way. That's the part of us that the Holy Spirit works on throughout our lives, bringing our soul and bodies into line with God's word through our obedience and faith and thus bringing us restoration and freedom. Just as a tree that is planted in good soil and watered well naturally bears fruit, so when we simply walk with God and yield ourselves to him, we will naturally bear the 'fruits of the Spirit,' which are love, joy, peace, etc. And thankfully, God is loving, forgiving, and patient with us during the whole process. He promises us his *grace* is sufficient for us, and his *strength* is made perfect in our weakness."

"So where does deliverance come in to all this?"

"Right...well, the devil knows that he can't touch our born-again spirits. They are bought by the blood of Christ and home safe. We are part of the family of God and that is that. But as I said, our souls and bodies are still being 'conformed to the image of Christ'—they are still in a battlefield. It's here that the devil can cause havoc, if he's allowed to have access or go unnoticed."

"I'm not sure I'm following you," Zara said, puzzled.

"Just as God has innumerable angels working with and for him, so our enemy, Satan, or the devil, has his beings—his demons—working on his side. The difference is their aim is to destroy and foul up every good thing of God's—namely this world and all that is in it. The Bible is written for our teaching, growth, and comfort, but also for our protection. The many principles found there are for our safety and well being. If we ignore them or are just plain ignorant of them, the enemy feels he has a legal right to take advantage of us. For example, God is clear in his instructions that we should not involve ourselves in any occult activity: horoscopes; séances; divining; tarot cards; new age healings—you name it. When we do involve ourselves with these things we open a door for the enemy to come in to our lives. We also give him access by repeatedly giving in to sin and deliberate disobedience."

"And when you say, 'come in'—you don't mean literally, do you? I mean, you're not talking about demons literally entering our body and living there, are you?" Zara looked slightly alarmed.

"Yes, Zara, I mean exactly that. The only way the enemy and his demons have more effective power is through a human body. So he's looking for legal ways of access so he can manipulate us and cause torment and trouble. That's why the Bible encourages us to walk closely with God so we don't have to fear or worry. Believe me, this is very real and it's a fact the devil does not want you to know. God himself has said 'My people are destroyed from lack of knowledge' (Hosea 4:6, NIV). He warns us to put on the armour of God as described in Ephesians 6, so that we might stand against the enemy."

"Wow, that's all news to me. I thought casting out demons was just something Jesus did in the New Testament when he was on earth—not in the twenty-first century! But hang on a minute...what does that mean we are going to see tonight?" Zara looked worried.

But Beth laughed reassuringly. "That's the best thing about it all. As Christians, Jesus has given us full authority over the enemy and his demons. When we recognise our mistakes or where spiritual doors have been opened in our lives to let the enemy in, and we *repent*, we then can cast out the enemy in Jesus' name—hence the term 'deliverance.' Believe me…the demons are more nervous than you are tonight about this meeting! Just go with the flow and don't be worried. It's not something you should be frightened about. And of course, there is much more to this subject than I've been able to tell you tonight. Consider this as an introduction."

"I've got a feeling I'm going to know a lot more about it all by the time tonight's meeting is over," Zara mused, looking up at the Performance Hall as the car finally pulled up beside it.

"I'll let you both off here while I find parking. Save me a seat," Tim called as they climbed out of the car and headed up the stairs.

The Performance Hall was a luxurious building, to say the least, and many international performers of theatre and ballet came here from all over the world to use the excellent facilities. Deeply padded seats tiered down to a wide open stage and the imposing ceiling was structured in such a way as to gain the best acoustics possible. As at the Town Hall meeting, the atmosphere was electric with excitement as over one thousand people waited in eager anticipation.

The meeting began with triumphant and joyful singing and praises to the Lord, and once again Zara was lost in awe and exhilaration. The speaker was a seasoned veteran of the demonic from New Zealand, a man well known for his knowledge and experience on deliverance. His message was powerful and enlightening, adding more depth of understanding to what Beth had already shared with Zara in the car on the way over. Zara was once again amazed at how little was ever mentioned of this subject at the church of The Light. Perhaps they had no understanding of spiritual warfare. Yet this was strange, considering they preached so often that they alone possessed the whole truth. This proved again to Zara the sad state of deception The Light truly was in.

The speaker had now paused and in silent meditation gazed

into the audience as though looking right through them. Then one after another he spoke out names of illnesses and infirmities and asked those who were suffering with such to come forward for prayer. He then began to point to different people asking them to stand, saying he could see a spiritual oppressor or demon surrounding them, even sitting on their shoulders. And then he began to pray. He prayed like Zara had never heard before, with authority and power, and things began to happen. All around the auditorium something began to stir. Unseen and sinister, a dark and foreboding presence was growing restless, weakened by the praise and prayer of the saints, knowing that its hour had come. Yet Zara did not feel scared. For another, more powerful presence was here. The presence of almighty God! Tears flowed freely down Zara's cheeks as she sensed the warmth and love of her God, and witnessed so many being delivered and healed. She stared in amazement as a man's shortened leg began to grow before her very eyes; as a woman leapt, healed, from her wheelchair; as a boy writhed on the floor in torment, only to be completely freed at the mention of Jesus' name. People were surging forward for prayer, and Zara could contain herself no longer.

"Beth—I want to go down there!" Zara's eyes were bright with excitement as she whispered to her friend. "I've never been able to talk in tongues and I want to…tonight!"

Beth squeezed Zara's hand. "I'll be praying for you. Go for it!" she whispered back delightedly.

Zara stepped out into the aisle and joined the many that were making their way down toward the front of the stage. Her heart was pounding and her legs felt weak, but she was determined to do this; in her heart she had never felt such a certainty, such closeness to God, and she knew this would be her night. As she waited quietly amongst the crowds, her head bowed, she eventually felt the light touch on her shoulder of one of the counselors, and the whispered prayers of several others around her.

"Is there something in particular you would like prayer for?" a young man asked kindly as Zara looked up.

"Well...I would like to be filled with the Spirit and speak in tongues," Zara managed a little nervously.

The counselor grinned. "It would be my pleasure. Have you been born again yet?" he asked inquiringly, to which Zara nodded. "Then you are already filled with the Spirit of God. Tonight we'll just ask for his empowering and gift of tongues," and softy he began to pray.

It was some minutes later, however, that he stopped. Gently he leaned forward and whispered in Zara's ear. "Has anyone in your family ever been involved with freemasonry or the occult that you know of?"

Zara thought for a moment in surprise. "Well...yes—my father was a mason, and actually my grandfather before him. My grandmother used to dabble in reading tea leaves and fortune telling if you call that the occult—but, how does this affect me?"

"A spirit of witchcraft has come down your family line, harassing you from birth and hindering you from moving farther into God. We're going to break that off you now," he said matter-of-factly.

He began praying again, softly laying his hands on Zara's head. In Jesus' name he commanded the spirit of witchcraft to be broken. Zara felt a tingling sensation from deep within. Her head began to spin and she felt an overwhelming urge to cough, as though her very insides were turning out. Still he commanded in Jesus' name for her to be delivered, and moments later Zara's hands began to numb and tingle as though something were exiting through their very tips. At last she relaxed, feeling a huge weight had been lifted off her shoulders. And then it happened. An intense heat surged through her body and an overwhelming sense of joy and peace. Tears welled to her eyes again as suddenly her lips began to move.

"Speak it out—speak out your new language," she heard someone encouraging in her ear.

Surprised, Zara began to mumble. Then she began to speak with more confidence as she realised the words pouring from her mouth were not in English. In fact, they were not in any language that she had ever heard before. It sounded so fluent, so melodic and flowed effortlessly off her tongue. She felt a new strength and her tears were now mingled with laughter as those around her began to clap and praise God in thanks. Her prayers had been answered! She, Zara Williams, was speaking in a heavenly language—she was speaking in tongues!

※

It was late that night before Zara eventually arrived home, trying desperately to open the front door quietly in the darkness, so as not to be seen or heard. She could remember before she was a Christian stumbling home late from parties, drunk and disorientated, and Zara smiled to herself as she took stock of her present situation. Her legs were still weak and wobbly, and she did indeed feel "high," though not with intoxicating chemicals. No, this was a new high—this was an exhilaration and deep contentment that surpassed all drugs and alcohol. For she was, as the Bible called it, "drunk in the Spirit."

Pushing the door open and stumbling in, Zara was surprised to discover that the kitchen light was still on, visible under the crack of the closed door at the end of the darkened hall. Kate had obviously forgotten to turn it off before retiring to bed. Creeping softly along the passageway she gently pushed the door open, reaching in to switch off the light. But, much more to her surprise, she found Kate sitting at the table, obviously waiting for her.

"Hello, Zara," Kate said coolly, her face serious and strained.

Confused, Zara sat down at the kitchen table, "Kate? You're up late."

But Kate remained as stone. "Brother Henry was asking after you tonight at the meeting," she uttered coolly. "I looked for you everywhere—I couldn't even find your car."

"Kate—before you get angry, let me explain . . ." Zara held up her hands in protest.

"You weren't at the meeting, were you, Zara?" Kate burst out. "Do you know what happened tonight?" Kate pushed her chair back and paced agitatedly back and forth across the floor. "The leadership somehow got word that Dan stayed on too long with me at my parent's house on the engagement night. Remember, he stayed on to help clean up and went home about 2:00 a.m.? They said this was not a good 'testimony' to the other young people of the church and that we had been a bad example." Kate's eyes began to well up with tears. "Tonight at the meeting they made Dan stand up in front of everyone and give a public apology."

Zara stared in disbelief as Kate continued. "I have never felt so *humiliated* and *embarrassed* in all my life!" She broke down and sobbed.

Zara was quick to get up and place her arms around her friend. "I'm so sorry, Kate."

But Kate pushed her aside. "The thing that really gets to me is…my best friend was not even there to support me. After all my pleading with you to keep out of trouble…where were you tonight, Zara?" Kate stared at her again with fiery, wet eyes and flushed cheeks, demanding an explanation.

Zara hesitated. How much should she tell her? "Kate…I've had the most amazing experience. I went with Beth and Tim to . . ."

"You did what?" Kate exploded, her anger and anxious frustration spilling out. "I don't believe this. They'll find out… they'll cancel our wedding…I can't believe you would do this to me!"

"But Kate, listen…I spoke in *tongues* tonight. I felt God's presence. People were being healed and delivered. It was amazing and . . ."

"*I don't care!*" Kate screamed, thumping her fist on the table to emphasise her words. "How can you call me your *friend?* You have *ruined* my life!" Sobbing, she ran from the room, overwhelmed by emotion and confusion. She slammed her bedroom door shut with such force the windows shook in their frames.

Zara stood for a moment in stunned silence before slowly sitting down again at the table. She had never seen Kate so distressed, and she felt desperate for her. Yet as Zara sat alone in the quiet of the night with her head in her hands, listening to the gentle ticking of the kitchen clock on the wall, another emotion began to rise within her. She began to feel anger. Anger at what the church was doing. Anger that Kate could not see how wrong this all was and be prepared to do something about it. Anger that their lives were being so manipulated and controlled. Tonight had been one of the most precious experiences of her life and she couldn't even share it with her friend for fear of the church's backlash and their threats of punishment. Well, she'd had enough. She would not submit to this control. Zara lifted her head with new resolve. Beth had invited her to a morning meeting at Grace Chapel this Sunday and no matter what, she was going! She would *not* let the church of The Light destroy her life.

# GOING HOME

The day was grey and wet as a shroud of black umbrellas surrounded the entranceway of the small, yet quaint nineteenth-century cemetery chapel. One by one friends and family had solemnly arrived to say their last farewells to Rhys, and after briefly comforting each other, quietly entered the church to take their seats in preparation for the funeral service. Leonard and Marjory were among the first to arrive yet they had hesitated to enter the church just yet. Anxious to support Yvonne and Paul on such a difficult and heartbreaking day, they waited patiently in the damp and drizzling rain for the hearse to arrive carrying Rhys' coffin.

The family had been forbidden to hold the funeral at the church of The Light on account of Rhys' recent withdrawal. Instead they had been forced to hold the service here in this little-known part of the town and in unfamiliar surroundings. Even the florists within the church had self-righteously refused to arrange flowers for the occasion and so Marjory, out of the kindness of her heart, had organised befitting bouquets from the local florist herself—and at her own expense. These striking displays of lilies now sat tastefully on pedestals—one adorning the entranceway, and two placed strategically around the pulpit area. She had also arranged the soft music, which could be heard piped gently through the sound system, and clusters of candles which burned brightly in alcoves, bringing a soft ambiance to an otherwise drab and sorrowful setting.

Finally, the slow procession of funeral hearse and family cars appeared at the bottom of the winding hill and eventually took their place outside the chapel. Marjory felt a lump rising in her throat as her dear friend alighted from the car looking strained and pale. What could she say to comfort her? Moving quickly to her side, Marjory silently embraced Yvonne for several minutes before allowing her to follow her distraught family indoors and to the front of the church. With tears in their eyes, Leonard and Marjory looked on as Rhys' coffin was carefully lifted on to the shoulders of the bearers, who slowly made their way through the arched stone entrance and down the narrow aisle. How hard it was to imagine that the child they'd known, who was so full of life and energy, now lay still and forever silent within this polished and flower-bedecked box. Sadly they followed into the church, where sniffling and stifled weeping could be heard, and discreetly slipped into the back row to join in with the first hymn.

As Pastor Whitfield had declined to take the service, it was Brother Henry who took his place on the platform to perform the ceremony. His face looked stern and unyielding, and fearing what he would say, Marjory reached for Leonard's hand, holding it tightly for support. Surely they would put aside church politics for one day and think of the dear family before them, so pained at losing their precious son and grandchild.

Brother Henry cleared his throat, and turning to his Bible, started reading from Ephesians.

> Children, obey your parents in the Lord: for this is right. Honour thy father and mother; which is the first commandment with promise; that it may be well with thee, and thou mayest live long on the earth.

He paused for a moment, peering over his glasses at Rhys' parents before going on.

And, ye fathers, provoke not your children to wrath:
but bring them up in the nurture and admonition of
the Lord. Servants, be obedient to them that are your
masters according to the flesh, with fear and trembling,
in singleness of your heart, as unto Christ.

(Ephesians 6:1–5, KJV).

Brother Henry closed the Bible resolutely as he looked slowly
around the room. "We are gathered here today under very sad
circumstances. A young man, once a member of our church, has
passed away—his life snatched, as it were, from him before it
had even started. God has a plan for each one of our lives, and
he had a plan for Rhys. That plan was to *obey* his parents and
the leadership of the church, and to *submit* himself to them.
I believe if Rhys had done this, we would not be here today.
Unfortunately Rhys stepped out from God's anointing and plan
and therefore from God's protection. By leaving The Light he
endangered himself, and sadly we see before us the result. May
this be a warning to us all—and may God have mercy on his
soul."

A stifled sob reverberated from the front of the chapel as
Rhys' mother let out a cry of grief. Yvonne was quick to put
her arms around her daughter-in-law, while staring stonily up at
Brother Henry. An awkward tension settled over the audience
as they waited to hear more. But Marjory felt angry. She could
not believe what she was hearing. How could the church be so
cruel, so condemnatory at a time like this? She could not sit and
listen to another word. Rising from her seat she excused herself
to those around her and made a hasty exit out into the crisp
afternoon air.

"Lord, how can this be right?" she whispered in prayer as she
paced the cobblestone pathway in her distress. "Surely these
are not your words. I will *not* believe that you are this harsh
on your people. Please surround Rhys' family with your *love*,
despite what they are hearing today. Lift them above the abuse

of men. Shelter and comfort them at this desperate time," she wept. "And despite all—let Rhys be home safe with you!"

✤

Kneeling down on the floor, Ruth opened her kitchen cupboards and began carefully wrapping the neatly stacked crockery into newspaper before placing them into a cardboard box. Since her decision to leave the church of The Light, she had been happily packing and cleaning the house, and the kitchen was now the last area to be done. The job had not been difficult as Ruth had scarcely unpacked the boxes from her last shift, when she had been so abruptly moved from her home and husband by the church. These boxes had been stacked for some time both in her lounge and in the spare room as she had been unable to bring herself to deal with them, and it was perhaps just as well, for it meant she was now able to move all the quicker. Deb's husband had a small van, and after work the last two evenings he had been calling by to collect as many of the boxes and pieces of furniture as he could. Deb had also been a gem, unpacking the boxes as they arrived at the flat, and several of Deb's friends had also offered to come across on Saturday morning to help Ruth give the house a final clean before escorting her to her new home. Later Saturday afternoon Deb planned to have a housewarming party and had invited as many members of Grace Chapel who could attend. It was all most exciting.

There were some matters, however, that were not quite as exciting, and in fact, being still unresolved, threw somewhat of a shadow across the proceedings. Ruth still had not found the courage to inform the leadership at The Light of her decision to leave, nor had she told Leonard and Marjory that after today Emily would no longer be living with them. In fact, Ruth had not even told Emily herself, as she feared she would fret unnecessarily. Instead she simply planned to pick Emily up after school this afternoon and take her to their new home in the basement

flat of Deb's house. Ruth sighed as she placed a china water jug
into the box. Wouldn't it be wonderful if she and Emily could
just disappear without telling anyone at The Light? How much
easier it would be for them both. But she knew it would not
be possible. The church of The Light had an uncanny way of
finding things out and dealing "appropriately" with them. No,
it would be much wiser to be up front and tell them of her decision to leave. After all, the church was not a prison and there was
no law that said she had to stay. They could not control her freedom of choice...or so you would think. Yet she could not help
but feel apprehensive. Only those who had been involved with
such a church as The Light would know that leaving was never
as simple as just walking away. Stopping partway from wrapping a sugar bowl in paper, Ruth stared at the floor in concern.
She knew it would not be wise to face Pastor Whitfield alone.
In all likelihood he would try to frighten or bully her into staying—and she could not have that. No, there had to be another
way and silently she hung her head in prayer as she asked for
wisdom.

※

It was at around three that afternoon when Ruth climbed into
the car beside Deb, who had offered to escort her to her daughter's school. Deb glanced across at Ruth, knowing how nervous
she must be feeling.

"So—the next big step, my friend. Picking up Emily," she
smiled encouragingly.

"I just hope she understands," replied Ruth tensely as she
donned her seatbelt. "She's had so many changes in her life
lately. I hope she can cope with yet another."

"Oh, but this is a great new change. She'll be coming home
to live with her mum again. I'm sure she'll be delighted."

"Yes, but leaving the church—all her friends are at The Light.
She's spent most of her life there. It'll be a big adjustment."

"An adjustment that will be healthy for the two of you. Just you wait until she meets some of the young people at Grace. There are some great kids there—really on fire for God. I know they'll take her under their wing and help her settle. I'm sure it's going to be fine, you'll see."

The car slowly approached the school gates where many other parents were also jostling for parking spaces as they waited for their children. They did not have to wait long, however, as the shrill sound of a bell soon signalled the end of the school day, and a surge of green uniforms hurriedly spilled from the classrooms as the pupils eagerly escaped. It was a good ten minutes before the initial flood of bodies subsided, and apart from a few last stragglers the courtyards soon became empty. Ruth scanned the area apprehensively, looking for her daughter. Where could she be?

It was some time later before a solitary figure eventually appeared through a side door. Her hands were thrust deep into her pockets and her shoulders were slumped well forward as she shuffled dejectedly along. Ruth's heart sunk. It was Emily—but how different she had become. She looked so sad and listless, so devoid of life and joy, and tears of pain welled in Ruth's eyes. Gathering herself together, she opened the car door and called her daughter's name.

Emily lifted her head and looked around in surprise. Had someone called for her? She stopped, peering toward the gates. Was that her mother? No, it couldn't be. But as she walked closer she realised that it *was. What was she doing here?*

"Mum!" Emily called as she quickened her pace toward the car. "You know you can't be here—you'll be seen!" She glanced hastily around her in alarm.

But Ruth placed her arm reassuringly around her daughter's shoulders and held her close. "Emily...I've got something to tell you. Get in the car and I'll explain everything to you."

Emily still looked alarmed. "Mum, what's happened. Is everything all right?" She leaned down and looked anxiously into the car.

"It's okay, sweetheart. This is Deb. We were in the hospital together. Remember?"

"Oh, sure. Hi." Puzzled, she climbed obediently into the back seat.

Deb smiled kindly back. "How are you doing, love? Did you have a good day at school?"

"Well, you know. It was school, what can I say?" Emily shrugged, smiling weakly. "What's this all about? Where are we going, and...does the church know about this?" Emily's voice was tense as she glanced once again over her shoulder, fearful of being seen.

The car pulled slowly away from the school and headed in the direction of their new flat at Deb's. Drawing a deep breath Ruth turned to her daughter. "Emily," she said softly. "I've left the church. I've left the church of The Light and I'm not going back."

Emily stared at Ruth in stunned silence, a mixture of emotions crossing her face. But it was not long before a barrage of questions was forthcoming.

"Am I coming with you? I...I mean am I still living with Leonard and Marjory, or you or...am I living at your house and...have...have you told the church about this yet? You know you just can't *leave*—there are rules. Mum, what if they find out . . ."

"Emily—it's okay." Ruth reached for Emily's hand and patted it reassuringly. "Deb has kindly offered us a flat under her house and we've already moved all my furniture in and set everything up. You'll be living there with me, too—in fact we're going there now. We'll be going to a new church called Grace Chapel. I haven't told the church anything yet. Just as soon as we're settled I'll ring up Leonard and Marjory and explain everything to them and arrange to get your things. We'll proceed from there."

"What about Dad? Does he know? Is he coming to live with us too?"

"Well...one step at a time. Let's just get settled ourselves first."

Emily stared abjectly out of the window. "I guess that means I'll never see my friends again," she said in a small voice.

Deb glanced in her rear-view mirror and noted that tears were trickling down Emily's cheeks.

"Emily—on Saturday we are having a party at my house as a way of saying 'welcome,'" Deb chipped in. "I've asked several of the young people from our church to come over and spend some time with you. There's one girl in particular that I'm sure you will like. Her name is Charlotte, and she's about your age. Would you like that?"

"Thanks," Emily whispered weakly, wiping her tearstained face with her sleeve.

Moments later, Deb swung into her driveway and pulled up to the door of the basement flat. "Well here we are. Home sweet home." She removed a key from her key ring and handed it to Ruth. "I guess you'll be needing this...and now I'll leave you two in peace as I'm sure you've got plenty of catching up to do. Just call me if you need anything, won't you?"

Ruth reached out and put her arms around Deb. "Thanks for everything. You've been a real friend."

Once inside the little flat, Ruth quietly closed the door and turned to her daughter, anxious for her reaction. Emily gazed silently around the tiny lounge and kitchenette where many of their belongings had been neatly arranged. A bowl of daisies was on the table and familiar photos hung on the walls. The flat was small but it felt like home, and looking back at her mum she could not suppress the emotion that arose from deep within her. Stumbling into her mother's arms, the pent-up tension of the past few months released itself like a damn and she sobbed uncontrollably.

"I...I'm so sorry, Mum...for everything," she wept.

But Ruth stroked her hair lovingly, tears of relief dampening her own cheeks. "Sweetheart, it was *not* your fault. You were not to blame for any of this," she reassured her. "You're home now, Emily, and we can start to put the past behind us. From now on things can only get better. And if we are patient…I'm sure we'll soon all be a family again."

# An Ultimatum

Peering into the oval mirror of her bedroom dressing table, Marjory powdered her nose and applied a pale pink lipstick while Leonard knotted a silk tie and pushed it into its place. Both were getting ready for the Sunday morning service at The Light, but how strange it felt this morning to be getting ready alone. Emily would normally have her music on while running the shower, and they'd grown accustomed to the opening and shutting of drawers and cupboards as she tried several outfits on, deciding what to wear. Then there'd been the array of cosmetics, sprays, and perfumes in the bathroom, and the fluffy slippers beside the fireplace, but all these had gone. Although they had spent their entire married lives in this house alone and without any children, it had never felt as empty and devoid of life as it did now that Emily had left, and they knew they would miss her.

It was Friday afternoon when Ruth phoned Leonard, explaining that she had taken Emily with her and left the church of The Light. She told him they both would be joining a small Pentecostal fellowship called Grace Chapel, and thanked them sincerely for all their help. As an elder, Leonard had felt it his duty to talk at length to Ruth about her decision to leave, but in the end agreed that she, indeed, made the right choice—and deep in his heart he could not blame her. He also agreed that going alone to inform Pastor Whitfield of her decision would not be wise and would only cause further pain, and had instead offered to tell the pastor himself on her behalf. Ruth had been greatly relieved, as this matter was weighing heavily on her mind, and emotionally she thanked him once again for his kindness. Although Leonard was not looking forward to telling the pastor of Ruth's decision, knowing how he reacted to those leaving the fellowship, he was quietly pleased and relieved for Ruth. She had been reunited with her daughter again and maybe now, at this new church of which she spoke so highly, Ruth and Emily could find the peace and healing they so desperately needed; although he certainly would never voice this to anyone except Marjory.

It was Saturday morning when Leonard had phoned Pastor Whitfield to convey to him the news and, as expected, it was not received well. The pastor had been livid with Leonard for not doing more to stop Ruth from leaving, and he was furious that Ruth had taken Emily without his consent. Leonard had to remove the phone from his ear several times as Pastor Whitfield shouted his disapproval down the receiver. When Leonard eventually hung up, he felt browbeaten and exhausted, but somehow satisfied that he had shielded Ruth from yet another unpleasant experience and had taken the brunt of the pastor's ire upon himself.

Now, as he pulled on his suit jacket for the Sunday morning service, he wondered just what would be said from the pulpit. It seemed each time a member of The Light managed to escape the fortified walls of the church, they were consequently the topic of several weeks' bitter sermons. Names were never mentioned directly, but it was always blindingly obvious to all who was being referred to, and Leonard sighed as he reached for his Bible. Nothing ever seemed to change. Year after year it was always the same.

⚶

Bob Everitt stood imposingly in his usual place outside the

church doors, his arms folded and his hawk-like eyes scrutinizing all activity around him. After several weeks of being inconveniently laid up with illness, he was keen to resume his surveillance to make up for lost ground. He noted each person that entered—who they were with, what they were wearing, who they spoke to. But perhaps more importantly he noted those who were *absent* from the meeting. Very few things happened in this church without Bob Everitt knowing and he prided himself on this fact. He also prided himself on being Pastor Whitfield's right-hand man, the latter depending on him to seek out and relay all information as and when necessary, and he took his role very seriously.

However, this Sunday morning he felt somewhat distracted. Glancing at his watch he noted that the service was about to begin, and a frown suddenly creased his leathered brow. The majority of members were accounted for this morning, but he noticed that one particular person was not. Zara Williams appeared to be missing. In recent weeks he had not been able to keep as close an eye on her as he wished and her absence now bothered him. With growing agitation he peered around the nearly deserted foyer, allowing five more minutes to pass. When still there was no sign of her, Bob made his way to the car park. Scanning the cars before him he looked in vain for the unmistakable, bright canary-yellow VW, but it was nowhere to be seen. Bob narrowed his eyes in annoyance as he stood for a moment contemplating his next move. Apparently she had not been seen at the mid-week meeting either, and he had his suspicions as to where she might be. The pastor had demanded he keep an eye on her and he could not let her absence go unheeded yet again. He must find out where she was. Quickly he made his way to his car.

It was a twenty minute drive to the quiet outer city suburbs where Grace Chapel was situated. As Bob slowly approached the church he brought his car to a stop just short of the driveway, positioning it so he was partially hidden by a flowering privet hedge. From here he could clearly view the parking area that surrounded the church's frontage. Lined by birch trees, the dappled sunshine filtered through onto the cars below. The car park was full, but there was only one car that Bob was interested in. Shielding his eyes from the bright sunshine that reflected on the paintwork, he scanned the area for the yellow VW with its familiar number plate—and as he had suspected, there it was.

Bob sneered in sarcastic contempt. "So, Zara Williams. Betraying your church and doing so behind our backs. Did you really think you could outsmart us? Will you never learn that we have our ways of controlling the rebellious? Oh, we may have recently allowed Ruth Henderson to slip through our nets, but only because she and her daughter were nothing to us. They were weak—unlike you, Zara. You have more strength of will, and once moulded will be an asset to our church. But there are lessons to be learned first and your weakness is obvious. Your friends! How unfortunate that they must suffer because of your foolishness. Well—let's see what the pastor has to say about this, shall we?"

⚥

The resplendent, glowing sunshine of spring streamed in through the large picture windows of Grace Chapel, warming Zara's face as she sat contentedly next to her friends, Beth and Tim, while waiting for the service to begin. Zara had managed to slip away early this Sunday morning from the flat without being noticed, for Kate was still reluctant to talk to her after her outburst last week and had remained brooding in her bedroom. If she did hear Zara leave, she would have assumed she was attending the early-morning prayer meeting at The Light in an effort to make amends for her recent behaviour, and Zara couldn't help but feel a little guilty. Her emotions were truly torn between wanting to be with her friends, Beth and Tim, in a life-giving place of worship, and being with her friend, Kate, no matter how difficult things were between them at the present. She wanted to support Kate during this important time of her life and hoped that all would soon be forgiven. Yet she still felt anger at the unnecessary control she perceived the church was wielding over its members, hence her taking the risk of attending Grace Chapel today. Still, Zara hoped her absence from The Light would not be discovered this morning, and that Bob Everitt's attention would be diverted elsewhere. Surely after his own absence from church he had more important matters to attend to. Anyhow, for Kate's sake, if at all possible, she wanted to avoid complicating things any more than they already were.

Looking around her, Zara noted two other familiar faces in the crowd—those of Ruth and Emily Henderson, who apparently, having just recently left the church of The Light themselves, were attending their first official service as members of Grace. Zara couldn't help but feel a little envious of them both as she watched them being greeted and embraced, and looked forward to the time when she, too, could safely call this church her home.

Moments later the worship began. A skilled team of musicians led in with a jubilant introduction on keyboard, guitars, and drums before the congregation stood to their feet and joined in with clapping, praise, and song. Zara beamed with delight. *This* was what church should be like.

> Come, now is the time to worship,
> Come, now is the time to give your heart,
> Come, just as you are to worship,
> Come, just as you are before your God,
> Come.
> One day every tongue will confess,
> You are God,
> One day every knee will bow,
> Still the greatest treasure remains for those,
> Who gladly choose you now.

Glancing around her she noted a young family near the front of the church. Both parents had a young child on their hip as they each stood with one arm raised, praising God. The children were clapping and laughing and Zara could not help but compare this scene to that of The Light. There, children were forbidden to attend the services, instead being closeted away to colour pictures or play with blocks. They were seen as a nuisance and a blemish to the image of perfection, and on the odd occasion when a child had been present in the meetings, the pastor had had them removed the moment they uttered a sound. How refreshing that here they were included as part of the family of God.

As the singing continued with great gusto and passion, Zara's attention was drawn to the young woman on stage who was song leading. Fascinated, Zara watched her for some minutes. It was not so much the clothes that she wore, or the quality of her clearly trained voice that was so captivating, but rather the extraordinary expression on her face. She was positively glowing. Her eyes were closed and her face was tilted toward the heavens as she sang in genuine love and praise to her God. This was not something Zara had ever witnessed in the dry, religious services of The Light, and she found that she *longed* for a similar relationship with God. How wonderful to know him in such a way. Surely this was what Christianity was all about.

As the worship drew to an end, Brian Somerville bounded enthusiastically on to the stage. Although in a shirt and tie, his manner was casual and friendly and immediately Zara felt at ease. She had not met Brian personally, but she had heard much about him and his wife, Lynn, from Beth, who spoke highly of them both.

"Good morning, folks!" he grinned, as he took up the hand-held microphone. "What a great day to be worshipping in God's presence, amen?" Everyone chorused a joyful "amen" in reply, as Brian continued.

"Well, this morning we have three special announcements to

make. Firstly, Angela and Mike gave birth to a lovely baby girl during the week and today we are going to dedicate her to the Lord."

The room broke into clapping and cheering as everyone turned toward the happy couple to offer their congratulations. As the exuberance died down, Brian went on.

"Secondly, we have two new members with us this morning—Ruth Henderson and her daughter, Emily, who are living with Deborah and her family in their basement flat. Many of you met them on Saturday at the welcome party that Deb hosted, but if you haven't made their acquaintance yet, be sure to do so at the end of the service. And last but not least—our dear friends, Gordon and Madeleine, are leaving us today. They feel the Lord is leading them to another fellowship across town, and we want to make sure we release them with our blessing and love. After the service we will be having a luncheon in honour of all three couples, so do stay and join us. Meanwhile, why don't you folks come up the front and let us pray for you now?"

Zara watched in amazement as members of the church surrounded the couples and prayed for them, speaking out words of encouragement and prophecy. She had never known new members to be welcomed, nor babies dedicated to the Lord, but most of all she had *never* witnessed those leaving the church of The Light being prayed for, nor blessed. In fact, quite the opposite. They were instead negatively preached about for weeks to come and all were forbidden to fellowship with them ever again. How wrong it all seemed now.

After a stirring message delivered by Brian, the service concluded and all arose to ready themselves for the luncheon served in the adjoining room out back. Tantalising smells of pastries and savouries drifted into the main auditorium and Zara realised just how hungry she was, having not had time to eat as yet that day. But she was also aware of the time.

"So, Zara. Will you stay to have lunch with us?" asked Beth, seeing Zara look at her watch. "You know you are more than welcome…there is always plenty of food. Or do you think you should be heading back?"

Zara was about to answer when she felt a hand on her shoulder and looking around saw that it was Ruth Henderson.

"Zara, isn't it? Hello, I'm Ruth." Zara stood to her feet and they both embraced. "I didn't realise you came to this church. When did you leave The Light?"

"Well…the truth is, I *haven't*," Zara grinned. "Just checking out the opposition, if you know what I mean." They both laughed, feeling an immediate bond, although they had never actually spoken to each other before. "I see *you've* made the plunge, Ruth. Any advice you can give me?"

"Only that you need to be very careful. Do they know you are here this morning? They seem to have eyes everywhere. All I know is that they can be very hard if they suspect you are going against them in any way."

Ruth looked toward Emily who was mingling with a new group of friends and Zara followed her glance. She recalled seeing Emily's name in the confidential file in the church's office, and although she didn't know the circumstances could tell from the look on Ruth's face that there had been pain in acquiring this knowledge.

"Anyway, if you do decide to leave, then let me know so I can cover you in prayer."

"Thanks, Ruth…that's really kind of you. But I won't be leaving until my best friend gets married. I'm supposed to be her bridesmaid, and we both know that won't happen if I'm at another church."

"We also both know that you may not even get that far if they find out you are here today," Ruth warned.

"I guess I'm hoping they'll overlook me," Zara sighed.

But Ruth was not so sure. "Look—if you ever run into trouble there is someone you can talk to at The Light. Do you know Leonard McKenzie at all?"

"The elder? I know of him, but have never actually spoken to him. Why?"

"He was a great help to Emily and me when we were going through difficult times. Of all the elders at The Light he somehow seems to be the most sympathetic and understanding. I would love to see him and his wife freed from that place. I'm sure you could go to him for help and advice if things get tricky."

"Thanks, Ruth, I'll remember that…but you may need to define 'tricky' for me. I don't like the sound of that." Turning to Beth who had been waiting patiently some distance away, she called her over. "Ruth and I have just been talking about The Light. Perhaps I will stay for lunch, Beth. It seems I have some catching up to do with my new friend."

It was late in the afternoon before Zara eventually turned her car into the driveway of her flat and made her way into the house. Throwing down her keys and bag and kicking off her shoes, she headed for the kitchen to make herself a coffee, humming to herself and noting that the house seemed deathly quiet. Kate must have gone out for the afternoon. Zara was still on a high from the vibrant atmosphere of Grace and feeling a need for music, she pushed open the sliding doors between the kitchen and the lounge to turn on her CD player. Stopping short, however, she was astonished to find that Bob Everitt, Brother Henry, and Kate were sitting silently on the sofa, awaiting her return.

"We've been waiting for you." Bob smiled like a self-righteous Pharisee. "Please, take a seat." He motioned toward an empty armchair.

Zara looked in bewilderment across at a pale Kate, seeking an explanation but Kate only stared at the floor, unable to meet her eye. Zara hesitantly sat on the edge of the chair. "What is this all about?"

"Maybe you could tell us, Zara. Where were you this morning?" Brother Henry demanded with the air of one interrogating the enemy.

"I…I . . ." Zara stumbled.

"You were at that *Grace Chapel*, weren't you? There is no point denying it. I saw your car in the car park." Bob interjected smugly, looking pleased with himself.

"You mean...you followed me?" Zara was indignant. "I don't believe this. This is just about as good as listening in to my telephone conversations!"

Kate looked up sharply at Zara with a puzzled expression on her face. This was news to her. But Bob chose to ignore the statement, quickly moving on.

"As we have informed Kate this afternoon, Pastor Whitfield is tired of this obvious continued rebellion and betrayal. You have been with us long enough, Zara, to know the rules of the church. You have already been disciplined for having lunch with that Bethany girl who was excommunicated from our fellowship. Yet you continue to speak with her on the phone and . . ."

Zara was quick to interrupt. "Yes, but how do you *know* I've been speaking to Beth on the phone?" She was cut off again.

"...and, *as* I was saying," Bob continued coolly, glaring at Zara, "you have now been caught attending another church. The pastor does not take these things lightly." He sat back in his seat and crossed his legs looking skyward, his finger poised on his cheek in contemplation. "But, perhaps we have not made ourselves very clear. Let me try to make you understand now." Bob turned to Kate and leaning forward stared stonily into her eyes. "Pastor Whitfield will *not* be marrying you and Dan. The wedding is off."

Kate gasped in disbelief before letting out a cry of dismay. "You can't *do* that...I have done nothing wrong. Why are you taking this out on *me?* It's so unfair." Weeping, she placed her head in her hands.

Zara felt sick in the pit of her stomach as she watched her distraught friend and longed to comfort her. No wedding! There had always been the danger of this happening, but she didn't actually think it would.

Seeing both girls distressed, Bob continued smoothly. "Zara, you have one week in which to make up your mind. Stay or leave. If, at the end of the week, you decide to repent of your actions and submit to the leadership of the church, we *may* reconsider the marriage of Dan and Kate. It would mean, however, several things. You must from that point on be obedient to the rules of the church; you must attend all meetings without question; and you must promise *never* to visit another church, nor make contact with ex-members outside of the church of The Light ever again. It would also mean that you cannot be a part of the wedding party." Bob paused for effect as he allowed this information to sink in before continuing. "If, on the other hand, you decide to leave us, I must be very clear of the consequences. You *will* be excommunicated," Bob threatened. "You will have no fellowship with any member of The Light, including Kate, and you *certainly* will not be attending her wedding. You will lose your job at the office and will be asked to leave this flat immediately. But perhaps more importantly than all of the above, your soul will be in danger of going to *hell* for disobedience and rebellion. I must also caution you that as was witnessed at a recent young person's funeral in similar circumstances to your own, you will very much be in danger of sickness or accident befalling you, having chosen to remove yourself from the protection of God. It is with the utmost care, therefore, that you should make your decision."

Everitt and Henry rose with slow deliberation, aware of the chaos they had caused and revelling in the sense of heady power they now felt. "We will be in contact with you again, Zara. You have one week."

As the door closed behind the two men, Zara and Kate were left to stare at each other in confused silence, each struggling with their own thoughts and emotions, aware of the other's pain, yet unable to find the words to heal.

Outside, Bob was quick to call the pastor. "She won't leave," he muttered into his phone. "She's too scared."

"Good work," Pastor Whitfield congratulated him before murmuring, "It's good to know *someone* is obeying my orders."

That night, unable to sleep, Zara rose from her bed and stood in the darkness of her room. Her spirit was heavy and her mind troubled by the day's events, and walking to her window she stared out at the moonlit sky. She had argued once again with Kate that evening, the latter blaming Zara for the woeful turn of events, and nothing Zara could say or do would pacify her. Emotions had been raw and tempers frayed, and Zara now wondered if their relationship would ever be the same. She dabbed at her eyes with the corner of her nightdress as they overflowed with tears. Kate had grown so distant and hard, so wholly uninterested in listening to what Zara had to say. To add to her sorrow she rehearsed over and over in her mind the words of Bob Everitt as he had threatened her with so many things, and in particular with his saying her soul was in danger of going to hell. Surely this was not true, yet his words continued to nag her with fearful persistence. Would she really be out of God's will by leaving the church? Would her life truly be in danger by making such a move? Turning, she walked back to her bed, perching on its edge with shoulders drooped dejectedly. She felt so naive, so foolish. Kate had warned her all along that the leadership would act harshly, just as they had done with Beth—yet somehow she had felt immune; angry and resistant to their control. Although all the warning signs were there, she had hoped they would do nothing to her. Today she was proved wrong. The iron rod of discipline had come down heavily and those closest to her were harmed in the process. Slipping to her knees and burying her head in her arms, Zara cried out to God.

"O Lord, help me. What should I do? Please show me what I should do." Hot tears continued to flow down her cheeks. "I long to know your will and to know your plan for my life."

In the still quietness of the night, Zara's mind was suddenly filled with the memories of the meeting that morning at Grace. She remembered the worship, the prayers, the uplifting message of Brian Somerville, the acceptance and love shown by all toward her. She reflected on the young woman whose face had been so aglow with the presence of God. And she felt the gentle reminder of the Lord that these were not the actions of a people bound for hell. Zara lifted her head as she heard the words of Ruth Henderson echo in her mind. *"If ever you need someone to talk to, Leonard McKenzie will understand."*

Sitting upright next to her bed, Zara stared up at the moon, so still and tranquil. For months she had struggled and questioned, comparing this fact with that, wondering what she should do, and yet somehow, deep in her heart, she had known the answer all along. A sudden peace settled gently upon her as though a soft quilt had been draped around her shoulders, and all her struggling and turmoil slowly eased away. Calmly pulling back the bedcovers, Zara climbed serenely between her sheets as though a huge weight had been lifted from her shoulders. In her mind, at last, the decision was made.

# THE PATH OF CHANGE

Devonshire Park had long been a favourite of Leonard and Marjory's. Not far from their home, yet set on forty acres of rambling farmland, one would hardly know they were in the centre of a bustling, cosmopolitan city. With its tree-lined walkways and wide open spaces it was the perfect place for both families and business folk alike to escape from the pressures of the day.

Leonard spread out a red tartan rug beneath the shade of an aging oak. The day was perfect for a picnic with its clear blue sky and crisp spring breezes, and this spot had the added advantage of an unhindered view. As Marjory unpacked the picnic basket, Leonard settled back to survey his surroundings. Always the keen gardener, his attention was first drawn to the carpet of flowers spread out before him: daffodils, tulips, cro-cuses, and freesias, their scent filling the air with heady sweet-ness. In a paddock just beyond, newborn lambs were bounding around their hassled mothers with newfound energy, and not far from them again was a playground where mums pushed squeal-ing toddlers on swings and dads played ball with their sons.

"Tea, Leonard?" asked Marjory, a thermos flask poised in her hand.

Marjory had always insisted that tea should be drunk from fine bone china cups and so Leonard was not surprised to be handed a delicate rose cup and saucer. By now the rug was covered in home-baked delicacies and Leonard felt spoilt for choice. This day was just what he needed. Leonard dunked a home-made shortbread into his milky tea and leaned back against the trunk of the oak for support. He had much on his mind right now and this would be the perfect time to sort through his thinking.

Earlier on in the week he'd had an unexpected visit from Zara Williams. She had phoned and asked to see him, and on the Monday night, as planned, came to his house to share her concerns. She told him of her decision to leave the church of The Light, but was insistent that he knew her reasons why. Leonard listened with interest and at times dismay as she relayed her story, feeling particularly troubled over the recent visit of Everitt and Henry to her flat. He was angry at their threats and harsh words, but unfortunately knew this was not the first time such tactics had been used. Threats and abusive bullying had regrettably become a way of doing things at The Light, and it was something Leonard was wholly against. Zara had then handed him the two pamphlets given her by Beth with information on spiritual abuse and religious cults, urging him to read and consider their contents. And after she had left, so he had done. With a heavy heart he had realised there was little within the pamphlets that he disagreed with and had, in fact, observed such behaviour within the church for some time. Regrettably these pamphlets served only as a confirmation of that which he had known in his heart all along; concerns he had only shared, however, with Marjory.

Leonard glanced across at Marjory now, sipping tea from her china cup with her white hair glistening in the sunshine. She had always been so gentle, always so supportive; even when he was away so often at meetings or doing the pastor's bidding here, there, and everywhere, she had never complained. She had been a precious companion and friend to him for so many years and he loved her. Yet he could tell that she, too, was tiring from the burden and pressure of life at The Light. What once had been such a joyous place of fellowship now had become difficult and oppressive, and it was taking its toll. Leonard felt an ache in the depths of his being as he watched his wife. Who could say how many more years they would have together. Neither of them was getting any younger. Surely these years should be the happiest times of their lives—not one of fighting the leadership every step of the way and being involved in never-ending politics.

He remembered a time when things were different. Many years ago Milton Whitfield and he had been good friends— Milton had even been Leonard's best man at his wedding. Marjory and Nancy, Milton's wife, had been the best of friends as well. He remembered when they all had been at the Baptist Bible College together. Nancy had been so vibrant and full of life, and together with Leonard and Marjory they had all dreamed of doing such great things for God. When Milton had first started the church of The Light he was passionate and on fire for God, and the numbers quickly grew, as people were drawn to his charismatic style and anointing. Leonard had happily worked at his side, and they had witnessed many wonderful meetings where people had been genuinely saved and set free. But then had come the tragic and untimely death of Milton's wife and child...and without Milton's beloved Nancy by his side, things had changed. Leonard sadly recalled the many nights they all had gathered around her bed crying out in prayer for her cancer to be healed. Those seeming unanswered prayers had been a bitter blow for Milton, one from which he never seemed to recover. In the years that had followed he had grown more inward and bitter, cutting himself off from all the known "Pentecostal type" movements. He fell out with many of his former pastor friends in the area and his control on the congregation tightened. His charismatic personality had all but disappeared. Leonard tried to talk to him on so many occasions, but Milton pushed him away, their friendship growing more and more distant.

Wearily Leonard sighed, reluctant to face the inevitable, but knowing he needed to confront within himself that which had been nagging at him for some time. Now, while he still had the strength within him, he had to make his move. He owed it to his wife, to himself, and to those who had so recently confided in him. He had always thought he would happily live his life out at the church of The Light, but now it seemed that may not be possible. Too much was weighing on his mind—there were too many things that he disagreed with and believed were not scripturally correct. Zara's visit had only aroused within him again his conviction to act and had served to renew his resolve to do something about the situation. He knew his time had come. Slowly, Leonard reached over and helped himself to a blueberry muffin. He knew what he must do. Like it or not he must find the courage within himself to call a long overdue meeting with the leadership of the church of The Light. He could put it off no longer. On Saturday he would confront Pastor Milton Whitfield and the elders and make them accountable for their actions, no matter what the consequences—and he of all men knew those consequences could be severe. He could not even conceive in his mind what life outside of the church of The Light would be like, having been a part of its system for so long, and he wasn't even sure if he and Marjory would cope with such change. But he did know God was with him, faithfully guiding his footsteps, and would never let him down. Besides, he had heard good reports about the little church called Grace Chapel and would be interested in visiting it, if the worst came to the worst. But perhaps it would not get that far. Perhaps this time Milton would listen to him, just like in the old days, and by some miracle change his ways.

Marjory had been studying Leonard's face for some time as he quietly drank his tea while deeply preoccupied with his thoughts. She saw the worried lines on his forehead, the hunched and tensed shoulders, as though he were carrying the weight of the world. And she worried for him. A genuinely kind and compassionate man, he took so much to heart, suffering inwardly with his emotions more than most knew. But *she* knew him, and something today was deeply troubling him.

Gently she placed a hand on his arm. "Leonard, sweetheart. Is there something you would like to share with me?" she asked kindly.

Leonard looked up quickly, jolted from his thoughts and realising how absorbed he had been to the exclusion of his dear wife. He smiled at her knowing gaze. How did he expect to hide anything from her? She knew him practically better than he knew himself. Reaching out, he squeezed her hand. "Sorry for being such poor company today, Marj," he apologised. "I've had a few things on my mind."

"What, just a few?" Marjory teased good-naturedly. But then growing serious again, she urged, "You know what they say…a problem shared is a problem halved."

Leonard looked into his wife's concerned, clear blue eyes. He didn't want to burden her, yet he knew his planned actions could have serious repercussions that would impact them both. In all fairness she needed to know his intentions.

"How about we pack this picnic basket up and go for a stroll through the woods." Leonard suggested. "You're right, Marjory. There is something I need to tell you…and I think you should prepare yourself. For I strongly feel I need to do something that may change the direction of our lives."

⚥

Wiping the dust from her old, brown suitcase and placing it into the middle of her unmade bed, Zara prepared to dismantle and pack her few, meagre belongings. The irony of the situation did not escape her, for she remembered that the last time she had used this case was on holiday with her friends Kate and Bethany. How quickly her circumstances had changed—and now she found she was homeless, jobless, and apart from Beth and Tim, friendless. Yet her peace remained. Despite all, she knew she was doing the right thing. And it was not all so bleak, for Beth had reassured Zara that she could stay with them for as long as it took to procure another flat, and Tim had heard of a position at his work that would soon be opening up. Ruth and Emily had also sent their love and assured Zara they would be praying for her; and Lynn Somerville, the pastor's wife at Grace, had phoned to invite her to a church barbeque at the beach on Saturday afternoon. All that remained then was for her to pack, and reaching into her wardrobe she removed several articles of clothing from their hangers and began folding them neatly into her suitcase.

There was still one issue, however, that had not been completely resolved. Although she had visited Leonard McKenzie earlier on in the week, she had not been so inclined to tell Bob Everitt of her decision to leave. Instead, she had chosen to write a letter to the leadership, which they should, by now, have received. Yet, there had been no telephone call, no acknowledgement, and Zara felt uncomfortable at the silence, confused as to its meaning. Either they were already giving her the cold shoulder for rejecting their church, treating her as they did so many other ex-members of The Light; or they were still planning to make their disapproval known to her or Kate—and she was not sure which she should be more afraid of. Certainly, her decision had not reached the general church populace yet, for she was still receiving phone calls about her rostered cleaning duties and her teaching syllabus for Sunday school. Even Kate was unsure as to which course of action she had decided to take. The truth was the atmosphere in the flat had been so strained and tense that Zara had been unsure how to tell her.

Zara moved to her side cabinet and opened the drawer to remove a white, sealed envelope that simply read "Kate." She had thought long and hard about what to write, and hoped her words would find a place in her friend's heart. She had genuinely meant no harm to Kate or Dan, and begged for their forgiveness, hoping they would understand her decision to leave.

She had wished them all the very best in their new life together and had also expressed her desire to see them again, but feared that it would not be so. How desperately she wanted Kate to see that she was leaving The Light because this *was* God's will for her life. She was not in danger of going to hell as the elders had threatened, nor would any ill befall her. How she wanted Kate to comprehend there *was* life outside of the church of The Light, and that there could be a wonderful future for both her and Dan; a future of freedom, healing, and teaching such as they had not had before; a future of ministry and joy together. Dan and Kate had both tasted the legalism and control at The Light firsthand, they could not deny this. Surely they did not want this suffocating domination to continue for the rest of their lives? Yet, sadly, it seemed they had blocked their minds to the truth, becoming deeply conditioned and indoctrinated by the church's teachings. Well—at least one thing was for sure. Zara's leaving would mean their marriage could go ahead unhindered—that is, minus one bridesmaid. With a heavy heart, Zara laid the envelope down on her bed as she continued emptying drawers and shelves and throwing shoes into plastic bags. She would leave the letter for Kate to find when she came home from work, for Zara intended to be well gone by then. This way they both could avoid the painful goodbyes that would be inevitable.

Her bedroom complete, Zara wandered out into the kitchen with an empty box to claim anything else that was hers. She picked up a set of mugs, a vase that had been a gift, and a bizarre fruit bowl that she'd taken a fancy to and purchased at the market one day. She smiled to herself. It really was hideously ugly and she couldn't remember what she'd seen in it, but it was hers and she was sure Kate didn't want it. Glancing around the kitchen, her gaze stopped at a plaque on the wall. Walking across the room, Zara removed it from its place and fondly held it in her hands. She chuckled at the words *"Born to Shop"* and at the frenzied woman pictured with many shopping bags and parcels. Kate had bought this for her, knowing her passion for shopping, and Zara sighed. She would miss the good times they had had together. Next it was on to the lounge where she gathered her favourite silk embroidered cushion; a small selection of classic books she'd been collecting; and some CD's. Passing the oak cabinet, however, she hesitated as she gazed at the silver frame in which sat the photo of herself, Kate, and Bethany. This was, by right, hers—but she could not bring herself to take it. Perhaps it would be a constant reminder to Kate of the friendships she had once had—but now lost.

Her work at last complete, Zara gathered her things together and struggled out to her car. Several trips later, her small vehicle packed to its hilt, she returned again to the flat for one final time. Carefully, she propped the white envelope which contained her letter next to the coffee maker, knowing this would be Kate's first port of call on returning home. Then moving around the flat, she paused to look in each room as though memorising its every nook and cranny. This little house had been her home for over two years and she had had many happy times here. She stood for a moment in silence before finally pulling the front door closed. Walking slowly to her car, she looked back sadly at a place she knew she would never be welcome to again. Kate had been like a sister to her—but a sister to whom she must now be estranged. With her heart aching, Zara started the engine and pulled away from the curb. A chapter of her life had drawn to a close…but just as surely, another was beginning.

# SPIRITUAL WARFARE

Contentedly lying back on her blue and white striped beach chair as the afternoon sun gently warmed her skin, Ruth closed her eyes and soaked in the welcoming sounds and smells of the secluded bay around her. She could hear the rhythmic waves gently lapping the sand, sounding calming and peaceful, and in the cloudless skies above seagulls squawked and squabbled as they circled endlessly, seeking fish and scraps of food. In the distance children laughed and squealed as they played in the warm rock pools, and the aroma of sausages, steak and onions cooking on the barbeque floated on the gentle breeze. Ruth liberally rubbed more sunscreen lotion onto her arms and legs then laid back again, the smell of the lotion, mingled with that of the salt sea water bringing back many happy childhood memories of time spent at the beach. She smiled serenely. It had been the perfect day for a church picnic.

"Mind if I park my chair beside you?" Deb's friendly voice interrupted her slumbering solitude, but Ruth was not perturbed. She and Deb had grown close these past few weeks, and Ruth was glad for her company.

"This is the life," Ruth sighed as she made room for her friend beneath the sun umbrella, adjusting the position of her chair and putting on her sunglasses. "I could get used to being a lady of leisure; reclining on the golden sands beside the deep, blue sea; dinner being cooked and served by the men folk; sipping cold lemonade whenever you fancy."

"Waxing a bit poetical there, aren't you, my dear?" laughed Deb. "Come back to reality and pass me some of that sun cream for my nose. I don't mind eating lobster, but I don't want to end up looking like one."

As she was about to reach for the bottle, a cackle of laughter and delighted squeals suddenly rang out from the grassy meadows behind them and, recognising one particular voice, Ruth turned to watch. She smiled as she saw Emily with a group of friends, being chased by mischievous boys of similar age who were brandishing buckets of icy cold water. It was all so natural and fun, and Ruth could not help but compare this to their days at The Light where, for Emily, all such contact with the opposite sex had been totally forbidden. Ruth was surprised Emily even knew *how* to relate to a boy, so closeted had been her upbringing. Yet she had seen such a change in her daughter of late, and her heart felt gladdened and relieved. Emily was beginning to relax and had started to smile again and, although it was early days yet, Ruth could see a glimmer of her daughter's old personality returning. She knew the traumatic experiences of the past few months had left their scar and would take some time to heal, yet Ruth felt comforted that they were both now in the right church for that healing to take place and she thanked the Lord for his goodness.

From under her wide-brimmed, straw sun hat, Deb watched Ruth with interest. "It's great to see Emily enjoying herself, isn't it?" She followed Ruth's gaze. "That tall boy with the dark hair—the one that has just thrown a bucket of water over your daughter—is a really nice lad." She chuckled. "Although it looks like he may have to find another way of enchanting the ladies! His parents are lovely folks too. We've known them for years. He'd be a great friend for Emily."

Ruth nodded. "They went to the cinema together last week. It all takes a bit of getting used to. The Light taught us to be so wary of places like the cinema. I'm finding it hard to get my head around it. We won't be getting a television for a while to come yet, but I'm glad for Emily's sake that at least she's having more of a normal life now."

Deb nodded as she continued to watch Emily. She wanted to say something to Ruth but was unsure if now was the time. "Ruth?" she questioned thoughtfully, relaxing back in her chair as she applied sun screen cream to her nose and cheeks. "Talking of partners…have you contacted Jack yet?"

Ruth turned toward Deb, a look of uncertainty crossing her face. "He's been on my mind a lot lately." She sighed, not knowing how to express what was on her heart. "I know I should phone him to let him know our change of circumstances. The truth is…well…it's been so peaceful with just Emily and me at the flat, I've been hesitant to do so. Before Jack and I split up, Jack's drinking was getting to the stage that I often didn't know what state he would be in when he returned home from work each evening. The strain of it all was really playing on my health—along with other things. I guess I didn't appreciate how unwell I was until I started to get better, if you know what I mean. I admit when I first left I couldn't bear to be without him and wanted so desperately to be back together again. But now…I feel so much stronger. I know I have a long way to go— but can you understand that I don't want to go back to the way things were? I'm not sure that I know what to do." Ruth looked pleadingly at Deb, hopeful for some guidance and input, and as always she was not disappointed. Deb reached out and gently took her hand.

"I sensed you were struggling with this issue."

She turned to look out toward the sea, but seemingly gazed beyond it—and Ruth knew what her friend was doing. She had become familiar with Deb's ways and knew she was quietly praying; seeking God's guidance and counsel…seeking a word of knowledge from the Lord.

"I think you need to be at peace about this," she eventually said, turning back to Ruth. "Phone Jack. Let him know that you are both safe and happy, you owe him that much. But don't be in any hurry to get back together again—not just yet anyway. Emily does need her dad, but give yourself and Emily time to heal first. Jack will see the change in you both and, who knows, he may be up for some change himself. Invite him to some of the meetings, or if he prefers, to just mix with some of the folks here—no pressure. I imagine he has some bitter feelings toward all things religious, and I can't say I blame him—so don't push the subject. But rest assured, my friend. God has not finished with your little family yet. I have a feeling things are going to work out just fine...you'll see."

As ever, Ruth was thankful for the simple, practical advice she received, so full of common sense and wisdom. Deb had not had to run to the pastor to find out what needed to be done, nor had she religiously sought to apply the letter and the law to this situation, insisting that she submit to her husband as head of the home and allow the abuse to continue. She had simply asked her God and he in turn had shown the path of reconciliation and healing. Why was it that everything had been so complicated and twisted at The Light? Why was the leadership so afraid of the common person having intimacy with their God? Maybe because they would have to yield all power and control of the church back to him—something they were obviously reluctant to do.

While Deb had been speaking, two slim and attractive figures had been making their way down the beach toward them, one a brunette and one a redhead. Colourful sarongs were wrapped around their swim suits and sand clung to their tanned legs. As they drew closer, one waved enthusiastically and called out Ruth's name. It was Zara and Beth.

Ruth was quick to stand and welcome them. "I heard the news, Zara," she said warmly as they both approached. "Welcome to Grace!" Ruth embraced her young friend. "How are you coping?"

"Not too badly—thanks to my dear friend Beth, here, who has taken me in and listened as I've talked for hours." Zara put her arm around Beth's shoulder and squeezed in appreciation.

Ruth winked at Deb. "Where would we be without such good friends?" She beckoned to Zara and Beth. "Come and sit under our umbrella and have a cold drink with us if you like."

The girls were quick to oblige. The afternoon sun was still bright in the sky and the temperatures were high. Sipping their cold drinks gratefully, Zara turned to Ruth.

"I must confess, Ruth, that Beth and I have sought you out today to share with you some news."

Something in her tone instantly had Ruth's attention. "What is it? Is everything okay?"

"Well, I'm not sure it will be," Beth chipped in. "This morning before we left for the beach, we received a phone call. It was from Leonard McKenzie."

Zara explained. "Remember, Ruth, you told me that if ever I needed to talk to someone at The Light, Leonard McKenzie would be a sympathetic listener? Well, I took your advice and went to see him just before I left the church. I shared with him openly about all of my concerns and he really took it to heart. Actually, as you suspected, Ruth, I think he's had his doubts for some time and my visit was the straw that broke the camel's back, so to speak. Anyway...apparently after I'd gone he really thought long and hard about what to do and decided it was time to call a meeting with Pastor Whitfield and the elders to confront them. They are going to meet tonight! He rang to ask my permission to share some of the concerns I had mentioned to him. He also intends to confront them over their treatment of you and Emily. Actually, I get the impression he has a few things he wants to get off his chest—but I think things could get messy."

"We felt very concerned for him," Beth concluded. "We all know only too well that he's going into a den of lions. Pastor Whitfield does not welcome confrontation at the best of times, and especially not from one of his elders. Interestingly he has been very careful to surround himself with a group of men who are either very passive or, like him, just as hungry for power but either way, all do his bidding without question. He'll not, therefore, take kindly to this meeting and they'll be few others that will dare to stand with Leonard's convictions. I think he is in for a hard time."

Deb had been listening intently and now spoke with concern. "Do you know when the meeting is going to take place?"

"I believe around 8:00 p.m. tonight."

Deb looked at her watch. "Good—that gives us time to organise some prayer. We need to find Brian and Lynn and as many other members of Grace who are here this afternoon. We can't let Leonard go into that meeting tonight without first entering into spiritual warfare!"

The sun had begun to set by the time everyone finished their barbeque dinners and settled themselves in the warm sand before the roaring flames of the bonfire. Apart from members of Grace, the beach was all but deserted now and ever quick to worship, Brian encouraged anyone with guitars to strike up a chord and start the singing. As darkness fell, Zara, Ruth, and Beth linked arms as they swayed in time to the music while perched on top of an old weathered log, and the flickering flames reflected on their faces the joy they felt deep inside. But a serious task was at hand and after singing several rousing songs, Brian stood on the beach to talk to all gathered. With the dark waves gently lapping the shore in the distance, and the fire crackling cheerfully in their midst, he explained the situation with Leonard McKenzie and asked that all join with Zara, Beth, and Ruth in prayer for their friend and elder at the church of The Light.

Huddled together now in the centre of the circle Zara, Beth, and Ruth bowed their heads, overwhelmed by the love and support they were receiving. Ruth reached up and wiped a tear that had slowly trickled down her cheek as she silently prayed in earnest for her dear friends Marjory and Leonard. One by one other prayers were uttered around the circle: prayers for Leonard's protection; prayers that he would know the wisdom of the Lord; prayers that the walls of division and abuse would be broken down. And then began something new to Zara and Ruth. Spiritual warfare. United in prayer and linked arm in arm around the fire, the small gathering began to tackle the spiritual strongholds and demonic powers behind the church of The Light. They bound up a spirit of deception, of religion, of control. They came against mind control and the spirit of fear; of pride and of oppression. They tore down the spirits of witchcraft and rebuked Jezebel. Nothing was left untouched; no stone left unturned. They spoke with authority in the name of Jesus and left Zara and Ruth in awe.

Finally Brian lifted his head with a triumphant grin, quoting a scripture from the Bible. "Remember…'Rejoice not, that the spirits are subject unto you; but rather rejoice, because your names are written in heaven' (Luke 10:20, KJV). Isn't that right, folks? Let's believe in faith that tonight God's angels are watching over our dear friend and that *his will* may be done. Be blessed, and have a great weekend loving Jesus and each other."

# GATHERING OF THE SCRIBES
# AND PHARISEES

The air was heavy with oppression as the sombre group of ten elders gathered around the large mahogany table in the centre of the pastor's office, ready for the meeting called by Leonard McKenzie. Bob Everitt sat staunchly with his arms folded, his face stony and unresponsive; his stance on the meeting already obvious. Others shifted nervously in their chairs as they waited for Milton Whitfield to enter the room, many unable to look at Leonard. It had been rumoured he intended to confront the pastor tonight over his dictatorial dealings with the church and it was feared the meeting could get ugly. Never before had an elder questioned the pastor's actions and, with the exception of Bob, all were apprehensive.

Leonard sat at the head of the table, strangely calm and serene as he contemplated the scene before him. He had known the men that surrounded him for many years and they were to him as brothers, yet tonight they could barely meet his eye. The fear of the system and of an authoritarian leader had overwhelmed them and far outweighed the years of friendship. They were afraid to admit the truth, afraid to speak their minds for fear of the consequences, and Leonard was saddened to see these men of God reduced to such a state. He knew they were good men, men who sincerely loved God and desired to serve the people, yet their vision and direction had become clouded by the whims of one man and they had lost their conviction and strength. Many, like Leonard, were growing older, their families and loved ones having been firmly rooted in the church for several generations, and they were unwilling to rock the boat lest they lose all. Instead they chose to ignore what they must surely know to be wrong. The truth had become dangerous to them, and so they had convinced themselves that they were doing God's will by blindly following their pastor's every order. Leonard tightened his grip around the brown leather journal he held in his hand. It was well worn by time and much use, for over the years Leonard had diligently recorded in these pages every question, every prayer, every concern for the church and its leadership. It was from this journal that Leonard intended to speak tonight and it was like his weaponry. The last entry had been of Zara's visit, which he had faithfully recorded, and silently he prayed for God's strength and wisdom to say what was needed. He was thankful, at least, for these few extra minutes to compose himself before the pastor arrived; word had reached them that he would be delayed on account of his watching a football match on television. Interesting, considering how vehemently he preached against both television and sport. Leonard sighed. It was just another example of the hypocritical pharisaic behaviour displayed here.

Voices from the adjoining office suddenly signalled the imminent entrance of Pastor Whitfield, and an unspoken apprehension caused all present at the table to sit erect in their seats at attention. The heavy oak office door swung open, and with an air of gruff impatience and displeasure Milton Whitfield took his place at the opposite end of the table from Leonard, placing his glasses on his nose and peering around the room like a sergeant major inspecting his troops.

"Where is Henry?" he snapped abruptly.

"Brother Henry can't be with us tonight, pastor," replied Bob quickly, suddenly smooth talking and animated at the chance to impress.

Milton huffed in displeasure. "He'd better have a good excuse." He opened his notebook and took up his fountain pen, poising it in his hand as he at last looked up at Leonard. Coolly he studied Leonard's face for several minutes before writing pointedly in his notebook, but Leonard remained still. He knew that Milton meant to deliberately unnerve and intimidate him, but Leonard determined within himself to remain settled and unperturbed. He *would* have his say tonight and nothing would put him off. The tension in the air increased as all waited for Whitfield to speak, and the room became uncomfortably warm, despite the fan that whirled gently behind them. Certainly the evening outside was one of glorious late spring with the sun only just having set and its heat still lingering around them. Yet had they had more discernment they would have known that the suffocation they felt was not only from the warm weather. It was from the gathering heavy spirits of religious oppression that fed on deception and fear.

Finally Milton put down his pen, glaring around the circle as he sized up each man before him. His unnerving gaze once again paused on Leonard.

"As I am sure you are all aware, I have agreed to hold this meeting tonight at the request of Leonard McKenzie." His voice betrayed a bitter resentment. Rising abruptly from his chair he clasped his hands behind his back and began pacing the floor as though in thoughtful contemplation as he continued to speak, weighing each word carefully.

"The church of The Light has always been a unique church. Unique in its superiority, its knowledge of the truth, its quality of leadership and people. And as such will always come under persecution from those on the outside…" he paused and looked momentarily at Leonard, "…and perhaps even from those on the inside. Yet we must not lose sight of what we are building here. We are building *a new level of society*…and as such we must have rules, regulations, and strong leadership to govern. The people are fickle. They are easily led astray and rebellious. This is why we must keep them busy with the work of God. It is why we must issue rules and demand that they be followed. We must keep the people disciplined and focused and not allow them to question. They don't know their own minds and must be told what to do, how to do it and what to believe. Independence must be squelched at all times. It is our responsibility to oversee this; it is our duty to ensure the safety of our unique society."

"Hear, hear," muttered Bob Everitt, to which Whitfield looked quietly pleased.

Spurred on, Milton placed both hands on the table and leant dramatically forward as though to emphasise his next statement. "No one on the outside will ever understand this. It is up to us. We are in charge and we are accountable *only* to God!"

Leonard had been writing in his journal with grief and disagreement as he took down notes on Milton's brief speech in order to respond to his statements accordingly. When he came to Milton's last statement, however, he was tempted to change the words to, "*I* am in charge and *I* am accountable only to myself, Milton Whitfield," for that surely would have been more accurate. Closing his journal he now cleared his throat and prepared to speak.

"Pastor Whitfield, elders...friends. Thank you for coming here tonight," he began as he quietly looked around the room. He paused for a moment as he stared at the table, collecting his thoughts and contemplating where to begin. Pastor Whitfield sullenly took his seat.

"When I first started attending the church of The Light many years ago now, I was impressed with the level of godliness I saw here. The people were content, the sermons were excellent...Milton, you and your wife, Nancy, were on fire for God with energy and enthusiasm that I admired. I remember a conversation I had with you both where you shared your dream of working on the mission field—in Africa, wasn't it?"

All heads turned toward Milton in amazement. This was hard to imagine. Milton dropped his eyes. He had not heard Nancy's name mentioned in public for many years, and for the smallest of moments a look of pain crossed his face. Raising his head again he narrowed his eyes. "Things were different then," he muttered, shrugging his shoulders almost callously in an effort to cover his emotions.

Noting the change, Leonard softened his voice, feeling compassion for the man who had once been such a good friend. "Over the years I have witnessed a change...a sad change. Just now, Milton, you have talked of building your empire, your new society—its image of perfection seemingly more important than the people that are hurting within it. Unlike the early days when you spoke of faith and hope, you now give harsh rules and impossible hoops to jump through that are destroying the people and their relationship with God. You inflict punishment on all who question; you purge anyone who disrupts the status quo. Milton, what has happened to your love of people and your God? Where are the compassion and the grace? Where is the focus on God? Tell me, Milton. Who is really in control of your empire—is it God or yourself?"

Shock registered on the faces of all present at such bold proclamations and feeling attacked, Milton's expression hardened. Any trace of vulnerability that may have been evident moments before had vanished, and he now became stony and cold.

"Leonard, I wonder if it is *you* who is confused," he laughed mockingly. "The 'empire' I refer to is, of course, the Kingdom of God, not my own. I am merely a humble administrator of that Kingdom. What I do, I do under the direction of God and nothing has changed. In fact—I wonder if the change you speak of is not perhaps within you! Maybe you have grown lukewarm and open to delusion. Perhaps the problem lies within *yourself!*"

Leonard was quick to reply, choosing to ignore the personal attack. "Under God's direction? No one can think or act independently in this place without gaining your consent first, you have just said so yourself. Mistakes are not allowed; negative feelings can never be expressed; questions are frowned upon.

This does not sound like the God I know! The leadership appears to have more control and direction over the people than God himself does."

"We are the administers of God's will, and the people trust our judgement!" Milton fired back. "If they didn't, they would leave."

"And face eternal judgement and hell fire? You have placed so much fear into the people they are terrified of leaving."

"Yet everything I have preached is based on Scripture!" Milton retorted indignantly with the air of a religious Pharisee.

"Yet twisted to serve your purposes."

The elders in the room had remained completely quiet, nervously looking from Leonard to Milton, and back to Leonard. Now Arnold Wilson, a meek and gentle man with white, thinning hair and almost transparent complexion, suddenly spoke up.

"I...er...I have at times wondered myself, pastor, if we were not being a little too harsh on the people . . ." he spoke in a small, sheepish voice.

Whitfield turned his attentions to Arnold; the latter sinking slightly in his chair and wishing he had kept that thought to himself.

"If you had *your* way, Arnold, there would be *no* discipline at all and the place would be in complete chaos; a fact that is blindingly obvious from the state of your own family! Besides, if we lifted the rules today and all abandoned the church tomorrow, who would pay for your retirement fund?" he snapped.

Arnold dropped his eyes and shuffled in his seat, his pale cheeks flushing. The others looked sympathetically toward him and an awkward silence fell once again. Leonard turned to his journal and began flicking through its pages.

"Recently I had a visit from Zara Williams . . ."

"Oh...you're not telling me you listened to the stories of a wayward girl who has only just become a Christian, are you? I thought you had more sense than that!" Bob Everitt suddenly scoffed, though a little nervously, Leonard thought.

"If what she said was untrue, then you have nothing to worry about." Leonard replied coolly. "Ah, here it is." He took up the journal and began reading his notes. "She claims that she has been: threatened, followed, spied on, telephone conversations have been bugged, plans have been interfered with, she has lost her job, her house, and been excommunicated from the church, and to top it all, has been told she will go to hell or suffer a dreadful illness or death for her rebellion and abandonment. Does that about cover it, Milton?"

There was a murmur around the room as the stark realities of the church's actions were plainly laid out before them, some familiar to them all, some not.

"Ah, excuse me...*bugging*, pastor?" Elder Blackmoor ventured with concern.

Milton Whitfield looked quickly at Bob Everitt, a small glint of panic in his eyes. "No, no," he laughed uneasily. "Where did she get that idea from . . ."

"Maybe from this receipt found in your filing cabinet." Leonard pulled the white slip from his journal and placed it on the table for all to see. There was again a murmur of disapproval and Milton visibly paled. But he was quick to regain control. Leonard may have found a small area of vulnerability, but he would not get the better of him. No one questioned Milton Whitfield.

"How did you get that?" he snapped. "Zara? I never trusted that girl. I always knew she was a rebellious division maker," he muttered angrily.

But Elder Kirby spoke up anxiously. "Is this true, pastor? Have conversations been bugged? This could be considered by some as illegal. I am not sure I am comfortable with these tactics," he whined, as he looked around at his colleagues who were nodding in agreement.

But Pastor Whitfield suddenly thumped the table, startling

them all. "We are accountable to a higher law! We must do what we see fit to govern the people. Does not the scripture say, 'Obey them that have the rule over you, and submit yourselves, for they watch your souls, as they that must give account' (Hebrews 13:17, KJV)? Is not the Master pleased when we are able to correct a child of God by using creative means? Zara Williams was strong willed, deceptive, and stubbornly rebellious, as her present course of action has proved. We sought only to help her."

"Perhaps you could explain the 'help' you offered, then, to Ruth Henderson and her family?" Leonard asked pointedly.

Milton huffed as he again stood to his feet and began pacing the floor. All elders' eyes were upon him, waiting for his reply, for many stories had circulated regarding this family, and the truth had become hard to discern.

"The answer remains the same. We will not tolerate insubordination!" he stressed with hostility. "This…Henderson woman's daughter was wayward and of the world. She was a stumbling block to others of her age. She needed to be disciplined and we sought to do so by teaching her submission to authority. The alcoholic husband certainly had no authority as he was a heathen who had no place here—and as for Ruth, she was weak. We did what we thought was best before God."

"And before God are you willing then to take accountability for the consequences of your help? Did you all know that both Ruth and Emily Henderson tried to commit suicide because of the harsh and uncaring 'help' that was offered them?"

A small gasp of concern sounded around the room as the elders looked at each other and shook their heads. Milton stopped in his tracks.

"They were both trying to gain sympathy and attention!" he yelled, noticeably shaken by this last statement. "This Ruth woman was full of self-pity and foolishness, and pampering to her needs would have been unthinkable. The same applied to her daughter. Discipline; rules; obedience—that is what this church is all about!" He pounded the last three words with his fists on the table.

Leonard shook his head wearily. He could see that Milton Whitfield was defiant and intractable over the release of power he held over this church. He would not yield that control to anyone—not even to God.

"Then, Milton," he said slowly—painfully. "You will have the church that you desire. A church full of broken people who long for healing; a church who has lost a personal relationship with their God; a church whose image of their Maker is that of a tyrant, ever expecting perfection that can never possibly be achieved. They will become drained, ill, and numb. They will fall by the wayside, desperate for spiritual food, or they will simply burn out. Is this the way you really want it?"

Whitfield scoffed. "Anyone in that category is not walking in faith and victory," he said smugly with stubborn self-righteousness. "They must work harder, in my opinion, to compensate for their lack of faith and weakness. The truly faithful are free of such problems."

Leonard looked long and sorrowfully at the pastor, his heart in anguish. Milton was a bitter and wounded man, and Leonard no longer knew him. He closed his diary, realising there was no more to be said—there was no point in proceeding any farther. Milton's face was hardened, his heart cold, his love of God confused and darkened. His ego and need for power had consumed him, and he seemed no longer able to hear the truth. Leonard looked down, and with some deliberation slowly removed a white envelope from inside his coat pocket. He felt strangely calm and at peace, as though a huge burden had suddenly fallen from his shoulders.

"I was hoping I would not have to give this to you...but it seems I have no choice. I can no longer stand by you in clear conscience; I can not be party to the spiritual abuse I see evidenced in this place. It is with much regret and sadness, therefore, that I give you...my resignation." He slid the envelope into the centre of the table.

Whitfield's eyes narrowed in anger, his face grew dark, his hands trembled with rage. He picked the envelope up and with calculated exaggeration slowly ripped it in pieces and scattered it on the floor as he stared pointedly at the men around him.

"*I* will say who is, and who is not on the council of the elders," he seethed through gritted teeth. "You are right, McKenzie. You will no longer be an elder of this church—but only because I have said so. As from tonight you will lose all authority in this place, and any funding that we have so generously bestowed upon you will stop forthwith. You can tell your wife, Marjory, that she too will be stripped of any responsibilities she holds, and neither of you will be permitted to have your say ever again. What's more, you will both join me on the platform tomorrow at the morning service so this can be announced to all. *Have I made myself clear?*" Whitfield's voice had been growing stronger and louder and his whole body was now shaking.

Leonard slowly rose to his feet. In comparison to the pastor, a mantle of tranquillity had descended on him and firmly he stood his ground in the face of raging anger and threats.

"I fear you have misunderstood me, Milton," he replied quietly, yet with a boldness he had not known before. "I did not mean I intend to resign as an elder of this church...but as a *member.* From tonight my wife and I will no longer attend the church of The Light."

A tense silence filled the room. In the history of the church this had never happened before and its impact on the fellowship was therefore immeasurable. Fearing his kingdom was under attack and his control was eroding before his eyes, Milton sneered, "How *dare* you...you can't do this . . ."

But Leonard walked resolutely toward the door. "Milton, let me quote to you from the book of Acts," he said coolly.

Whether it be right in the sight of God to hearken unto

you more than unto God, judge ye. For I cannot but
speak the things which I have seen and heard.

(Acts 4:19–20, KJV)

And with that, Leonard McKenzie turned and walked out of
the office.

# WEEDS IN GOD'S GARDEN

The morning sun had barely risen in the amber sky when Gladys Jones pulled her cardigan around her shoulders, closed the door of her small wooden bungalow and climbed into her car. A brisk breeze rustled the leaves of the trees above her, where a chorus of birds noisily welcomed the dawn; but Gladys scarcely noticed either. Unlike most sensible people who were still soundly sleeping in their beds this Sunday morning, Gladys felt energised, alert, and raring to go; not only because she was on flower duty this morning and out of necessity must gather buckets of flora from the many willing donors, but also because of the news she had received from Peggy Percival late last night. It was not often that an *elder* left the church. And a senior elder at that. What could he have done to have resulted in such radical action? Word had it that Pastor Whitfield and the remaining elders had had to ask Leonard McKenzie to leave after some secret meeting that had been held last night. A *secret* meeting. Gladys shivered with delight. Things had not been this exciting for some time.

Her first port of call was to Cynthia Blackenbury, a widow and friend, who lived nearby and who had offered to provide gladiolus for Gladys' display. Cynthia's cottage garden was a picture, and as Gladys walked briskly up the cobblestone pathway she couldn't help but admire the handsome hollyhocks and delphiniums that grew under her windows. Anticipating her arrival, Cynthia threw open the door.

"Come *in*, my dear. I have the flowers in a bucket here already for you to take," she said enthusiastically. "You *will* stay for a cup of tea, Gladys, won't you? It is so early in the morning."

"That would be lovely, Cynthia. To tell you the truth I've had some upsetting news and would appreciate someone to talk to," she sighed with exaggerated heaviness and looked sideways at her friend to see if her words had had the desired effect.

"Gladys? What has upset you? Come and sit down, my dear, and tell me everything." Cynthia bustled around Gladys, fussing with cushions and rattling cups and saucers as she prepared the tea.

"Then...you haven't heard?" Gladys asked innocently. "Leonard McKenzie has been asked to leave the church." She dabbed her eyes in mock distress.

"No! Elder Leonard McKenzie? And Marjory? My sweet Lord!" Cynthia turned to stare at Gladys, her eyes wide with shock. "But...Leonard is a senior elder and has been with the church for as long as I can remember. He and Marjory are such lovely people. Marjory used to visit my sister in the retirement home, and she always brought muffins or some sort of home baking for her. My sister said she was a very nice lady." She turned again to prepare the tea. "It just shows you, doesn't it, that you don't always know what is going on with people. Does anyone know *why* they were asked to leave?" She poured steaming hot tea into a china cup and handed it to Gladys.

Gladys took her cup and saucer and began sipping her tea gingerly. "No...I've not been able to discover the reason, but you can be sure it will be serious. I know that a special meeting was held last night where the decision was made. Peggy Percival mentioned she thought the scene was ugly and Leonard had been made to leave the room. Poor pastor, after all he has done for that man."

"My, my," Cynthia murmured. "You just never can tell."

A tap at the door interrupted their thoughts. "Cynthia? It's only me—can I come in?"

It was Eugena Gibson from across the road, also a member of The Light.

"I saw Gladys' car in the driveway and I had to come and speak to you both. I've just heard that Leonard and Marjory McKenzie have been asked to leave the church! Isn't it dreadful?"

"It's *terrible* news. We were just talking about that very same thing. Come in, my dear, and sit down. Would you like to join us with a cup of tea?"

It was some time later before Gladys finally emerged from her discussions with Cynthia and Eugena, during which time the phone had rung constantly. News was spreading fast and as Gladys hurried off to her next contributor of flowers she wondered just what would be said at this morning's meeting. She shivered with excitement. Now *that* would be a meeting worth attending!

⚜

All eyes were fixed solemnly upon Pastor Whitfield as he took his place on the platform that Sunday morning. The atmosphere in the large auditorium was tensely expectant as everyone waited for the response or possibly for the answers as to why such a well known and well liked senior elder of the church had been excommunicated. No one could imagine what events could have transpired to cause this course of action and to add to their many questions, the remaining elders were acting most unusually. They hung their heads almost guiltily and some shuffled awkwardly in their seats. What did they know that was making them so uneasy?

"I would like to begin this morning's meeting with a reading from Matthew 24:4- 13," Pastor Whitfield's voice boomed acrimoniously over the congregation, and en masse all obediently turned to the scripture. Instinctively they knew from the tone of his voice and the expression on his face that he was most displeased with the recent turn of events. From past experience they knew that this morning's message then was to be one of bitter doom and gloom, and no doubt as a consequence there would be the legalistic tightening of the already harsh laws of the church. His voice was gruff as he began:

> Take heed that no man deceive you. For many shall come in my name, saying, I am Christ; and shall deceive many...Then shall they deliver you up to be afflicted, and shall kill you: and ye shall be hated of all nations for my name's sake. And then shall many be offended, and shall betray one another, and shall hate one another. And many false prophets shall rise, and shall deceive many. And because iniquity shall abound, the love of many shall wax cold. But he that shall endure unto the end, the same shall be saved.
>
> (Matthew 24: 4–13, KJV)

Whitfield closed his Bible heavily with a thud, and stared out over the congregation sullenly.

"We are truly in the last days. A day when those you thought were close to you, those you trusted and served side by side with for many years, suddenly turn on you and persecute you. Jesus himself said such days would come, and I tell you, these days are upon us. Your very brothers and sisters in Christ will deliver you up to be afflicted, thinking they are doing God a favour, but *they* are the ones who are being deceived. For I tell you, when you are doing God's will, there will be those who will hate you, who would even desire to kill you. When you preach faithfully from the word of God year after year there will be those who are offended at the word. They will be offended at the truth and the way that truth is carried out in this place of worship. They will start to question the standards here and the methods of disciplining the family of God in our midst. They will start to undermine the leadership. These same people will betray you and hate you, and their love for you will grow cold. They will be attracted to false prophets in other churches and desire fellowship with these false prophets over the fellowship of their own true brethren here at The Light. But the Bible tells us we must endure all such persecution and if we do so *we* will be the ones that will be saved."

Although, as usual, Pastor Whitfield had mentioned no names, it was not hard to imagine who he was referring to. Reading between the lines the congregation quickly came to the conclusion that Leonard McKenzie had turned on Pastor Whitfield and the elders, attacking their doctrine and faithful "shepherding of the flock" over the many years, though why it was hard to tell. How odd for such an upstanding man of this community to do such a thing. But then, as Pastor Whitfield said, such things would happen in the last days and as he stressed on many occasions these *were* the last days, when even the most righteous among them could be deceived. This was a time when they must all stand together and support the leadership. There was a need for all to be strong against persecution and resist it in all its forms. After all, the church of The Light was elite and had been granted the uttermost revelation and truth. God surely favoured them highly and placed them above all other churches. They had a responsibility therefore to guard this truth and fortify themselves against all attacks from the outside—even from those on the inside who questioned and caused division.

Pastor Whitfield's voice droned on and on as he turned his attention to the church laws, expressing his displeasure over what he felt was a loosening of the discipline and a falling of the high standards of the church. He rebuked the young ladies over their makeup and jewellery and what he felt were inappropriate hemline lengths and insufficient head coverings; and he admonished the men for their incorrect haircuts, forbidding them to grow beards or moustaches. "We are a holiness ministry and must separate ourselves from those of the world," he stressed irritably. "We must show those who stand against us that we are a people of excellence."

Many in the congregation nodded their heads in agreement

and resolved to improve their performance. Others looked weary and defeated, but resigned to the fact that this was the Christian life and there was little choice in the matter if they wanted to please God.

Whitfield continued with his admonishing. "When married couples enter this church, I want them to hold hands and smile at each other, no matter what has gone on at home. We must show the world who looks on from outside our gates that we are happy and our marriages are successful. We *must* allow God's discipline and the discipline of the church to control our lives if we are to stand against the world." With this Pastor Whitfield began thumping the pulpit to make his point. "In short *we will not tolerate insubordination!* And, as I have said before on many occasions, if there are those who would abandon us, we must treat them as *rats* that have run from the ship—as *weeds* that have been plucked from God's own garden! *Do I make myself clear?*"

⚡

It was hard to remember the last time that Leonard and Marjory had attended another church and it was, therefore, a strange sensation to draw up in their car outside of Grace Chapel. They had heard so many good reports of this little church that they thought they would come along and see for themselves. Besides, they had nowhere else to go this Sunday morning. Unsure of the meeting times they had arrived at 11 a.m., but it appeared that the service was already under way, for they could hear vibrant singing and clapping even from where they had parked on the roadside. They only hoped they would be welcome and would not be turned away due to their late arrival. Reaching for Marjory's hand Leonard squeezed it reassuringly.

"It is a day of new beginnings, my dear," he sighed, both with apprehension and anticipation. "Who would have thought we would be starting again at our age?"

Marjory looked out of her window as the sun reflected brightly off the modern building. The rows of birch trees that surrounded the church swayed gently in the wind as though moving in time to the joyful music that resounded from inside its walls. In total agreement with her husband, she had been preparing for this moment for some time, suspecting this may be the outcome of Leonard's encounter with the pastor and the elders. Yet, now that it was upon her she felt a great sense of loss, for in fact a whole lifetime of friends and experiences were left behind her to be returned to no more. She knew they couldn't stay at the church of The Light, not with the way things had become, but as she sat in the car looking out at what could possibly be their new church, it suddenly struck her. They had been part of such a tight-knit community for so long and one that had shunned everything and everyone outside its walls. Would she and Leonard be able to survive on the "outside"?

"I suppose we are starting again, aren't we?" she whispered wistfully.

"Well, we'll need to find new friends, as by now our old ones will have been told to have nothing more to do with us. And I suspect we'll be learning new doctrine here as well—so in that sense we are starting out again. Let's just hope this old dog can learn a few more new tricks," he sighed.

Marjory turned to Leonard and looked into his soft grey eyes, seeing the pain and weariness of the years behind them. Dark rings betrayed a lack of sleep and his face was drawn and lined from carrying the weight and responsibilities of the church of The Light for so long. Besides which he was still hurting from the harsh confrontation of last night's meeting. He was a good and kind man who didn't deserve to be treated this way, and she loved and respected him deeply.

"Oh, I think you've got a few more good years in you yet," she smiled affectionately, patting his arm. "Besides," she said with more confidence than she felt, "we've got each other. We'll get through this together and it'll all work out fine, I'm sure."

She looked back one more time at the church. "I just wish I knew if I should be wearing a hat or not. Do all churches wear hats as do The Light?"

Leonard chuckled. "I can't say that I know, my love. But…I think it's time we went and found out."

Hand in hand they walked down the narrow, tree-lined pathway that led to the back entrance of the church and unobtrusively made their way into the auditorium. The meeting was alive with singing and praise and no one noticed as they slipped quietly into the back row. They stood together as two small children on their first day of school, looking awkward and somewhat out of place; Marjory with her blue-feathered hat, and Leonard with his three-piece suit. They had been obedient to their God and had followed his leading, even though it had meant losing so much. They had bravely stood up for what they felt was right and had faced the fire, confident that their God would come through for them. And they were not to be disappointed. For as they stood in this new place soaking up the atmosphere, a gentle peace began to descend upon them as though God himself had placed his arms around them, and all their uncertainties began to dissipate. As Leonard began to open his mouth in praise, he felt the burden of many years begin to roll off his shoulders and an inner strength begin to return. As Marjory, too, tentatively lifted her hands in prayer, she felt the quiet assurance that they were in the centre of God's will, and her heart began to rejoice. With tears in their eyes they listened to the words of prophecy and encouragement around them, and watched as people's lives were touched by the presence of God. How often they had longed to see this happening at the church of The Light and how desperate they had been for the leadership to see it. But the door had been firmly closed on them and the truth had been rejected. Now, as they silently watched, it seemed, a new door was opening, and with quiet excitement in her heart Marjory took Leonard's hand in hers.

"God is so faithful," she whispered. "After all our battling…I believe he has led us to a new home!"

❦

It was halfway through the Sunday morning meeting at Grace when Emily's attention began to wander, and she began glancing around the room. In truth she was looking to see if a certain young man was attending church today, for she'd been seeing a lot of Chad Hamilton of late, and although it was early days, his feelings toward her were growing obvious. Yet Emily was unsure about such a relationship. Having had so much unwanted attention already from the opposite sex she was beginning to feel confused and vulnerable. Chad seemed like a nice guy and one with whom she was having a lot of fun, yet still she was eager to take things slowly. How could she tell him what she'd been through? Would he even understand? This was all so new to her, for at The Light she had been forbidden to even talk to boys, let alone go out with them. What should she do? It was as she was anxiously scanning the auditorium looking for Chad, however, that her attention was suddenly drawn to a certain familiar blue-feathered hat at the back of the room. Had she seen right? Gasping she turned to her mother.

"Mum!" she whispered excitedly. "Leonard and Marjory are sitting at the back of the church!"

Ruth looked at Emily in surprise then turned quickly, straining to see past the many people who were seated in the auditorium. Sure enough, there they were. Elated, she tapped Zara on the shoulder, who was sitting in front of her with Beth and Tim.

"Zara, look behind you to the back row," she whispered softly. "Leonard and Marjory are here!"

Discreetly, Zara and Beth turned to catch a glimpse of the couple as they sat unsuspectingly listening to the sermon. Zara returned her attention again to the front, although her thoughts were racing. She was overjoyed to see Leonard and Marjory, but was equally concerned that their presence here meant the meeting last night with the leadership had not gone well. Had they been excommunicated? Had the pastor been harsh with Leonard for the things she knew he had planned to say? How she longed to talk with them and offer them the support and love they would surely need. Thankfully she did not have to wait long. For as was customary, Brian stopped his message part-way through in order to give the people a chance to meet and greet each other before re-gathering again. Zara, Ruth, Emily, and Beth were quick to make a beeline toward the couple, Emily being the first to reach them.

"Uncle Len—Aunt Marj!" she cried with delight.

Marjory's eyes were damp with joy as she hugged Emily and then embraced the others one by one. "Oh, it is so good to see some familiar faces," she beamed.

Zara turned sombrely to Leonard. "I gather the meeting didn't go down too well then?" she questioned with concern. The others turned to listen attentively.

"I'm afraid Pastor Whitfield is a very stubborn man," he shook his head sadly. "He is so determined to keep the people under his control and rule them with legalism. In the end I could see it was no use trying to make him see differently. I handed my notice in, so to speak, although I suspect a different story will be told to the masses. I can imagine they'll be having a field day this morning dissecting it all. Gladys Jones will be in her element."

They all laughed at this thought, each knowing well what Gladys was like. Yet behind the laughter there was an unspoken understanding of the ordeal that he had been through, and a deep bond of friendship that only those who had experienced such suffering could possibly comprehend.

"You know we all spent some time last night covering you in prayer." Zara went on to describe the gathering at the beach and the spiritual warfare that had taken place.

Leonard was visibly moved. "Thank you all so much," he said, his voice breaking slightly. "You've no idea how much that means to us."

"Why don't you all come around to our place for lunch?" Beth suddenly offered. "We'd love to have you, and I think we all could be a help and encouragement to each other at this time, don't you?"

It was agreed, and after deciding amongst themselves what food each would bring and the directions to Beth's house were given, they all returned happily to their seats as the meeting continued.

As the message drew to a close, Zara was experiencing butterflies in her stomach. Being her first Sunday as an official member of Grace Chapel it would soon be her turn to be prayed over, and while she felt nervous, it was a moment Zara had looked forward to for some time. Sure enough, as the last scripture was read and the last amen uttered, Brian called her up to the front with Beth and Tim and introduced her to the congregation. Much to Zara's delight, a group of young people in the corner of the room began to clap and cheer. She'd meet them yesterday at the beach and now Brian called several of them up to pray with her also. However, as the folks gathered around to pray, Zara suddenly leant over to Brian and whispered something into his ear. Nodding in understanding he turned to the congregation once again.

"Before we pray, Zara has just brought something to my attention. I do believe we have two special people with us this morning, Leonard and Marjory McKenzie. As many of you will recall, we prayed for these folks just last night around our church picnic bonfire. Leonard has been an elder at the church of The Light for many years but has recently suffered some real hurts at their hands—as have a few of the folks who have joined us. So, as we come together in prayer this morning, welcoming Zara into our midst, let's also lift this dear couple up to our God and ask for his peace and healing to flow through them." Brian raised his eyes and looked toward the back of the room. "Leonard and Marjory…welcome to Grace Chapel!"

# NEW BEGINNINGS

The mid-summer's sun was high in the sky and the deep ocean was as blue as sapphires as the sleek white launch cut through the water with ease. A trail of foaming white waves billowed out behind and squawking seagulls circled above. The busy docks were fast disappearing from sight and far in the distance a sandy beached island beckoned. It was an idyllic day to be out on the water.

Ruth held tightly to the chrome rails as she stood alone at the back of the launch, allowing the cooling breeze to flow freely through her hair. She had been looking forward to this day, though admittedly with a little apprehension, and she hoped all would go well. The boat belonged to a retired doctor from Grace by the name of Adam Brooks and he had kindly invited a small group of friends aboard, including Brian and Lynn Somerville, Leonard and Marjory, Ruth…and Jack.

Ruth had been in contact with Jack over the last few months, slowly building new bridges of friendship with him. Jack had been surprised at her leaving The Light, yet deeply respectful and appreciative of the courage it had taken her to do so—a fact that had helped in healing their relationship. They were not living together as yet, having agreed to give each other as much time and space as was needed. They were just taking things slowly. However, of his own accord, Jack had been attending some of the Alcoholics Anonymous meetings for his drinking, and seemed intent on getting his life back together again. He had been truly shaken by the departure of his wife and daughter, and deeply regretful of his actions—even if his bitterness over the intrusion of the church of The Light into his family affairs still lingered. The wounds imposed by this religious institution would take much longer to heal and so today, understandably, would be a big step for Jack. This would be the first time he would be mingling with folk from Ruth's new church and she couldn't help but feel a little nervous.

"Isn't this just a gorgeous day?" Marjory sighed contentedly as she joined Ruth at the stern. "Jack seems to be getting on well with the men folk up at the bow. They're already talking about doing a spot of fishing before heading out to the island for some lunch and I've heard him laughing heartily several times."

Ruth turned to Marjory looking visibly relieved. "Really? Thank goodness. I deliberately came back here to give him room to get to know the men. I admit I especially want him to get to know Brian. I just have a feeling Jack will be able to relate quite well to him—well, that's what I'm praying anyway."

Marjory put her arm kindly around Ruth's shoulders. "You just relax and enjoy the day, my dear. It's all in God's hands."

"Would you both like a cold drink?" It was Lynn, with an armload of cans from the icebox. "This is the life, isn't it?" She placed the cans down on the table and relaxed into the padded seats, admiring the view. The others soon joined her. "The island we're headed for is a favourite of Brian and mine. We used to bring our children here for picnics and fishing when they were younger."

"Do you have a boat then?" asked Ruth with interest.

Lynn chuckled with delight. "Not on a pastor's salary! No, we've got friends who have a boat—although not as luxurious as this one."

Ruth was a little puzzled over this last statement, especially as she reflected on Pastor Whitfield's position in life. He had a grand home overlooking the sea in the best part of the town, he drove the latest car, had a holiday home at the beach, and had several boats of his own. What sort of salary must he be on? Seeing her questioning look, Lynn went on to explain.

"Brian is a great one for giving. He'd give the shirt right off his back to anyone in need if necessary. He's used a lot of his own money to establish many Christian endeavours. At the moment he's busy establishing a Bible college at Grace, which he plans to launch internationally. He's started initially doing night classes with some of the folks from church, but is all set to begin a day school very shortly. He's already arranged to sponsor ten eager Fijians to come across and billet with us as his first batch of students. His vision is to train these ten up, then release them back into their villages to start their own Bible schools there. It's just one of many ideas that he has." Lynn smiled affectionately. "Brian has more ideas before breakfast than most people have in a lifetime!"

It was hard not to like Lynn. Soft-mannered and ladylike, she had a good sense of humour and had her feet solidly on the ground. And unlike the leadership that Ruth and Marjory had known, she was approachable and ready to listen. Lynn studied the two ladies before her, aware of their recent hurts and troubles.

"What do you both see yourselves doing, now that you've left The Light?" she asked kindly. "In what way would you like to get involved at Grace, or are you happy just 'being' at the moment?"

Marjory and Ruth looked at each other in surprise. It was not something they had ever been asked before. At The Light they had been simply *told* what they should do—they had never been given an option and there was never the choice of just relaxing and being left alone. As a consequence they didn't know what to say.

"I...I hadn't really thought about it," said Marjory hesitantly, while Ruth looked on equally as puzzled.

"Well, I've been watching you over this past little while. Marjory, I see you have a real gift of hospitality and counsel. I notice young women especially are drawn to your kind wisdom and advice—you're like a mother hen gathering her chicks! When you feel you are ready, I'd like to give you an official role in that capacity if you'd like. Later on we may even get you up at some of the ladies' meetings to do some teaching. What do you think about that?"

Marjory was a little overawed. In all her years at The Light she had never been given any official roles and had not been allowed to teach, apart from Sunday school.

"I don't know what to say. I…I've never had to teach in front of a crowd before—I don't know if I could do it."

Lynn was quick to place her hand on Marjory's arm. "There's no pressure at all. Just think about it, and most of all pray and ask God for his guidance. He'll show you when the time is right."

Ruth could feel herself getting uncomfortable. Years of fear and unquestioning obedience to the leadership had taught her to do whatever she was told. What if Lynn suggested she also should teach? She knew she couldn't cope, yet how could she say no?

Lynn looked at Ruth kindly, sensing her fear. "Dear Ruth—don't be afraid. I didn't mean to alarm you. I see in you a woman of real compassion with the ability to encourage. I believe you also have a powerful gift for intercessory prayer, which may eventually flow into the prophetic and the gift of discernment. God has many good things in store for you and wants you to know you are loved and cherished!"

Ruth dropped her eyes quickly, feeling them burn with tears. Her heart was warmed with joy. How faithful God was to her. He alone knew her fears and anxieties and had met the cry of her heart.

Lynn glanced down to the front of the boat where the men were happily casting their rods out into the deep blue ocean, hoping for a catch. "Talking of good things being in store," she winked at Ruth, "shall we go and see how Jack and the others are getting along?"

Jack's line had been twitching on and off for some minutes, but as the ladies joined them it suddenly arched steeply, the reel zinging out of control. "Whoa—I've got a biggie here!" Jack cried excitedly. "Looks like we'll be having fish for lunch after all!"

Jack slowly applied the brakes to the reel, trying to tire the fish out, but it continued to struggle frantically. Brian quickly grabbed the straps of the angling chair and belted Jack in, while Leonard helped him hold the rod. Adam jumped to the controls of the boat and brought her to a slow pace. Amidst whoops and cries from all involved they finally reeled in a beautiful two-hundred-and-fifty-pound marlin.

"What a beauty!" Brian exclaimed. "There's more than lunch here—in fact we could feed a whole tribe! Good on you, Jack!" He gave him a friendly slap on the back while Jack beamed with delight.

Leonard and Adam had already armed themselves with sharp knives, ready to gut and clean the fish. "Any of you ladies like to do the gutting?" Leonard joked.

Adam looked up as he chopped through the marlin's head. "Lynn? Could you do something for me? Do you mind keeping the boat in low gear and gently steering her around to the landing? We're nearly at the island."

As the launch chugged gently into the bay and made its way toward the wooden jetty for mooring, Ruth quietly came up behind Jack and whispered in his ear. "Quite the hero, aren't you?" she teased. "So, how are you getting along with everyone?"

Jack turned and put his arm around her waist. "Actually…I have to say, not bad…not bad at all. Especially Brian. He's not a bad guy," he said reflectively, "considering he's religious!" Jack winked at Ruth with a grin.

The afternoon was spent lazily relaxing in deck chairs on the beach, drinking ice cold Coke and feeling the warmth of the golden sands between their bare toes. Occasionally they would slip into the cool, lapping waves before returning again to dry off in the sun. And of course the hamper of food they'd brought with them was dipped into regularly. The men talked seriously about business, sports, and politics, while the woman chatted lightly about family and friends. It was not long, however, before the sun began to set in the western sky.

"I love this time of night," sighed Lynn, looking out at the sun slowly disappearing beneath the horizon as it left a trail of bright oranges and reds across the sky. "Anyone want to come for a walk?"

Adam stood to his feet, dusting the sand from his shirt. "You couples go on if you like," he smiled. "I'll stay here with our things and start packing up the boat. We'll need to leave in about half an hour."

Arm and arm, Brian and Lynn, and then Leonard and Marjory, walked on ahead, their images glowing in the setting sun. But Jack held back. Silently he watched as they made their way down the beach, happily talking while enjoying each other's company and soon branching off as couples to be on their own. He turned to Ruth and quietly took her hand. "Would you like to walk with me?" he asked almost tenderly.

Together Ruth and Jack walked slowly along the shoreline, the waves lapping at their feet, the dappled light dancing on the water. At first they walked in silence, each deep in their own thoughts. But then Jack stopped and turned slowly toward his wife.

"Ruth, I can't help but notice you have really changed. You are so much more at peace and seem…content. It's as though a weight has been lifted off your shoulders. I suspect it's got something to do with this new church." Reflectively he turned and began slowly walking again. "I've never said this before… but I am really sorry for the way I have treated you . . ." His voice began to break. "I want things to change." He looked up at the couples now some distance from them. "I really like this

Brian—and Leonard too. Do you think they'd have one more place at this Grace Chapel for me?"

Ruth stopped in the sand, her heart racing. Had she heard right? "You'd come to Grace? With me and Emily?" she asked gently.

Jack nodded.

Tears of joy running down her cheeks, Ruth quietly embraced her husband in the fading light of the summer's day. They held each other for some time, allowing healing and forgiveness to flow between them. Then, in the shadows of the twilight evening, they gradually made their way back to the boat to join the others. The sun may have gone down upon this day, but for them a new day was dawning!

# OUTSIDE THE WALLS

The weeks and months that followed held many new experiences for Leonard and Marjory, Ruth and her family, and Zara. To say that the years of legalistic control and spiritual abuse had taken its toll would be an understatement, yet they all rejoiced in the new church they had come to with its sound doctrine and balanced teaching, and felt confident that in time their healing would be complete. Not that Grace Chapel was perfect, for wherever man is involved there is imperfection. Having never experienced spiritual abuse themselves, there were often times of misunderstanding and even impatience between the members of Grace and those ex-members of The Light as they learned to grow together in the Lord. But the spirit at Grace Chapel was different from that of The Light, and it was never long before any troubled waters were soon calmed. In fact it was these very differences that prepared Grace for the many more ex-members who would find their way into the safety of their fold. Over time many wearied and troubled souls from The Light would make their way to Grace Chapel's door, hungry for life and spiritual food, and all would be welcomed with open and understanding arms.

Although several months had passed since Leonard and Marjory had left The Light, their phone still had not rung. Oh, it rang endlessly with people from Grace Chapel, checking that they were managing all right and inviting them to meals and on outings, but they never again heard from anyone at The Light. Even Paul and Yvonne Pritchard, their oldest and dearest friends, kept their silence and it had all seemed so strange. After all Leonard's years of service as an elder it would be thought that someone would phone and wish him the best, or at least ask what his side of the story may have been. And even with Marjory, one small "thank you" for all the work she had put in over the years would have sufficed. But yet there was only silence. The peculiar thing was, even if the congregation had been told they were both bound for hell's fire, surely, you would think, *one* person would ring to try and save their souls. Surely *someone* would knock on their door and try to convert them from the so-called error of their ways. But it was not to be so. A complete congregation of people turned their backs on the ones they feared would poison their minds and cause division. They had retreated into their fortified walls for protection and would not venture outside. For Leonard and Marjory, a whole way of life had disappeared in one evening.

Yet there were many new challenges to divert their attention. They were thoroughly enjoying it at Grace. The people were friendly and open, and they quickly made several good friends. They had their difficult times, for they were used to doing things a certain way—the church of The Light's way—and they found that old habits died hard. Nevertheless Brian and Lynn patiently took them under their wing, enjoying their maturity and dependability in so many other areas. In fact Brian had asked Leonard if he would teach at his Bible school during the day, offering him full training, and Leonard had accepted with delight. He threw himself into the task with great gusto so that on occasion Marjory had had to pry her husband away from his books just to spend time with him. She, in turn, became involved in counseling and thoroughly enjoyed her new found freedom, although she had never been more acutely aware of her own lack of knowledge and training in this field. As a result she had gladly accepted the much-needed assistance and guidance offered by Lynn, who became a close friend.

Leonard and Marjory had drawn much strength from each other and from their God. They had travelled a difficult path and had stood unwaveringly for what they believed to be the truth—no matter what the consequences, nor how fierce the opposition. Yet they found the journey was not over. Even though they were of an age when most folk would be retiring, they found that God had not finished with them yet. The book that was their lives had not been closed. Instead, a new chapter was well on the way to being written.

❦

Zara applied for university that she might put to rest her desire to study law and gain a bachelor's, even a master's degree. At The Light this could never have been a possibility, for women were discouraged from pursuing such a career and the worldly atmosphere of university was preached against often. Yet the teaching was so different at Grace. Here she was encouraged to seek God's plan for her life, no matter what path it took, and spurred on by constant encouragement and a deep sense that anything was possible with her God, she had taken the plunge. It was not without reservation, however. The negative messages she had received into her spirit during her time at The Light had gone deeper than she had anticipated and would take some time to heal.

She never heard from Kate again. There had been no response to her letter, no phone call or visit. Through the grapevine Zara learned that Kate and Dan had married, though with Dan's two sisters as bridesmaids. Zara had sent a small gift with a card wishing them all the best in their new life together, but she had not received a reply. Even years later she would think of her friend and grieve for the friendship that was lost.

Yet life moves on, and soon Zara found her own flat which she shared with two new friends from Grace. Her attention was also soon taken with a young man called David, whose zeal and passion for God she greatly admired. Together they planned to take a short mission trip with a group from Grace to the Philippines and life began to take on a whole new meaning.

Of all the ex-members, Zara had spent the least amount of time at The Light. Did this mean, therefore, that she had been unaffected by its influence? True, she had not had years of indoctrination and legalism, yet The Light had been her first church experience, and consequently, she had formed most of her concepts of God from The Light's teachings. The idea that God was an overwhelming power not to be reckoned with was deeply ingrained within her, and the concept of God's grace versus the Law was new and confusing. Often she fell into the trap of performing to gain God's approval, yet with time and correct teaching, these concepts would be reshaped and replaced, and by experiencing God's presence first hand, she would soon conquer her feelings of fear. What would be harder to deal with, perhaps, was her deep suspicion of leadership and her constant struggle with issues of control. Zara indeed had not realised the power the church of The Light had held over her, even in the short time she had been there.

⚥

For Emily and Ruth the journey would be harder. The deep wounds inflicted upon them from the harsh dealings of the leadership of The Light, and the abusive treatment of some of its members left deep scars. Emily would always struggle with relationships, finding it hard to trust again and rarely would she feel "safe." She would find that the deep psychological pain in her life would have other, more dubious outlets. And although Ruth was much improved, she would often struggle with anxiety and depression. In fact, disorder and dysfunction would become words they were both familiar with.

Yet God was so faithful. Jack gave his life to Christ and he and Ruth eventually got back together again. Every step of the way God was there to guide and to direct; to teach and to heal. Although the path was long and the healing so often seemed slow, God never let them down. Despite all, his hand of love and power were there to lift them above the pain, never allowing them to suffer more than they could handle. It was through him and the love and support of his people that they had a hope and a future.

꣎

And as for Gladys Jones...

She was last seen at the supermarket with her nose so far in the air on account of self-righteously avoiding Zara and Beth that she ran her shopping trolley into a neatly stacked pile of cans, and followed herself into the pile shortly thereafter. Zara had tried to conceal her great amusement, quickly offering Gladys a helping hand, yet this was piously rejected. Gladys' face had remained so cold and her demeanour so icy that from that point on Zara had affectionately referred to her and other such sad members of The Light as "The Frozen Chosen"!

There is one thing we can be certain of, however. Our God does not so callously reject us. His stance is toward us; for us. He sent his son, Jesus, to save us. He is in the business of healing, restoring and lifting burdens. His words echo down through the ages and are as true today as ever...

> For I know the plans I have for you, says the Lord, plans for good and not for evil, to give you a future and a hope.
>
> (Jeremiah 29:11, Living Bible)

# BIBLIOGRAPHY

Hassan, Steven. *Combatting Cult Mind Control: Rescue.* Rochester, Vermont: Park Street Press, 1988, 1990.

Johnson, David; VanVonderen, Jeff. *The Subtle Power of Spiritual Abuse.* Minneapolis, Minnesota: Bethany House Publishers, 1991.

"Seeing God In New Ways; Recovery from Distorted Images of God." Juanita R. Ryan. The National Association for Christian Recovery. 6 May 2005. http://www.nacronline.com.

"Spiritual Abuse: Rules & Characteristics of Harmful Faith Systems (Part 5)." Adapted from "Faith that Hurts, Faith that Heals" by Arterburn & Felton by Steve Cadman-Neu. Christian Counselling/Counselling Inner Healing; Art & Play Therapy. 6 May 2005. http://www.christiancounselling.on.ca/articles_spiritual_abuse_rules_&_characteristics.htm.